MIDNIGHT EMBERS

L.S. PULLEN

Copyright © 2021 by L.S. Pullen

Midnight Embers

Text copyright © 2021 L.S. Pullen

All Rights Reserved

Published by: L.S. Pullen

Beta Read by: Kirsten Moore

Edited by: Liji Editing

Proofread by: Crystal Blanton and Amber McCammon

Cover Design & Formatting by: Leila Pullen

Photo: Licensed Adobe Stock

The right of L.S. Pullen to be identified as the author of the work has been asserted by her in accordance with the copyright, Designs and patents act 1988.

No part of this book may be reproduced in any form or by any electronic or mechanical means, including information storage and retrieval systems, without written permission from the author, except for the use of brief quotations in a book review.

All characters in this publication are fictional and any resemblance to real persons, living or dead is purely coincidental.

"There is a stubbornness about me that never can bear to be frightened at the will of others. My courage always rises at every attempt to intimidate me." — *Jane Austen, Pride and Prejudice*

Chapter One

Meghan

Finally, I get to have a girl's night with Clara. It's been too long—between her having Jacob and her controlling arse boyfriend, Emilio. Tonight is an infrequent occurrence, and I intend to take full advantage of the fact.

We used to frequent Rattlers almost every weekend before we were even old enough to drink. Terrible when I think about it now, how I'd lie to my dad about being at Clara's and vice versa... How we never got caught is beyond me. We'd go to the George pub first, share two bottles of wine and then walk across the road for dancing and shots.

It's not even the best pub or bar in town, but it's not far from me in Winchmore Hill or Clara in Oakwood, and the music is good. Don't get me wrong, the floor is always sticky, and there's only ever one toilet in the ladies' restrooms that flushes by the end of the night, but it's familiar, and I love the atmosphere. We've spent our time sitting at the bar before stepping onto the dance floor. The place is pretty much a hole in the wall, so it is always packed.

The aroma of alcohol and body odour, mixed with the aftermath of tobacco from the smokers, assails my senses.

"One more dance," Clara shouts in my ear—to be heard over the music. "And then you can treat me to another shot."

I nod, and she pulls me in for a sweaty hug.

"Thank you for this," she says, squeezing me hard. "Don't get me wrong, I love Jacob, but I miss being carefree. You have no idea how lucky you are."

Yeah, right... I'm still trying to come to terms with being dumped and living and working with an overprotective dad.

She squeals when *'Never Let You Go'* blares through the speakers, and we both get lost in the music. I love to dance, but around strangers, not so much. It's easy to pretend I'm an extrovert on the outside and not the introvert I work so hard to hide. At work, I'm confident. I have to be, and as a personal trainer, it's part of the job. But the truth is, it doesn't come without effort. I've always been insecure, being on the heavier side growing up.

It began with fat girl taunts, and I thought not eating was a way to fix it, but I was wrong. And that's when I began training. But then those taunts about my weight turned to ones of men objectifying me instead—and girls being bitchy.

Maybe it's how I've always managed to situate myself well into my environment. It becomes tedious at times, but it's how I cope. It helps to be here with Clara. She's so outgoing, the yin to my yang.

A guy grabs her around the waist, and her eyes go wide. I step forward and pull her to me, shaking my head to the guy over her shoulder who shrugs it off and moves onto someone else.

"Eww," she says, laughing as she grabs my hand and drags me towards the bar, both of us breathless as we perch on the free stools and get the bartenders attention. She orders us both a shot of whiskey sour, and I tap the card reader. I already know I'll regret this in the morning, but whatever.

"Cheers," we say in unison. She clinks her glass with mine and it spills over the rim, but we each tip our heads back and down our shots.

"Well, I'll be damned." I turn in my seat, and Faye, a girl we used to go to school with, leans in and greets us both with a kiss on the cheek.

"It's been forever since I last saw you both out," Faye says, waving her hands around in excitement. She always was overzealous.

She pulls up a stool and situates herself between the two of us, and before I know it, she orders another two rounds of shots. She's giddy with excitement over a threesome she had last weekend. We've always taken what she says with a pinch of salt.

"I guess those days are over for you, now you're a mum," she says to Clara, and then she zones in on me. "And you're still pining over your ex, no doubt."

I look past Faye and see Clara rolls her eyes, and I try not to laugh when she shakes her head.

"Ohh," Faye squeals, almost bouncing in her seat and slapping the counter. "I knew there was something I always wanted to ask the two of you."

I look at Clara quizzically, but she shrugs. No doubt Faye is about to enlighten us.

"Have you ever wondered if Henry and Ethan played the old switch-a-roo while you dated?"

"What?" I ask, wondering how much she's drank tonight.

"You know, where they pretend to be each other to get a taste of the other girlfriend in bed…"

Clara almost chokes on her vodka and coke and begins coughing. I'm pretty sure my mouth is gaping open.

I don't even know what to say or how to answer that as my cheeks burn with embarrassment and an uncomfortable silence ensues as Clara stares back at me, and then she is full-on laughing at the audacity of the question. The worst part is that I can't ignore the fact that I have indeed thought about what Henry would be like in bed, even though I'm fully aware that's all kinds of wrong.

"I need to pee. I'll be right back," I say before standing up.

Clara's expression hardens ever so slightly as I move to go past her. "Wait, don't tell me you thought about it?" she asks.

I shake my head and make a hasty retreat to the toilets. I take a moment to try and cool my face, the colour unforgiving as I stare at my reflection in the mirror.

Trying to squash down the desire that courses through me when my mind wanders, I get caught momentarily thinking about Henry—who happens to be my best friend's ex and my ex-boyfriend's twin brother.

Shaking my head, I mumble to myself, grabbing the paper towels and dabbing my sweaty face—my flushed response a dead giveaway.

Exiting the toilets, I walk straight into a wall of rock-hard muscle. And immediately, I tense at the unmistakable and pungent smell of Emilio's aftershave. I have to hold back the urge to gag.

Sinister eyes stare down at me.

"Clara said you'd gone to the lav," he says, blocking my path in the poorly lit hallway as he reaches to swipe hair from my temple.

I swat his hand away and step back to put distance between us.

"Yeah, and you had to check, I take it? What are you even doing here? You couldn't even let her go out for a few hours, could you?" I retort.

He raises an eyebrow. "I was meeting my crew here before moving on somewhere else," he says, sucking his bottom lip into his mouth. "Don't act like you aren't pleased to see me."

I lean back further. "Hardly," I reply.

"Come on. You're always around Clara. I know you want me."

I scoff at that; he is delusional.

"I do not. Clara is my best friend, and Jacob is my godson. It's the only reason you see me."

I don't add that he puts on a façade to keep his temper in check when I am around them, but I know it's there boiling beneath the surface. I've seen the bruises Clara tries to hide. His lip twitches in a way that makes my skin crawl, and my pulse begins to race. I attempt to step around him, but he cuts me off, pushing me back against the wall—hard.

"What do you think you're doing?" I say, trying to hide the tremble in my voice as my adrenaline spikes.

"You can deny it all you want, but I know you're playing hard to get."

He leans closer, his aftershave now overwhelming. I turn my face to the side.

"I'm not interested," I say with as much confidence as I can muster.

He grips my chin, forcing me to look at him, and I react instinctively and slap his hand away, but he's fast and grabs my throat, tight… too tight.

I might be a personal trainer, but he's a professional MMA fighter, and I know I'm no match for him. It doesn't matter that I train hard or that I've been doing it for years.

His eyes turn dark, almost soulless. "You'll eventually give yourself to me, and I always get what I want, one way or another."

I shove his chest with as much force as I can, causing him to let go, and I quickly dart past him and back into the sea of people. My pulse is racing as I try to calm my breathing. Any other time, the corridor would be full of girls queuing for the toilets. I hold my hand to my throat, knowing there's no way he hasn't left a mark.

"I was just coming to find you," Clara says, shoving my coat into my arms, and it's not lost on me that her hands are shaking. "The sitter just rang. I'm sorry, I need to get back to

Jacob." And I wouldn't put it past Emilio if he told her she should go home.

I nod, pulling on my jacket. Her eyes zone in on where Emilio grabbed me. She turns her back to me and starts in the direction of the exit.

Passing Faye, I wave bye, but she's engrossed in something one of Emilio's cronies is whispering in her ear and barely acknowledges us as we leave.

I let out a sigh of relief once the cool air hits me when we get outside. After what just happened, I'm ready to get out of here too. Thankfully, there is an Uber less than a mile away, so we don't even have to wait long.

"Did he do that?" she asks, her nostrils flaring.

"Yep. He came on to me and grabbed me by the throat. He doesn't like the word no," I reply, raising my eyebrows.

Clara nods as she types frantically away on her phone, not even surprised by her boyfriend—and that's even more disturbing.

"I honestly don't know how much more of him I can put up with," she whispers, her glistening eyes glancing over my shoulder in case anyone is in earshot.

"He told you to go home, didn't he?"

She looks up from her phone. "Yeah, pretty much."

"You need to leave him," I reply, tucking my arm into the crook of her elbow.

"I'm sorry, but you know it's not that simple. You know what Emilio's like."

I can't control the shiver which rolls down my spine, because I do, and it's all the more reason she needs to get away from him once and for all.

Neither of us says anything else. The buzz we were feeling less than half an hour ago has since diminished.

The driver drops her home first, and she offers for me to stay, knowing I'll decline. Spending a night under the same roof as Emilio is a hard no for me.

Besides, I have work tomorrow, and I smile to myself at the thought of seeing Henry training at the gym. It's one of my guilty pleasures and a perk of the job—getting an eyeful of his ripped body, as his muscles strain, and his olive skin glistens with perspiration from a hard work out. But it's mostly witnessing him in his element.

Chapter Two

Meghan

I haven't stopped all day. The gym has been heaving with members, and my classes have kept me busy. But it hasn't stopped me from going over the current situation with Clara, and I know just the person who might be able to help. As soon as my last client leaves, I shower and change, making my way to Ethan's. I have an idea it's probably crazy, but if anyone will understand, it's him.

My mind wanders to Ethan and the vivid memory of him dumping me. I was completely blindsided. It was the same night that ended his career and left him in an induced coma. I visited him every day, praying he'd be okay. Henry had called after he woke, saying Ethan wanted to see me. I couldn't help but hope that he'd admit that breaking up was a mistake, and that he wanted me back.

But of course, he didn't.

Ethan still wanted to be friends. Nearly losing him made me put things into perspective, and if that meant only having him in my life as friends, then so be it. We were friends before we started dating, and I had naively thought it would be easy to step back into the friendship zone, but I'd been so very wrong.

I ring the doorbell and bounce on the balls of my feet.

Janet, Ethan's mum, smiles wide when she opens the door.

"Oh, honey, it's been weeks. How are you?"

She leans in for a hug and then steps aside, waving for me to enter.

"I'm good. Work has been keeping me busy. Is Ethan home?" I ask as I toe off my trainers.

She nods. "He's out in the conservatory. Can I get you anything to drink, love?"

I follow her through to the kitchen. The smell of something in the slow cooker assails my senses, causing my mouth to water.

"No thanks, I'm just going to see Ethan."

Janet smiles as I pass her to open the conservatory doors. "Well, if you change your mind, help yourself," she says, going back to her stack of paperwork on her kitchen table.

Ethan is engrossed in something on his laptop as he types away with rapid precision without even having to look at the keys. I thought he was skilled in fighting, but this is on a whole other level.

His hair has grown out since I last saw him, even though it was only a fortnight ago. Entering the conservatory, I pull the sliding door closed behind me.

Ethan glances up, pulls his earbuds free, and moves his laptop to the table as he stands.

"Megs."

His smile is so wide, showing his brilliant white teeth. He opens his arms and pulls me in for a hug. I don't hesitate as I step into him, and he wraps me tight in a hug.

I breathe in his scent of fresh soap and white musk. And it's hard not to get lost in the nostalgia of being in his arms.

"I've missed you," I admit, unable to stop the words from spilling from my lips.

He kisses the top of my head—the gesture so familiar—before he steps back and clears his throat.

"Same, I was beginning to think you'd been avoiding me," he says.

I shake my head, but he's not entirely wrong.

"Of course not," I lie.

"So, what is it? What's going on?" he asks, searching my face.

I bite my lower lip. "It's a little complicated. Have you got time to talk?"

He arches an eyebrow and shakes his head at my question. "I always have time for my favourite girl." His fingers slip between mine and he leads me to the sofa.

If that were true, things would be very different right now. My stomach feels uneasy.

"Yeah, right," I say, unable to keep the sadness from my voice, trying to avoid his searching gaze.

His forefinger lifts my chin until we make eye contact. His other hand is firmly in mine.

"Don't... Don't do that."

"Do what?" I ask, licking my dry lips—Ethan's eyes following the action. I swear I see something in his expression.

"Act like you aren't one of the most important people in my life."

My heart stutters and my palms begin to sweat, but thankfully, he lets go of my hand, pulling me into his side. But I'm not sure if that's better or worse.

"Sorry," I say as my thoughts momentarily shift to Henry, but before I allow the guilt of our one indiscretion to rear its ugly head, I squash it back down.

"Don't be. Now, what did you want to talk about?"

I let out a deep breath before speaking.

"It's Clara."

He tenses and I move, so we're facing one another.

"Is she okay?"

I shake my head. "No, I need your help." Chewing my lip, I wonder if this is a bad idea. Maybe I should leave him out of this?

"Talk to me," he says, his voice coaxing. His fingers thread through mine like an anchor, but I can't ignore the all too familiar zing of electricity and heat that courses through me. Is it just me, or is it stifling hot? I reach for the zip of my hoody and he lets go of my hand. It's impossible to ignore the way his eyes dance over my face, his gaze so affectionate, as I slip out of my hoody. But if I thought it would help, I was sorely mistaken because when his fingers skate across my skin to move the hair off my shoulder, my stomach summersaults with desire.

Chapter Three

Henry

Olly successfully dodges my strike as we spar, and I amp up my game. He might not fight professionally, but he's quick on his feet. It reminds me how I need to bring my A-game for this upcoming fight. It's the biggest of my career to date, with more at stake than just winning. It's about taking down that son of a bitch, Emilio. I've heard the saying about there being a thin line between love and hate, yet I never quite grasped it until he betrayed me by sleeping with my girlfriend, Clara. I loved her, and he knew it. He was practically family, and we grew up together.

But what he did to Ethan, ending his career, it brings out a rage I never had before. It courses through my veins like lava.

I will do everything in my power to win this for Ethan.

But I know I need to keep my head in the game one hundred percent, no distractions… or should I say distraction… Meg.

She's my kryptonite. No matter how hard I try to appear indifferent around her, it's fucking impossible. And there are so many reasons I need to keep myself in check where she's concerned. Her working here doesn't help matters; seeing her every day and trying to ignore my physical reaction towards her.

"Umph."

I'm knocked onto my arse—hard—and air whooshes from my lungs.

I shake my head. "Fuck."

Olly winks, bouncing from one foot to another, and I can't even be mad at him. I had it coming.

"What the hell, H? Get your damn head in the game," Nathan shouts, throwing a towel at my face.

I'm fucking embarrassed. The way Olly just took me down was an amateurish stunt, and yet, he got one over on me. I can't let this shit happen. I need to keep my head clear and my mind on the fight.

"Want to go again?" Olly asks.

I shake my head. "Nah, I think I'm done for today," I reply, holding out my fist for him to bump. He nods, wiping the sweat from his brow.

Nathan hands me my water bottle and I take a gulp.

"Hey, man, what's with you today? You need to stay focused."

I click my neck.

"I know, and I will."

"Good."

He pats my back hard and then sends me to go shower. I need to remind myself why so much is riding on this fight.

When I arrive at my mum's, she smiles and mollycoddles me the moment I step through the threshold. I pull her into a bear hug, engulfed by orange blossom and vanilla, her bold signature scent. She's always worn the same perfume ever since I can remember.

"Henry, I know you're busy training, but I hardly see you anymore. Once a week isn't enough," she chastises.

Guilt swamps me. Of course, she's right, and yes, my training has a part to play, but it's not the only reason, not that I'd admit that shit out loud.

"I'm sorry, Mum, you're right. Is Ethan about?" I ask.

She nods her head towards the conservatory and I kiss her temple and make my way through the kitchen.

Pausing my hand on the handle, I peer through the clear glass. Ethan is saying something to Meg as she undoes the zip of her hoody and shrugs out of it, leaving her in a tight-fitting T-shirt. My eyes flit to him; maybe its adrenaline from the sparring still waning through me, but it gets my back up the way he studies her face like that, his lips stretching into a smile as he reaches out and pushes the hair off her shoulder.

I stamp down the feeling and slide the door open. Meg's beautiful grey eyes rise to mine, and her smile fades. She leans away from Ethan, but his hand on her shoulder tightens.

"What can I do for you, brother?" he asks.

I swear he's smirking. "Does there have to be a reason for me to visit?" I reply, crossing my arms.

"Nope," he replies, popping the 'p.' His eyes going back to Meg, mine follow, and that's when I notice her neck.

"What the fuck is that?" I ask, stepping forward. I clench my fist to stop the overwhelming urge to reach out to her.

Her hand automatically goes to her throat. Ethan's eyes follow her movements, and I see the exact moment he notices.

"Meghan?" he questions, his voice firm.

She stands, along with Ethan, as he gently takes hold of her elbow. Her eyes dart to the door—the one I'm blocking—and I cross my arms and stand a little straighter.

"It was a misunderstanding, okay?" she says, staring back at Ethan.

"Then, by all means, do tell," he says.

"Fine. If you must know, Emilio accosted me outside the

toilets at Rattlers. He didn't like it when I turned down his advances. He has the twisted impression I want him, and that I only see Clara and Jacob to get closer to him."

Ethan's posture goes rigid, but his touch is gentle as he brings his hand up, his fingers skimming over her bruised skin, causing the light dusting of hair to rise on her arms.

"He's a cunt nugget," Ethan says, gritting his teeth. "No one touches you like that. I'm going to kill him." His tone is heavy and laced with anger.

She reaches for his hand and gives it a gentle squeeze, lowering it as she does. A silent conversation, one I'm not privy to, passes between them. I hate how their exchange makes my stomach roll with jealousy.

"No, you won't. I'll kick his arse in the ring. If anything will fuck with his ego more, it'll be losing to me." Emilio will pay for laying his hands on her, and I'll make damn sure of it.

Ethan is about to rebuke my response when Mum brushes past me, clapping her hands together. I didn't even hear the slide of the door.

"Are you both staying for tea? There's plenty," she asks. Her eyes are passing between Meg and me. Either she's unaware of the tension, or she's choosing to ignore it.

"I could eat," I reply, breaking the silence.

"What about you, Meghan? I can't remember the last time you stayed and had dinner with us as a family."

I can. It was the weekend before Ethan's last fight.

"Are you sure?" Meghan asks.

"Of course, I made plenty. I'll go dish it up."

And before Meghan can respond, my mum is already back inside faster than a whippet.

"This conversation isn't over," Ethan says just as his phone chimes. "Sorry, I need to take this." He releases his hold on Meghan to take the call. He steps out onto the patio, leaving us alone. She shifts uncomfortably, bouncing on her heels. For a brief moment, I see her vulnerability, the same as the night

Ethan dumped her. Gone is the confident woman I'm used to seeing at the gym.

But just as quickly, it's gone. She clears her throat and brushes past me, leaving a floral fruity apple fragrance in her wake.

I fucking hate apples.

I help set the dining table. We've had it since I can remember. Ethan and I even carved our initials into the wood. I glance over to him as he bumps his hip with Meg, causing her to let out a small chuckle, and it's a stab straight to the gut.

Once we're seated, our plates full, we dig in, and I inhale the smell of the buttery garlic bread. While we eat, there's a strained palpable atmosphere which my mum tries to make up for, and it works too. They're quickly chatting up a storm.

I glance at Meg and watch how she holds the stem of her wine glass, almost regal, her long fingers so elegant, with short nails painted in a pastel shade. Ethan says something, and she lets out a laugh, covering her mouth with her hand, and the sound goes straight to my belly. Her fair skin is now flushed pink, highlighting her cheekbones.

The way her long hair rests over her shoulder, makes me want to reach out and touch it to see if it feels as soft as it appears. Her current hair colour reminds me of ravens, both dark and luminous. Her eyes sparkle—bluer than their usual grey—as she talks about the young self-defence class she's been teaching so passionately. Her eyes have always changed colour depending on her mood.

She's animated using her knife and fork as she eats and talks intermittently. I've never noticed how someone eats until now, but I think I could watch her eat every night and never get bored.

"I saw your last post on Instagram," says Mum as she cuts into her food, interrupting me from my appraisal of Meg. "It already had well over ten thousand likes."

"Yeah, it's blowing up," I reply with a shrug.

The truth is… I never expected to become a social media influencer, but with the sponsorships and the fighting, it goes hand in hand. I'm blown away by the number of followers I have, and lucky for me, Nathan is good at helping me organise my content.

Who would have thought that me holding a protein shake would get so many likes?

Ethan says something to Meg and she lets out a laugh, and it's hard not to stare. She covers her mouth with the back of her hand—cheeks flushed. I almost forget myself and smile until Ethan rests his hand on her arm, and it's like a sucker punch to the gut. I swallow hard.

The way he touches her is intimate, familiar. And of course, it is, they were in love once.

Hell, I'm pretty sure they still are.

But Ethan ruined it. He threw her away like she was nothing.

And for what?

I stab at my new potatoes with more vigour than necessary.

"So, Henry, how's training going?" Ethan asks.

I look up, my eyes stopping where his hand still rests on her arm.

It takes me a few seconds longer than necessary to swallow my food before answering, "It's fine."

And then I concentrate on finishing my food.

"Come on, no need to be so evasive. I won't have a meltdown talking about your training."

Dropping my cutlery to my—now—empty plate, I look up.

"Never said you would. Training is training."

He and Meg exchange a look, and I push my chair back, the legs scraping against the tiles. I take a deep breath once I'm in the confines of the kitchen and busy myself putting my stuff in the dishwasher.

Ethan approaches me from behind. I know it's him from the sound of his bare feet as they hit the tiled floor. And it only irritates me more.

"What the hell is wrong with you, H?" he asks, carrying in the rest of the plates and nudging me out of the way so he can get to the dishwasher.

"Me? What's wrong with you?"

He straightens and faces me. Ethan has never been one to shy away or back down, least of all from me.

"Maybe I don't like the way you are with Meg."

Slamming the dishwasher door shut, he crosses his arms, one eyebrow raised.

"What is that supposed to mean?"

I lean in a bit closer.

"Leading her on for one thing."

His pupils dilate, and his jaw ticks. "You don't know what you're talking about."

"Oh, don't I? You dumped her, you left her. And yet, you still fucking touch her like you have some claim over her. What the fuck?"

The scent of apples catches my attention, and I smell her before I see her.

Meg clears her throat, and we both turn in her direction. Her cheeks redden as she focuses on Ethan.

"I need to make a move. I'll speak to you soon," she says.

He steps forward, whispering something I can't make out before kissing her on the cheek. She turns and leaves without even so much as a goodbye or a glance in my direction.

Shit. I hate this.

Chapter Four

Meghan

Adrenaline pumps through my veins as I start the engine. What the hell was that all about? And where does Henry get off making assumptions about Ethan and me, for that matter? I drive and try to make sense of it all and pull up to a red light, waiting to pull onto the dual carriageway, when my phone alerts me to a message from Henry.

Meg, can you come to mine so that I can explain?

Is he serious?

Bubbles appear, followed by another text.

Please?

Someone beeps me in the car behind, causing me to startle, and I look up to see the lights have turned green. Dropping my phone in the cupholder, I pull away, hitting the accelerator a little harder than intended, causing my wheels to spin on the tarmac.

I chew on my lip. Either I go and let him explain why he felt the need to give Ethan shit, or I carry on allowing this awkwardness to grow between us.

Go, let him say what he has to say and leave.

He has an important fight coming up, and I need to be there for Clara. It's not like either of us have time for anything else. I mean, it was one time, one damn kiss, on a night that changed everything, but the memory is so vivid.

Ethan asked me to see him right before his fight, and I thought it strange he never has before. Maybe he was nervous; this fight is a big deal and holds so much more weight with him going up against Emilio.

But what I wasn't expecting was him to dump me.

He blindsided me. His words were ringing in my ears as I tried in vain to get my words to form a coherent sentence. It's near on impossible, even more so when I've always thought him out of my league and couldn't understand why he was with me.

This though, I did not see coming.

How can he say both he loved me and that it's over in the same sentence?

He just dumped me and walked out of the changing room without a backwards glance. Leaving me standing there with my heart in my throat, like he hadn't just turned my world inside out.

I don't know what to do. Do I go home?

My dad would get suspicious. I just need to pull myself together long enough to get out of here without drawing attention to myself. Everyone will be busy watching the fight anyway. I grab a handful of tissues from the box on the side and blow my nose.

"Meg, I was looking for…"

For a millimetre of a second, I thought it was Ethan, turning to face him, but he and Henry have a distinct difference to the baritone of their voices, and maybe deep down, I'd hope he'd come back and tell me he had made a mistake, which makes me cry harder.

Henry is in front of me in two strides, his eyes grow a darker shade of brown as he scans my face frantically.

"What's wrong? What's happened?"

I shake my head and then try to answer, but it comes out as a choking sound.

He pulls me to his chest and wraps his arms around me.

"Are you hurt? Talk to me," he says, his tone pleading.

"Eth... Ethan broke up with me," I say on a strangled sob against his shirt.

He pulls back, his eyes wide, running his hand through his short dark hair, causing it to stick up in places.

"He did what?"

But I can't bring myself to repeat the words out loud. It's too raw.

I go to move away from him, but he pulls me to him again. How is it I fit so perfectly wrapped in his arms? Because they're twins, you stupid idiot.

They're not the same. They are mirror twins, yes, but they couldn't be more different. Even his aftershave is distinct. He smells like oak and hazelnut.

He rubs my back in a soft circular motion as I cry—his touch is so warm. When my breathing calms down, I pull away and try to sniff back my tears.

I raise my eyes to meet his, and I see something reflected in his I haven't seen before, something akin to longing.

No, surely not?

His calloused palms cup my face as he uses his thumbs to wipe at my tears.

I swallow, trapped in his penetrating gaze, unable to look away as he dips his face towards mine.

And then I feel the faintest whisper of his lips graze the side of my mouth, and I turn into the touch... and then we're kissing.

A rush of air escapes me as he pushes me into the metal lockers behind me. His body pressed against mine; I feel him everywhere. He moves a hand to the back of my head and fists my hair, tilting my face, claiming me as his own.

And for a few moments, I am completely lost to him. He is my centre of gravity, holding me together, and nothing exists beyond the two of us.

I don't know who pulls away first as reality comes crashing in around us. The sounds beyond the closed door grow louder as spectators cheer and clap.

Henry can't even look at me. I see it written all over his face, a pained *expression, and it speaks a thousand words but what stands out most of all is*—*regret.*

I park outside his house and switch off the engine, but I don't see his car when I look around. I'm tempted to leave, but when I stare into my rear-view mirror, he's already pulling up behind me. And I know I can't go without talking to him first.

He rushes over to me as I get out of my car.

"I didn't think you'd come. You didn't reply," he says.

I clear my throat. "I was driving. Maybe this is a bad idea," I admit.

He shakes his head. "No, it wasn't, and you're here now. Come in so we can talk."

"Okay, but I can't stop long." Sometimes I think my dad still sees me as a teenager. I need to move into my *own* place. I can't stay at home forever.

His hand hovers at the small of my back before touching me and ushering me forward, and I wish I could say it didn't give me butterflies, but I'd be lying.

I'm acutely aware of everything he does, from unlocking his door and allowing me to enter first, the way he fills the hallway, and his scent invading my senses to the point of intoxication. And I'm transported to the night of the kiss and how he felt beneath my palms.

I realise he just asked me something, and I completely zoned out.

"Sorry, pardon?"

His lips curve into a smirk. "Did you want a glass of wine?"

Biting my lip, I nod my head.

"Just a small one."

Following him into the kitchen, my eyes stray to his arse, and I quickly avert my gaze to what he's doing instead. His actions are so confident and self-assured as he pours us both a drink and passes me mine, tilting his head towards the back door.

"Shall we talk in the garden?"

I nod, unable to find my voice. Instead, I take a large sip of wine and follow him outside. Nothing about this place has changed. I used to spend so much time here with Ethan before the accident and always felt so comfortable before, but now I feel like an intruder.

"Where's Nathan?" I ask as he sits down on the grey rattan U-shaped sofa and pats the space next to him. Nathan is Henry and Ethan's cousin, but they're more like brothers.

"Helping out Lacey, something about boy trouble."

I can't hide my snort. "Isn't he usually the one causing the trouble where his sisters are concerned?" He's the youngest of three older sisters, but anyone would think he was the eldest.

"Yep, but this time she asked for his help," he says with a smile, his dimple prominent. Where Henry's is on the left, Ethan's is on the right. I can't help but notice their differences. And then I look away. It's not like I'm comparing the two.

"So, why did you ask me to come?" I ask, bouncing my knee restlessly.

Henry might train at the gym where I work, and we see each other often, but this is the first time we've been alone since that night. And I'm grateful to be holding the glass. I wouldn't know what to do with my hands. Being here alone, I feel exposed, more vulnerable.

"To apologise about what you overheard between Ethan and me."

I nod and finger the stem of my glass as he continues, unable to relax.

"I just hate how he gives you mixed signals."

I fix my eyes on him with a frown. "Mixed signals how? We're friends."

He raises an eyebrow. "Well, he touches you like you're more than friends."

I want to roll my eyes. Ethan has always been tactile, even before we started dating.

Secretly, I think maybe I crave the contact, even though I'd never admit it out loud—and least of all to him or Henry.

"Well, if we are, then it's news to me," I reply. Ethan doesn't want me, not anymore. "Why do you even care?" I ask, unable to ignore the curiosity clawing its way free.

"Because I saw first-hand how you were after he dumped you. How he broke your heart."

I lean back and shake my head. He went there. So he can talk about Ethan dumping my arse, but not the kiss the two of us shared? Moving to my feet, I place the glass on the coffee table, and my hand trembles ever so slightly. The birds are chirping up a rave in the trees overhead.

Why are they so damn happy?

"Yeah, well, he's not the only one to ever hurt me," I reply, stepping around the table. "I need to go."

Henry reaches for my hand, sending heat up my arm and through my entire body as he pulls me back and ushers me to sit. His knee bumps mine, causing my scalp to prickle, and I hate my torturous body for reacting to him.

"Meg, come on. I'm sorry... You deserved better then; you still do."

Do I, though? Maybe Ethan was right to dump me. I was never good enough for him.

Henry reaches out and wraps a lock of my hair around his forefinger.

"Believe me when I say I don't ever want to see you get hurt again." He trails his fingers at the base of my throat, where the bruise from Emilio still lingers.

"And as for Emilio, he won't get away with this," he says.

I let out an audible gasp. The pad of his thumb circles my skin, sending a pool of warmth deep in my lower stomach. His rich, honey brown eyes grow a shade darker, more hazel brown and I'm suddenly caught in a moment where everything around us begins to fade.

He leans closer and dips his head, his intentions clear.

"Don't," I whisper. "If you're going to kiss me and then punish me for the indiscretion afterwards, please don't."

I'm at war with myself, the push and pull of wanting to run and needing to stay.

"It was never my intention to punish you." His voice dips an octave.

My hand moves to his chest, ready to push him away—his heart is racing a rapid staccato beat that matches my own under my touch.

And then he makes up the distance, claiming my mouth with fierce abandonment. This isn't like the kiss we shared before. This is full of longing and want. I'm vaguely aware of him lifting me until I'm straddling his lap, drowning in his embrace. All conscious thoughts disappear as I move to my knees, taking his face between my hands—liquid fire courses through me. My entire body is blazing like molten lava. His hands cup my backside, holding me against him, and I moan into his mouth.

A car door slams in the distance, and whatever bubble we were just in explodes as he draws back, breaking the kiss, our ragged breathing the only sound I can hear.

"We can't," he says, squeezing his eyes shut.

And the heat I'm now feeling has nothing to do with the pleasure from mere seconds ago. I scurry off his lap and jump to my feet.

"Sorry," he says, and I hear the sincerity in his voice, but I can't bring myself to look at him.

"I need to go," I say, my throat thick, my voice hoarse.

This time he doesn't try to stop me. There's an echo of him saying something under his breath to my retreating back, but I can't make out his words. My head is thumping and my heart is racing as I rush through the house without a backwards glance. I am reprimanding myself for allowing it to happen *again*. How could I be so foolish?

Chapter Five

Meghan

Today is my day off, so thankfully, I didn't need to worry about running into Henry. After last night, I'm just not ready to face him. Things are awkward enough already.

I have no problem finding somewhere to park. I pull down the sun visor and check my reflection. Even the concealer isn't enough to hide the dark circles under my eyes. Taking a huge breath, I lean over and grab my bag from the passenger footwell.

Here goes nothing.

I've arrived a little early to meet with Ethan, so I'm not surprised to see he's not here as I glance around. The bar isn't overly busy for this time of day, and the ambience is chilled and relaxed. Soft music plays from the speakers overhead as I approach the bar. Spotting a familiar face, I smile when he glances up.

"Hey, Smeggy," Olly says as he steps up and leans over the bar to greet me with a kiss on the cheek. I have to stop myself from rolling my eyes at his use of my nickname, and if it were anyone else, I'd probably take offence.

"Are you ever going to let that nickname go?"

He winks. "Nope, never."

I perch on one of the stools at the bar.

He taps the top of the bar with his fingertips, slinging a dish towel over his shoulder.

"What's your poison?" he asks.

I chew my lip. "Umm, a cranberry and lemonade, please."

Olly prepares my drink, glancing up, his eyes curious. "So, what brings you here?" he asks.

"I'm meeting Ethan," I reply.

"Oh, a hot date?" he asks, winking as he drops a slice of lemon in my glass before sliding it towards me. I pull out my card, but he waves it away.

I lean over to grab a straw, shaking my head. "No, Oliver, it's not a date." He knows better than anyone that Ethan dumped me.

Taking a sip of my drink, the bite of the cranberry followed by the tang of the lemonade is refreshing. Olly watches me, evaluating me, his eyebrows furrowed.

"What is it?" I ask, placing my glass on a coaster.

He begins drying a glass. "You've not been yourself lately. Is everything all right?"

I tense a little, hoping he doesn't notice. "I'm fine, just a lot going on."

He lets out a sigh, and I think he knows that's the most he's getting out of me. His lips form a straight line as he leans on his elbows and gets eye level with me.

"I know I've been a bit preoccupied lately, but I'm always here for you, you know that, right?"

It's hard not to suppress my grin. "Yeah, I have noticed. Rachel's hot. You tapped her yet?"

He flicks me with the tea towel. "Behave. It's not like that."

And it's true. Olly's a flirt but not a womaniser. He's not

frivolous with women, never has been—it's like he keeps them at arm's length.

"Like what?" I ask, feigning indifference.

He blows out a puff of air and glances around the bar before answering. "We're friends. I like her," he says with a subtle shrug, and I swear the tinge of red spreads over his cheeks, causing me to sit up straight.

"Hold on, you like her, like her?"

Olly looks away, but I see how he's trying to suppress a smile before glancing back. "Something like that, but you're deflecting... we were talking about you," he replies, his face growing serious.

Being an only child and the youngest of our group growing up, they've always looked out for me, but sometimes, it's a bit suffocating.

"It's just girl stuff," I reply, hoping he backs off.

"I know a lot about girls," he retorts.

I snort out a laugh. "Ha-ha, hilarious, Romeo." I sip my drink and peer over my shoulder.

Where is he?

Looking back to Olly, his face is serious. "I wasn't trying to be funny. Stop being so mysterious. I know you, Meghan. Besides, I thought we were friends," he says, laying it on thick.

"Of course, we are, and don't give me that look."

He holds up his palms. "I was doing no such thing..." He cuts off mid-sentence and smiles over my shoulder. "E, my man."

Ethan stands beside me, his palm going to the small of my back, and holds out his other fist to Olly, who bumps it with his.

"Hey, man. Meg, you good?" Ethan asks as he leans in and kisses my temple. I suppress the urge to inhale his scent.

I clear my throat, holding up my glass. "Do you want a drink?" I ask.

Olly swats me with the tea towel *again*. And this time, I do roll my eyes.

"Hey, that's my job, Smeggy. E, what can I get you?"

"Just a coke, thanks, man."

Olly's movements are effortless as he prepares the drink. He's always so self-assured in everything he does. I envy that about him. He slides the glass towards Ethan and looks at me as he speaks.

"So, you here to find out why this one has gone all secret squirrel on our arses?"

Ethan laughs. The vibration rumbles through his palm and onto my skin, causing me to flush.

"It's why I'm here," he says, giving me a wink.

I swat his shoulder as Ethan pulls out his wallet.

Olly cocks an eyebrow. "Fuck off, man," he says, waving away the note Ethan extends towards him. Ethan shakes his head in response, shoving it back into his wallet, slipping it back into his jeans pocket.

"Thanks, man."

"Yeah, well, I barely see you. It's the least I can do."

Leaning back on my stool, I spot a table over in the corner and tilt my head in its direction.

"Go on, I get the hint," Olly says with a lopsided grin.

"Not funny," I reply, standing. Ethan already has our drinks in hand and follows me over to the table.

Sitting down, Ethan places down our drinks and sits next to me.

His shoulder brushes my arm and I let out a shiver.

"You look different. Has something else happened?" he asks, turning to face me, his knee knocking mine.

And my mind goes straight to last night and my kiss with Henry. I try not to fidget when I reply.

"No, nothing."

He leans away a fraction, his knee no longer touching

mine, and I let out a breath. But his eyes study me, and I wonder if my tone gave me away.

"Okay, so what's going on with Clara?"

I pull my lip between my teeth and his thumb comes up, pulling my lip free.

"Talk to me."

I take a deep breath. "I want you to help me get her away from Emilio."

His jaw flexes at the mention of the guy who ruined his career. There was a time when we were all friends. Hell, we were more than friends; we were family. But the dynamics changed. When Emilio became more popular in the MMA circle, so did his ego and attitude. The tipping point was when Clara cheated on Henry with Emilio.

I'm the only one who is still close with her. I disagree with what she did and told her as much, but when she fell pregnant, there was no way I was turning my back on her. Her flaws and bad decisions don't define her. She knows she fucked up, but I also know she doesn't regret having Jacob.

Ethan clears his throat, but his eyes remain dark when he speaks. "So, she's finally come to her senses and decided to leave the prick?"

I nod and reach for my glass, stirring the ice with the straw.

"It's not safe for her and Jacob," I say hushed. My eyes scan the bar, paranoia settling over me, and I shiver, bringing my hand to my throat. "I mean, look what happened to you." And Ethan is—*was*—a trained fighter.

The tension radiates off him in thick waves, but when he reaches for my chin and tilts my face to make eye contact, his touch is gentle yet firm.

"Is he hitting them?" he asks, his jaw flexing,

I reach up and take his hand in mine. It trembles under my touch.

"Her, yes. Jacob, no, not yet."

"But it's only a matter of time, isn't it?" He clenches his fist.

I nod and swallow the thought that makes me want to throw up.

"What do you need me to do?" he asks.

An audible sigh escapes me as relief washes over me, knowing I'm not in this alone.

"I want you to help me get them away from him. I have an idea, a night when I know his sole focus will be elsewhere, but I'm not too sure of the details."

He tilts his head, and then his shoulders slump as he begins to put the pieces together.

"You want to do it the night of the fight."

I nod, and my heart squeezes. No one knows me the way he does.

Letting go of my hand, he runs his fingers through his hair. I prefer this length; it suits him.

"Does Henry know?"

His question surprises me.

"No, of course not. Besides the less he's involved, the better." I bite my lip. "It's why I need your help."

"Henry isn't a fool. He'll figure it out."

It's irrelevant. This isn't about Henry.

"Maybe, but he already has enough training for this fight with Emilio." I don't miss the way Ethan's body goes rigid. It's bad enough Emilio is the reason he'll never fight professionally again, and now Henry will be the one facing off against him. His ex-best friend, the one who also ruined his relationship with Clara… it's so fucked up.

I wrap my arms around my middle, worrying my lip. What if the same thing happens to Henry?

"Hey, it's going to be okay. We'll work this out."

Emotions work up my throat, and I silently let my tears fall.

Ethan leans closer and his big strong hands cup my face as

he wipes my tears with his thumbs. I lean into his touch, close my eyes, and try to steady my breathing. The soft murmurs of the other patrons and the music fade into the background as I savour his embrace.

His lips press against my forehead before he pulls me to his chest, and I wrap my arms around his back. I bury my face into the crook of his neck, relishing the comfort of being in his arms.

"Thank you," I whisper, not even sure he can hear me until he replies.

"You don't have to thank me. I've got you, always."

I tense as guilt washes over me and I suppress the urge to cry again.

"It'll be okay, you'll see," he says, kissing the top of my head. I already lost him once... I can't lose him again. Even if this is all we'll ever have, he means too much to me. And I know I don't even deserve this much.

Chapter Six

Henry

Jase is standing outside the main doors when I arrive. He smiles wide and holds out his fist.

"Hey, man, long time no see," I say, smiling.

He lets out a deep laugh. "Yeah, the baby has been teething. She's like a bear with a sore head."

"Sorry, I can't help, I know fuck all about kids," I reply, and then I get that deep sinking feeling when I remember that might not have always been the case.

"Even after our third, neither do we, man."

Jase used to fight professionally but retired after a knee injury and now runs a security company. He still frequents the gym for workout sessions. It's how he knows Olly and who got him a contract working security.

Something catches his attention, and he pats me on the back as he steps past me. I peer over my shoulder to see a young guy getting a little handsy with a girl who isn't interested.

I wait for a beat to see if he needs my help, but as usual, Jase's presence alone is enough to make most men turn to jelly.

I walk into the bar; passing groups of people and couples milling about. It's still reasonably quiet, but something niggles at me as my eyes roam the room and land on Ethan and Meghan.

Unable to break my line of vision, I continue to stand here like a plank as I take in the sight of my brother and Meghan embracing. He has her wrapped up in his arms, whispering into her hair.

What the fuck?

I've never been a jealous person… until now… until her.

My pulse begins to race and my head pounds. I grit my jaw and clench my fists, but what can I do? She's not mine, but she's not his either.

"Fuck," I curse out loud, gaining attention from a couple at a nearby table.

I shake my head and turn on my heels before I do something foolish. No way can I bear witness to whatever that was. I only popped in to chat with Olly and run something by him, but it can wait. This is awkward on a whole new level.

Jase looks confused when he sees me leave but says nothing as I call out "bye" over my shoulder and make a hasty retreat.

What the fuck is going on? Meg and I shared something last night. And now what? They're back together?

I find myself back at the gym and hope Nathan hasn't left already. I let out a frustrated sigh until I spot him talking to some girl I've never seen before. He sees me over her shoulder and pauses as his eyes rake over my face. Leaning in, he says something to the girl and walks towards me, eyebrows raised.

"What the fuck is the matter with you?"

Sometimes I hate how intuitive he is. I prefer him when he's playing the clown.

"I just saw Meg with Ethan," I grunt out.

"Right, and your point?"

I clench my fists. "I didn't like it," I admit.

He smacks me hard on my shoulder. "Of course you didn't. Because you're into her and too much of a pussy to do anything about it."

He crosses his arms, feet apart. Is he seriously baiting me right now?

"Fuck off. He's my brother. And he's still in love with her," I whisper-shout, getting in his face. Nathan doesn't even flinch or withdraw. Sometimes it worries me, he has zero fear factor, and I'm not just talking about with me, I mean with anyone.

"Oh, okay, and you were just talking when I came home last night. I'm not an idiot, Henry. She left pretty fast after that. Were you thinking about Ethan then?"

I reach out and grab his T-shirt, yanking him towards me. He barely blinks as he pushes me off, and I release my grip, running my hand through my hair.

I need to get a hold of myself. I pinch the bridge of my nose, trying to rein in my temper. Fuck, I don't get like this —ever.

"You're a hypocrite and a fool, H, and maybe, dare I even say it, a martyr."

Nathan is one of the most laid-back people I know, yet he's not holding back even one iota right now.

"Damn, tell me how you really feel."

His stance relaxes. "Listen, I've got your back. You're my cousin and best friend, but so is Ethan. Hell, you're my brothers. But what's happening now is a fucking shit storm and you either both need to let the girl go, or you need to let her choose who to be with and get it all out in the open."

He rests his hand on my shoulder. Sometimes I don't understand him at all—coming from a guy who has never had a serious relationship, yet here he is, giving me relationship advice.

It's far from simple, and this whole situation has me

second-guessing myself. I worry deep down about whatever I feel for her; this overwhelming and agonising need will either vanish or consume me, and then what? It's all for nothing and will result in me hurting both Ethan and Meghan. I care about her—I always have.

And then Clara started paying me attention. Ethan told me to watch my back with her. Even though she was our friend, there was something about her he didn't trust. I was weak. She stroked my ego and wasn't afraid to come after what she wanted—me.

And yes, I was hurt when she cheated on me with Emilio because I loved her. I wouldn't have done that to her. We had our problems. No doubt we would have broken up eventually.

I shake my head and let out a loud groan.

"I need to focus on this upcoming fight, nothing more."

Nathan doesn't say anything in response, only nods in understanding.

"Right now, I just want to spar. No more talking. You game?"

"Of course," he replies to my retreating back as I make my way to the changing rooms to pull some training gear from my locker. I grit my teeth the entire time, ready to let off some steam.

When I join Nathan, he's warming up—or more like giving the other gym members an eyeful as he flexes his muscles. If I were in a better mood, I'd take the piss out of him and give him shit, but I don't have it in me.

"Headgear," I say as I pull on my gloves.

Nathan nods in understanding. With my training, I need to stay focused. It's why I've tried to avoid whatever is brewing between Meg and me.

I go in hard, and Nathan moves. He's always been quick on his feet, but I'm also fast; he gives me a cocky grin, goading me.

Breathing, I try to relax and find a comfortable boxing

stance, watching Nathan pivot, and then I attack, throwing a punch on an exhale.

Punch, exhale, repeat.

But I'd be lying if I said my mind didn't wander. If Ethan hadn't dumped Meg right before the fight, would the outcome have been different? Was his head not entirely in the fight? I could never understand why he didn't wait until after. It's something I've never asked.

We never spoke about the part he played in the break-up. I don't even know to this day what possessed him. When I saw how upset she was, I wanted to be the one in the ring with him to knock some fucking sense into him.

But then, when I saw the way he went down, seeing him not moving... I wished it were me in that damn ring. It took everything in me not to go after Emilio right there and then.

I thought Ethan being in an induced coma was the worst part, but when he did wake up, there was something different about him—he was more guarded. Our relationship shifted; he lost a part of himself that night, and in return, so did I. It's why no matter what happens, I intend to make Emilio pay. He's going down, one way or another.

Chapter Seven

Meghan

I've been staring at my phone for the past hour. I tried calling Henry, but it rang out. I get it, he doesn't want to talk, but the last thing we need is more awkwardness between us.

"Just text him already," I say to my empty bedroom.

I think we should talk, clear the air.

There, that's to the point, right? He can't keep ignoring me. Hell, he trains at *my* gym for crying out loud.

Ten minutes pass, the message shows as delivered, and it annoys me. He's read it and is choosing to ignore me, very mature.

Glaring at my phone, I drop it to my bed.

I stomp to my bathroom, strip out of my clothes and step into the bath. Emotionally drained, I let out a sigh and immerse myself under the cotton candy bubbles.

I don't understand why Henry is ignoring me. He ended that kiss, not the other way around. And yet, it's all I can think about. The first time we kissed was something else, but this time, it was more.

My stomach flutters to life and I clench my thighs together, wondering what the rest of him can do, but I shake the thought away. He doesn't want his brothers' sloppy seconds, and yet, he's kissed me twice now.

I touch my lips and try to ignore the fact I have this raw need that courses through my entire being when he kisses me. So different to the kisses I've shared with Ethan. I drop my hand, hating myself for the comparison. What is wrong with me?

After my skin begins to prune and the water becomes cool, I get out, dry myself, and dress in my sleepwear. I check my phone and I'm enveloped in disappointment—still no reply.

And now I'm getting angry.

The least you can do is text me back if you don't have the guts to take my damn calls!

I am pressing send before I talk myself out of it.

I refuse to play games, and I hate that I'm chasing after him when it's clear he doesn't even give a shit about our friendship. His silence speaks volumes.

Deep down, I had hoped what I felt for him was indeed reciprocated. And not an out of reach infatuation and mindless fantasy. My phone vibrates on my chest, and I wish I had some self-control.

And say what, Meg? That I fucked up, again? That I crossed a line, again?

I sit up, my fingers moving across my phone at double speed.

So what? You'd instead stick your head in the mud like a damn flamingo?

I close my eyes and lay very still, tapping my right forefinger to the back of my left hand—something I've always done ever since I can remember. I don't even know why I do it as I breathe in and out.

My phone vibrates again—this time, I pause before reading the message.

Like you, you mean? I saw you with Ethan!

What does that have to do with him ignoring me?

Bubbles appear, so I wait to see if he's sending another message.

He tries to hide it, but I see the way he still looks at you.

I squeeze my eyes shut, heat builds behind my eyelids, and before I can stop myself, I cry. Because no matter how much I wish things were different, they never will be, and it hurts to think I may never have the chance to open up to Henry—without fear of reprisals.

And what is that supposed to mean? Do you know what, just forget it. It's bad enough you ignored me, and now you're making me feel like shit. Thanks!

I hold the button on the side of my phone and slide right to power off. I need to face facts and get over whatever weird infatuation this is. Acceptance is a motherfucking bitch, but the sooner I do it, the better.

Reaching for the remote, I turn on my radio. The volume is down low and late-night love songs is the station I listen to when I'm feeling melancholy, which seems to be often lately. It somehow makes me feel better, knowing I'm not the only one listening, that somewhere out there are others feeling alone.

I'm not an idiot. I'm not heartbroken. It's not like I can grieve something I've never had, and yet, I find myself mourning it nonetheless.

Henry

The temptation to launch my phone across the room is very real right now, but I don't need shit from Nathan if I break the damn thing.

She's not wrong; I did ignore her calls. I'm a bastard. Why would she even want to talk to me? And what do I do? I tell her I saw her with Ethan, stalking her like a damn sociopath. Which isn't even the case, but now she knows, and I must look like an even bigger arsehole.

It's just... seeing her in his arms like that, after we kissed was too much, too soon. And yet, where do I get off? She's not even mine.

Fuck it. I bring up her number and dial, but it goes to voicemail.

I grind my jaw so hard my back molars are likely to fall out.

Anything I text her now will be a moot point. I know I fucked up *again*. I tried to put our first kiss down to shock, stupid as it sounds, but when I saw her in that state, I just wanted to comfort her. We never spoke of it afterwards, not with everything that happened to Ethan.

It was the guilt which consumed me, and not so much that I'd kissed her but that I'd kept it from Ethan, and yet, I didn't owe him a damn explanation. He made his choice. And that's what grates on me when I see him pawing over her, giving her mixed signals and leading her on. I need to come clean, tell him and be done with it; let me be the bad guy, but it wouldn't just be my fallout, would it?

I can't be that frivolous with Meg's feelings.

She deserves better.

She always has. I send her one last text.

I'm sorry x

Chapter Eight

Henry

I grunt as I lift the weight over my chest and hold it. Meghan never messaged me back. I let my jealousy get the better of me and did something I never wanted to do—hurt her. The last thing she deserves is my hostility.

Nathan takes the handle and places it back on the bar, and I sit up, snatching up the towel and patting my face. A noise catches my attention over and the low music coming from the speakers. Some guy narrowly avoids a dumbbell landing on his foot, clearly distracted, and I follow his line of sight to see what—no... *who* has drawn his attention—Meghan. Who just so happens to be mid-stretch, bending over, causing my dick to twitch.

I drop the towel to my lap. *Down, boy.* Meg stands and sees the man watching her in the mirror, and even from here, I can tell she's pissed. She turns her entire body towards him and props her hand on her hip, eyebrow raised, staring him out. My eyes scan back to him; he waits for a beat but soon looks uncomfortable, grabs his bottle of water, and turns towards the running machines.

I can't help but let out a snort, proud of her for holding her own. Why should she back down when he is openly appraising her like a slab of meat? *Bloody bellend.*

Nathan raises an eyebrow and I ignore him as I get back to my set, but my focus is now split between my workout and sneaking glances towards Meg. She's not once looked this way, and I wonder if it's intentional or if she hasn't seen us. But when she has to bypass us to go to the rowing machine, I know for a fact she's blatantly ignoring me—something she's never openly done before.

A weight settles in my gut. *Fuck.*

I'd be lying if I said it didn't hurt.

It wasn't fair of me to throw Ethan in her face as I did, but lately, my mind has been consumed with memories of those two stollen kisses. And how they aren't enough. I can't keep denying our sexual chemistry. Maybe we should find a way to explore whatever this is between us? I want her. But not at the expense of hurting Ethan.

I go into my routine hard as I try to push away my thoughts.

"Hey, man, I need to go pick my sister up. You good?" Nathan asks.

I nod. "Yeah, I'm almost done for the day anyway."

I move onto the dumbbells for the next twenty minutes but stop when I see Olly coming downstairs with Rachel on his heels.

Wiping my face, I finish my water before going over.

"Hey. Well, aren't you a sight for sore eyes," I say, smiling at Rachel.

"Why, thank you," Olly says, fluttering his eyelashes, causing me and Rachel to let out a laugh. "I'm going to set out the mats," he says to her, leaving us alone.

"So, you and him?" I ask, flicking my thumb over my shoulder, noting the blush is spreading up her throat and across her cheeks.

"A lady doesn't kiss and tell," she replies.

"I don't doubt it. Well, if you ever change your mind or he fucks up, I'll be happy to step in."

She rolls her eyes. "I don't think you could handle me," she says.

I clutch my chest with mock hurt. My scalp prickles, and I know when I glance behind me, I'll see Meg. She's talking to Olly with her hand on his arm. And there it is again, a wave of jealousy. I shake my head and turn my attention back to Rachel.

"Oh, I think I could handle you plenty," I reply smoothly, but her expression is one of amusement, and it's clear the only guy around here she's remotely interested in is currently whispering to the one girl I can't get out of my damn mind.

Rachel is quick with her retorts, and I like how she can hold her own, not backing down from a bit of banter, and I'm pleased for Olly, he deserves to be happy—maybe I do too?

Olly claps his hands behind us, gaining our attention.

"Okay, Rachel, you ready?"

She slaps me on my bicep and goes over to join him and Meg. Intrigued, I follow.

I hear the wariness in her voice when Olly asks if she's ready to spar, and I have the urge to help put her at ease.

"It'll be fine," I say.

Meghan's posture goes rigid before she begins to move on the balls of her feet.

"Are we doing this or what?" There is a hard edge to her voice, which is foreign for her, and Olly notices.

"Easy, Rocky," he says, keeping his tone light, but I also hear the underlining warning.

While he helps Rachel with her gloves, I give Meghan a curious look and mouth, "You okay?"

But she ignores me and stares at her feet.

Maybe I deserved that.

I move off to the side of the mat with Olly as he calls out

verbal instructions. I join in with a few of my own too, as we watch Meghan and Rachel spar.

An overwhelming scent of a pungent perfume hits my nose, and I have to restrain myself from groaning just as Melissa approaches.

Fucking marvellous.

Olly greets her with a smile, whereas I say nothing, but it's not lost on me how she's pushed her chest out. I keep my eyes level with hers as she mentions her yoga class and something about a downward dog. But I just want her to go away. Peering over my shoulder, Meghan catches sight of Melissa, and her eyes turn into slits as she focuses back on Rachel.

Melissa clutches my arm and leans in to whisper in my ear, drawing my attention back to her.

"If you want to get down and dirty again, I'm game," she says.

I shake my head. "I'm training," I say under my breath as if it's a get-out clause. We had a one-night stand—one being the operative word—and yet, she always comes back asking for more.

"Well, think about it," she says, strutting away.

Olly gives me a look and laughs, but I shake my head.

Chapter Nine

Meghan

I've felt Henry watching me when he thought I wouldn't notice. It's hard to ignore him when I get a visceral feeling in my gut whenever we're in the same room together. Even before I see him, I sense him.

Olly's concern over me is sweet, he's always been like a brother, so it wasn't lost on him when he found me staring at Henry as he openly flirted with Rachel, and I'm sure it's innocent enough, but it didn't stop the punch to my gut at witnessing it.

And I'm aware this is only light sparring. Olly had been teaching Rachel self-defence when I asked if she'd like to spar with me sometime. She seemed surprised that I'd ask, so I was pleasantly surprised when she took me up on the offer. I'd like to get to know her better; apart from Clara, I don't have many other female friends.

I show Rachel how to hold her stance. This is what I'm good at and what I love. She's nervous, I can tell, but soon enough, she'll feel more confident. This is about teaching her to better her reaction time and enhance her skills. Olly and

Henry both call out a few instructions, but I think it's more for Rachel's benefit; I am, after all, a trainer.

"Extend your arm and fist like this, then follow it with a kick like this." Showing her the motion—the punch Olly has undoubtedly already taught her—I add in a kick for good measure, and I have her do the same. She picks it up quickly, mirroring what I'm doing.

"That's it, just like that," I encourage. She smiles as we continue.

"Now, let's add a combination of offensive moves like this and defensive ones like this." Again, I show her a block and an attack, twisting my body.

"Wow, you're a good teacher," she says, her breathing a little heavier now.

I smile. "Thank you. You're a quick study. Now, keep doing that and try to anticipate when I come at you next."

She nods, her face full of concentration as I throw a light punch and she reacts with one of the defensive moves.

I glance over to Henry and Olly, noting how they've quietened from only moments ago, to find Melissa practically thrusting her breasts into Henry's chest, and it makes me feel sick to my stomach.

Rachel comes at me, but I sidestep her, my eyes springing back to Henry just as Melissa goes on her tiptoes, whispering in his ear. My heart hammers in my chest, and it's nothing to do with the sparring. It's just white-hot rage. Why do I even care? I turn and extend my fist toward Rachel, but I already know I'm too close right as my fist makes contact with her face, and she drops to the ground with an oomph. *Shit.*

Olly drops to his knees, coaxing Rachel into consciousness as I tear off my gloves and make a mad dash to the kitchen for an ice pack. I can't believe I just did that. Pushing down my tears, I rush back to Rachel. Olly has her sitting on a bench, accessing her face as I pass him the pack. He's livid and has every right to be. I could have seriously hurt her. Fuck, I probably have. So much for building her confidence.

I can't even bring myself to look at Henry if his reaction is anything like Olly's.

"Oliver, give me a second with Meghan," Rachel says, and I expect him to argue, but instead, he gets up and walks past me, and I don't miss the scowl on his face.

"I am so sorry, Rachel. Are you okay?" I ask, my voice cracking.

She smiles but cringes. She's going to bruise.

"I'm fine. You really do pack a punch," she says, and I know she's trying to make light of what just happened.

"You have every right to be angry with me. I'm annoyed with myself. I'm so sorry," I say.

She gently touches my arm. Her other holds the pack to her cheek.

"Accidents happen. I'm fine, Meghan, honestly," she says in a nurturing tone, and I wonder if she's the same way with her daughter, Molly, knowing how lucky she is to have a mother like Rachel when mine couldn't leave my dad and me quick enough.

I rest my elbows on my knees and stare at the floor. This needs to stop. I need to get my shit together. Denying how Henry makes me feel affects me in the workplace—somewhere I cannot afford another distraction. Maybe I just need to be forthright with him, put my happiness first for a change. I don't want to lose Ethan, but if things don't change between Henry and me, I fear losing him anyway, so what choice do I have?

Olly comes over and gently pulls the ice pack away from her face as I stand and watch their exchange.

"I am sorry, Rachel," I say one more time and then walk away. I can hear Olly giving her an ultimatum, the walk-in centre or his, and I sigh in relief when she says his.

What the fuck was I thinking? I wasn't, and that's the

problem. How Rachel was so gracious after me knocking her out is beyond me.

I'm a trainer. I know better.

It was meant to be light sparring, not throwing a hard enough punch for her to go down. She wasn't even wearing headgear.

I sit down in the empty kitchen and cover my face with my hands.

Shit.

"Meghan?"

Henry is the last person I want to see right now; I can't even look at him.

"If you're here to tell me that I fucked up, I'm well aware, Henry."

I sense his warmth before his fingers wrap around my hands, softly prying them away from my face. He crouches in front of me, his eyes roaming my face.

"I'm not," he says. "I know it was an accident."

"Oh, you do, do you?" My voice rises.

He lets out a heavy sigh, which makes me feel worse.

"I'm sorry, I don't mean to be a bitch to you. I'm just humiliated. I could have seriously hurt her, and my dad will freak if he finds out." I struggle to mask the croak in my voice. I will not let myself fucking cry.

"Olly won't say anything. You know he won't."

He's right. Olly is trustworthy, but this is different; he cares about Rachel, and I wouldn't blame him for outing me.

"I don't know what the fuck is wrong with me," I say, but it's a lie.

He squeezes my hands, and it's only now I notice he never let go.

"You know I'm not interested in Melissa, right?"

I draw back a fraction, but he holds firm, keeping his eyes fixed on mine.

"You don't have to explain yourself to me. You never have

before," I retort, and maybe it's a dig over the fact he never once tried to talk to me after our first kiss and then proceeded to avoid me after our second.

He grabs the back of an empty chair. The legs scrape against the floor as he drags it in front of me. His knee brushes against mine when he sits, sending an unwelcome flutter to my lower stomach.

"No, and just like then, I'm handling myself wrong, and I'm still doing a piss poor job of it even now."

One of his hands moves towards my face. His eyes search mine, and then he brushes his thumb, sweeping it over my cheek, causing me to let out a soft gasp into the quiet of the room.

"This isn't a game to me," he says, pointing between us. "I'll have to talk to Ethan if we have any chance of whatever this is between us going any further. But I need to know you're over him. I want to be sure that when you're kissing me, you don't wish it was him."

I cringe and pull away, getting to my feet. He does the same.

"Is that what you think?" I ask, crossing my arms.

His fingers run through his hair, and he eyes the ceiling before they land back on me.

"No, I mean… Shit… I don't know."

I shake my head; it will always come back to the fact I've been with Ethan.

"I need to go," I say, and before he can say another word, I rush past him. I keep my head cast down until I get to the changing room. I grab my stuff from my locker, foregoing a shower, eager to put distance between me and the gym, grateful today is indeed my day off. And that's another thing —I need to get another job somewhere else.

I drive with no real destination in mind until I'm idling along the curb and come to a stop and switch off the engine.

Deep breaths.

Staring at my mum's house, I wonder why I'm even here. I won't get out of the car. I never do, but once I found out where she lived, I was curious.

I've seen her a couple of times from a distance; she's even glanced my way, but I don't think she recognised me, or if she did, she was impervious to me.

I was twelve when she left us, no note or even a goodbye. She never even sent me birthday cards.

I don't understand how a mother can do that—leave their child.

My phone signals a notification. Leaning over, I locate it from the bottom of my bag.

A message from Henry.

I'm sorry x

This is ridiculous. We aren't even together, not really, and yet, when I saw Melissa flirting with him, it set off a trigger. I never felt jealousy like this with Ethan—hell, I've never felt jealousy at all. But this, it's not a healthy fucking reaction. How can he consume me so quickly?

Does this just prove Ethan was right to dump me?

It's a sour admission and one I don't wholeheartedly believe.

But when Henry kisses me, it's with reverence, it's all-consuming, everything else around us evaporates, together we implode, and all my thoughts disintegrate.

And yet, I can't deny that when Ethan woke from the coma… if he had told me that he had made a mistake, I would have taken him back in a heartbeat. He was—and still is—like a security blanket. I feel cared for when I'm around him, even now when we're no longer together. But it's becoming abundantly clear I don't get to keep them both.

If I do this, the thread holding me to Ethan won't just be frayed. It will be severed.

Chapter Ten

Henry

Meg never replied to my last text, and honestly, I can't say I'm surprised. I stayed at the gym until they closed—it's not like I had anywhere else to be. My social life is pretty shit between training and events, unless Nathan forces me out or has an impromptu house party.

When I pull up on my drive and climb out, I notice a figure on my doorstep they move and set off the motion sensor, so they are now cloaked in a halo of light. I see its Meg. I let out a deep breath as I approach her, worried she'll bolt at the earliest opportunity like a scared kitten.

She moves to the side, allowing me to unlock the door. I flick on the hallway light when I step inside and glance over my shoulder, tilting my head, gesturing for her to come in. I dump my gym bag on the floor and head towards the kitchen. The sound of the front door closing, followed by the soft padding of her footsteps, lets me know she's right behind me.

I swallow before turning to face her. She places her bag on the kitchen counter and wraps her arms around her middle.

It's as though she's attempting to make herself shrink, which is ridiculous with her being about five-foot-six.

She bites her bottom lip, her eyes bouncing around the kitchen before clearing her throat.

"Where's Nathan?" she whispers, her voice a little hoarse.

"He's helping my cousin move her stuff back to my aunt's house. He's staying there the night."

"Oh," she replies, her eyes meeting mine. Hers are red-rimmed and puffy.

My chest tightens. "Shit, Meg, have you been crying?"

She doesn't answer me, and my gut twists. "Come here," I say, opening my arms.

I hate that she hesitates before relenting and making up the distance between us. Her scent invades my senses as I pull her to my chest. Something about holding her in my arms and her being in my space settles me in a way I rarely feel.

I stroke the ends of her hair between my finger and thumb.

"I'm sorry, Meg. What I said about you, about Ethan… I never meant to hurt you," I whisper into the quiet of the room. The only other sounds are from our breathing and the electric buzzing coming from the fridge.

"Is that what you think? Do you believe I'd do that?"

I shake my head. "No, but you loved him." And there is a part of me that thinks she might still love him, and if she had the choice of him or me, I honestly don't know who she'd pick.

"Yes, and he left me." Her eyes glance over my face before meeting mine again. "But when I'm kissing you, it's just you and me. No one else."

She rubs her hands softly over my back, and my spine tingles from her touch.

"I'm terrified of whatever this is between us. Ethan is still my best friend. I don't want to hurt him, and if this goes wrong, it could end badly for all of us." Her admission is one I've thought about too, and it's a real possibility.

I squeeze my eyes closed. The last thing I want to do is hurt them. I know our relationship will be nothing like the one she had with Ethan. And yet, there is a part of me that would do anything for this woman. We are inevitable.

Drawing back, I glance down at her face, which is etched with worry. She's so conflicted. All I want to do is comfort her, ease her mind, promise her everything will be okay, and yet it's a promise I have no power over. I lean down and pause, inches from her mouth.

"Tell me what you want…"

She licks her lips, her throat rolls as she swallows, and I can't help the reaction I have towards her at this moment.

"You," she replies in a breathy whisper.

My heart skips a beat as I crash my lips against hers and a gasp escapes her, but as soon as the surprise wears off, she opens up to me, and I am a charged wire. She is the one who lit the fuse, and my entire body thrums with satisfaction.

I pull her closer to my body and try to slow down the frantic kiss, barely able to think straight while intoxicated by her taste and her soft, satin lips.

Our breathing is heavy when I find the willpower to draw back from the kiss, but my hold on her doesn't ease.

"If we do this, there's no going back. It can't be undone," I say, my gaze focused on her. If she wants out, there's still time for her to change her mind. For me, there is no going back.

"I know," she replies, her eyes vulnerable. She bites her bottom lip to still the quiver. "But I'm tired of fighting this."

I breathe a sigh of relief and can't hide my smile because the feeling is mutual.

"Me too," I admit, and I've never been more grateful to Olly for his suggestion of these spotlights in my kitchen until now. The way they're shining down around her highlights her radiant skin.

"Do you have any idea how beautiful you are?" I ask.

Her pupils dilate, and I take great delight watching the way her cheeks begin to heat. She shakes her head with a roll of her eyes. But before she can respond, I cover her lip with the pad of my index finger. And then I slowly run my finger down her chin, tracing her throat until I reach her chest. I can feel the rapid beat as I flatten my palm over her heart.

"Here... this right here is what attracted me to you. Your heart, your loyalty, the way you look out for the ones you care about."

Her breathing grows heavier and she goes up on tiptoes, her mouth connecting with mine with abandonment.

I grab her under the arse and she wraps her legs around my waist. Her lips trail a path over my jaw and down my throat. I thrust into her with a grunt.

Her fingers dig into the back of my neck.

"I want you," she says, her voice sexual and unrestrained.

I'm pretty sure something between a groan and a growl works its way up my throat. She bites my open mouth like a seductive temptress, and damn, it's enough to make my knees go weak. If anyone has the power to bring me to my knees, it is indeed this woman.

Her lips move to my neck. Her tongue sweeps over my flesh before she takes me in her mouth, marking me.

Meghan grabs my lower lip between her teeth and bites down. A thrill explodes through my entire body. She traces my lips with her tongue, pausing to kiss me softly—the craving I have for her increases with every stroke, every nip, every breath.

When she pulls back, I look into her eyes; they're full of the same desire that is no doubt reflected in my own. And now it's my turn to take over from her exploration. I grip her hair in my fist and tilt her face, giving me perfect access. Her mouth opens with a gasp as I take the lead and kiss her with soft, gentle strokes.

She shifts in my arms, causing welcome friction between us.

I rut against her, and she rewards me with a soft moan. My fingers sneak underneath her top, where I trace patterns up and down her spine. She shivers, her heartbeat pulsing in her throat as I pepper soft, wet kisses down to her cleavage. She unhooks her legs from my waist, her palms pushing against my chest, her touch searing. There's no way she can't feel how rapidly my heart is racing.

"Sit," she says, her tone a command.

I look over my shoulder at the high back, cream leather dining chair and drag it out.

Intrigued to see what she does next, I sit like an obedient puppy, keeping my eyes on her as she sinks her teeth into her bottom lip before stepping forward and straddling my lap.

I grip her arse firmly, pulling her to my arousal.

Her hands roam over my torso as she grips my top, pushing it up, baring my chest before she pulls it off and drops it to the floor.

She lowers her head, her lips meeting my bare flesh, her tongue sweeping from my throat to my nipples. She moves off of me as she kisses along my happy trail, hooking her fingertips into the waistband of my jogging bottoms. She tugs and I lift my arse off the seat as she pulls them down my thighs and off my legs.

My erection strains through my boxer briefs, pre-cum evident through the material. I reach down and cup myself hard. She moves my hand and grips the elastic before lowering them—my dick springing free.

On her knees, her eyes meet mine, and I'm caught in her web, unable to look away. She licks her lips, and before I have the chance to take a breath to prepare myself, she wraps her fingers around the base of my arousal and squeezes.

I reach down, placing my hand on the top of her head as she artfully begins kissing my arousal, her tongue working its way to the underside, moving up and down my shaft in light, gentle kisses. She familiarises herself with my size before her tongue darts out, licking my entire length from tip to base.

And damn if I don't go weak in the knees when she begins gentle flicks over my frenulum with the tip of her tongue. It's a torturous dance back and forth, up and down, slowly creeping her lips up and over my head and then backing off. I let out a deep groan. The heat from her mouth has my dick throbbing with anticipation.

It takes everything in me not to beg her to slide it deep into her mouth.

"Fuck," I hiss through clenched teeth, thrusting into her mouth.

Her fingers move to the underside of my balls, and I can't stop the feral sound which escapes me. I fist a handful of her hair but allow her complete control. She hollows her cheeks and takes me into the back of her throat, and gags, but she doesn't slow her assault. She works me into a frenzied state of helplessness.

I should tell her to slow down, to stop doing that thing with her fingers, but as her movements intensify and she speeds up, I throw my head back, squeezing my eyes shut.

"Shit, Meg," I say, tightening my tangled grip of her hair, driving her closer, spurring her on. The sounds coming from her as she takes me to the back of her throat have me at her complete mercy.

"Fuck, I'm going to come," I growl, and I swear I feel her lips tilt into a smile.

A raw and powerful sensation builds at the back of my spine, a white thunderclap explodes behind my eyelids as pleasure shoots through me, and I empty myself into her mouth and down her throat.

Chapter Eleven

Meghan

I'm irrevocably intoxicated by Henry. The texture of his skin against my tongue. The heady scent of his arousal, not to mention the sound of his pleasure as he calls out my name while I milk him for every drop of his orgasm.

My knickers are dripping wet from being so turned on by him. Maybe I should be embarrassed, but this is right where I want to be. Not thinking about tomorrow or the repercussions of what we're about to do.

I want to open myself up to him. Allow him to consume me. To feel the aftereffects of him being inside me—to know he wasn't some unattainable wet dream.

Wiping my mouth, I lean back and look up and over his rigid torso. My fingers dance over his thighs, and his—now—semi-hard dick twitches from my caress.

My scalp tingles when he releases his grip from my hair. He opens his eyes and stares down at me, his lips slanting into a lazy smile. A look, one I've never seen from him before, something private, just between the two of us. He sits forward, drawing my attention to his chiselled abs when they tighten with the movement. Reaching down, he grabs my upper arms and pulls me into his lap.

"Too many clothes," he says in my ear before his tongue darts out, eliciting a gasp from me. He pulls my top up and over my head, his fingers tracing the sensitive skin at my sides, and I'm unable to contain my giggle.

"Ticklish," he says, his tongue sweeping along my clavicle. "I look forward to exploring every fucking inch of your body and finding your most sensitive spots."

He grabs my hips and lifts me like I weigh nothing, his biceps bulging when he gently places me on my feet. His fingers dip into the material of my leggings, pulling them down along with my knickers. I hold onto his shoulders as I step out of them one foot at a time.

The chair scrapes loudly behind him as he stands. I'm naked, except for my bra, until he reaches around with a quick, deft flick of his fingers. He slips the straps down my shoulders, allowing it to drop to the floor with a soft flourish.

He lavishes me with his eyes—a long perusal of my body—making my insides squirm in anticipation. And it surprises me how my first instinct isn't to shy away from him or try to cover my body. I'm still learning to accept compliments when they come my way. When he said I was beautiful, I felt a mix of emotions.

I'm no longer the chubby girl I once was, and now with my job, my body is a focal point. And yet, my insecurities are still there. I'd be lying if I said I was no longer self-conscious. I'm more than what you see on the surface.

But the way he's staring at me so unabashedly, with his semi-hard erection between us still glistening from my mouth moments ago, has my nipples hardening.

Reaching out, his calloused hands grip my hips as he picks me up, pulling me flush against him. He pivots and sets me down on the kitchen table. I gasp, the surface cold against my bare flesh, causing the hairs on the back of my neck to rise.

He swings the chair in front of me and sits, his palms on my thighs, spreading my legs. I grip the edge of the table in anticipation.

I moan as he teases my entrance with his fingers, sliding them over the wetness of my folds. My breathing grows heavier, my arms shaking from the contact. Then, without hesitation, he glides a finger and hooks it inside me. I arch in response with a soft moan. His other hand is reaching up and pinching my nipple between his thumb and forefinger.

Fuck.

When his thumb plays with my clit, I huff out a moan of pleasure.

I bite down on my bottom lip when he inserts another finger and scissors me open, spreading me wider. The sound of my arousal is evident as he pumps them deep inside me.

Seeking more friction, I move into his touch, riding his hand harder.

And just as I'm getting lost in the sensation, he pulls them free.

"What the fu…" But before I have the chance to protest my discontent, his hands dip underneath my arse, and he pulls me forward in one quick motion. The air rushes from my lungs in a loud whoosh, his face aligned with my centre.

He blows onto my wet flesh, and my entire body shivers.

Oh my fucking God.

His tongue flattens and then swipes over my perineum right before he plunges it into my pulsing channel.

I arch into him, one hand on his shoulder as the other grabs his hair, and I throw my head back. His fingers dig into my arse almost painfully.

"More." I pant. My voice doesn't even sound like my own. My legs wrap around his shoulders, and my hands grip the table for leverage as I gyrate in his face.

Sliding a hand between us, I work over my clit, but he

stops me, slapping it away with a tutting sound and replaces it with his own.

His touch is so much more explosive.

I'm dripping wet, too consumed with chasing my orgasm to give a shit.

"Yes, Henry, right there, please."

He fucks me with his mouth until I'm calling out his name. My orgasm is ripping through me in mind-blowing waves. He drags my body onto his lap, so I'm straddling him, and his lips find mine. There is something erotic about tasting myself on his tongue.

Henry gets to his feet, knocking the chair to the floor with a loud thump—my legs still wrapped around his waist. I move my mouth to his throat, licking the sheen of sweat as he carries me upstairs and into his room, kicking the door shut behind us.

He lowers me to the bed, the scent of him on his sheets engulfing me, and I sigh in satisfaction. He releases my legs, and I scoot up the bed as he hovers over me, his hard length fully erect between us.

"I need inside you," he groans, leaning down to take a nipple into his mouth while palming my other breast.

He continues lower, his tongue making a path over my abdomen. My lower stomach pulsates with a heavy need. I grip his hair and tug him back up.

"I want you *now*," I say as his eyes meet mine, the colour so dark in this light that my desire for him intensifies.

And as if to drive my point home, I sit up, grab his hard length and move it up and down his shaft; at the same time, I begin to finger myself, arching my back into the palm of my hand.

"Fucking hell, Meg. You're killing me," he says, digging his teeth into his bottom lip.

My eyes follow him as he leans over to the bedside table, pulling open the drawer and fumbling inside.

"Shit," he growls.

He moves away further, and I let go of him and pause, touching myself as he digs through the contents of the drawer frantically. Then he sighs in relief, pulling out a condom. "Thank you," he says, his eyes going heavenward. I can't help but laugh.

He sits back on his haunches, his erection bobbing from the motion. Snatching the foil packet from his fingers, I move to my knees, ripping it open with my teeth. His pupils dilate as he watches me. Taking him in my hand, I give him three firm strokes. He exhales loudly, his eyelids fluttering closed as I slide the condom down his erection.

Positioning myself, I straddle him so the tip of his shaft is at my opening. Slowly, I ease onto him, holding my breath until he's fully sheathed inside me.

"Oh my God, finally…" I groan.

His warm honey eyes cast down, staring between us. Now connected, I wiggle a fraction, allowing myself to accommodate his size. Even turned on and wet, he's fucking packing.

I circle my hips and throw my head back, his hard length consuming me with an ever-growing need.

His hands dig into my hips as he lifts me and then pulls me back down in quick succession. I feel him everywhere. He leans forward, peppering soft kisses over my chest and up my throat, gripping my face, plunging his tongue into my mouth.

Shifting onto his knees, he lays me down, his weight bearing down on me in the most fulfilling way. My legs wrap around him and I press my heels into his arse, urging him on. As he pounds into me, my whole body moves with the motion.

"Faster," I say on a heavy breath, my nails scraping down his back—they're not long, but they'll likely leave a mark.

"Look at me," he grunts out.

He holds my stare, his eyes full of lust and wonder as he claims me with every thrust.

"Ah, right there, fuck me, harder, Henry."

I'm not usually so vocal, but I want everything he has to give me and more.

He smiles like the devil himself and hooks one of my legs in the crook of his arm.

"Ahhhh."

My orgasm is right on the precipice, ready to be set free. I writhe underneath him, desperate for the wave of release to consume me, but I also want to ride it out for as long as possible.

His lips come down to my neck, where his teeth nip the skin.

"Come for me," he grunts.

And just like that, I detonate, unable to hold back my muffled curses from the intense wave of pleasure that assaults every single nerve in my body.

I've never come like this, not during intercourse—never like this. He tenses and rears up deep inside me as he follows with his drawn-out release.

My hot channel is pulsing around him, wringing him out until he collapses on top of me. His weight smothers me momentarily before he rolls onto his side, with him still inside me, both of us breathing heavily.

When my vision returns, he's staring at me with a content expression, and his eyes sparkle with a weightless gaze. This man is beautiful. He leans forward and kisses my nose. The moment is so tender, I swallow back a sudden onslaught of emotions.

Slowly, he pulls out of me to dispose of the condom. I reach over the edge of the bed to retrieve my clothes, but they're not there. My cheeks heat as my self-consciousness tries to take over, but I push it away. Strong arms wrap around me, and Henry pulls me flush against his chest. He's still semi-hard, but it's the warmth and security of being in his embrace that makes all my insecurities vanish.

I feel like I've come home.

I relax into him as he manages to pull the duvet over us both.

"Will you stay?" he whispers.

I peer over my shoulder, his lips meeting mine for a slow and gentle caress.

"Stay?" he asks again.

I roll over, so we're facing, and I nod. "Yes."

He lets out a contented sigh and snuggles me closer.

"Good, because I'm not finished with you yet," he replies, his voice deep and full of promise, eliciting an excited flutter in my lower stomach.

Chapter Twelve

Henry

Meg's eyes drift closed, and I know she's asleep from the soft sound which escapes her slightly parted lips. Is it selfish of me, hoping it's just a quick nap? I'm in no way finished exploring her body. I'd be lying if I said I hadn't imagined what it would be like to be with Meg. And yet, having her naked in my arms is more than I ever could have envisioned. Meg pulls her arm free, causing the duvet to slip, exposing her torso.

I take my sweet time as I study her features, the double curve of her upper lip—Cupid bow. I recall Clara commenting how she wished she had her lips. I googled it one night after Clara and I had split up, telling myself I was just intrigued. It's where the upper lip resembles the bow of Cupid, the Roman God of erotic love. And that was the first time I touched myself while consciously thinking of Meg.

I run my fingers through her ebony locks before lightly tracing the dusting of freckles that covers her nose and cheeks as the crescendo of her breathing calls to me like a siren.

Cool air licks my bare flesh as the mattress dips beside me. I turn my head and see Meg angled away from me, as she types into her phone. I rub my eyes and check the clock on my bedside table to see its just after ten.

I reach out and stroke my finger down her spine. She shivers and peers over her shoulder.

"Everything okay?" I ask, my voice rough.

"Yeah, just had to message my dad," she says.

I roll onto my side and lean on my elbow, watching as she places her phone face down on the bedside table before laying back down facing me—her finger tracing over my abdomen. My dick twitches and she bites her lip as it thickens between us. I shrug. What does she expect? I've longed to have her like this in my bed for so long.

"Do you regret it?" she asks, vulnerability evident in her voice.

"No," I say, and it's true. "You?"

She shakes her head. "No, not even a little bit," she replies, licking her lips.

My stomach groans, distracting me from where my mind was about to wander.

She smiles at the sound.

"Are you hungry?" I ask, stroking my finger over her soft cheek.

"Yeah, I could eat."

I kiss the tip of her nose before getting out of bed. Grabbing myself a pair of boxer briefs, I pull them on, tucking my semi-hard cock inside. If I weren't ravenous for food, I'd be balls deep inside her, with her hair wrapped around my fist.

Shaking away my chain of thought, I toss her a T-shirt and she holds it to her chest.

"I'm just going to use the bathroom," she says, pointing over her shoulder. I nod and head downstairs, giving her some privacy.

I pull out a container, shove it into the microwave, grab

some cutlery, and place it on the table. The sound of her bare feet on the tiled floor draws my attention, and I have to stifle a groan. The T-shirt comes to a stop mid-thigh—her legs are long and toned, and it's hard not to be distracted by the dark red polish on her toes. This woman is heat and sin.

Her cheeks flame red when she looks past me at the table, and I don't think I'll ever be able to look at it again without thinking of how I had her perching on the edge as I feasted on her wet pussy.

"Leftovers okay?" I ask, clearing my throat.

She nods, her eyes following me as I move over to the fridge and grab us both a bottle of water, passing her one. Her eyes watch me as I drink mine.

I drop the empty bottle into the recycling bin. "I was thirsty," I say, winking.

Her laugh echoes as she puts her bottle down and then pads softly over to the cupboard to retrieve some plates. I love how comfortable she is in my space.

Or should I say *our* space—when Ethan, Nathan, and I all moved in together, Clara and Meg helped us, saying it needed a woman's touch.

She leans forward, placing a plate on the table, the T-shirt rising, and I stifle a groan.

"Do you want some wine with your pasta?" I ask to stop myself from taking her from behind and bending her over the damn table.

"Please," she says.

I pour her a small glass. I'll have to replace the bottle. It's for when Nathan has his "lady friends" visit. I grab myself a beer.

She takes the offered glass from me.

"Thank you," she says before taking a sip. Turning her back to me, she places it on a coaster. I can't resist this time, and I grab her from behind, pulling her to my chest.

I kiss the top of her head, the scent of coconut and sex engulfing my senses, the smell intoxicating.

I let out a groan as she wiggles her arse into my erection.

"Later," I say with a groan, and that's a promise.

I rest my chin on her shoulder. "I can't tell you how many times I've imagined being with you, like this."

She turns her face towards me, inches from my mouth, her eyes questioning.

"I never would've guessed. You always manage to act so indifferently around me."

And she's right, of course, but it didn't come without effort.

"I was trying to protect myself… and you," I reply honestly.

She lets out a soft sigh. "I understand, but it stung. Especially after our first kiss. You never spoke to me about it. You and Ethan both hurt me that night in equal measures."

I feel a twinge deep in my gut, and I hate myself. But I thought I was doing the right thing by not talking about it and pretending it never happened.

"I'm sorry, I thought I was doing the right thing denying my attraction towards you and the way you make me feel."

I lean in and give her a soft kiss; I refuse to deny myself.

"So, what changed?" she asks, her eyes back on me. "Why are you now giving into whatever this is between us?"

And fuck me if that isn't a loaded question.

"Seeing you with Ethan at my mum's," I admit with a cringe.

"Oh my God. You were jealous!"

She tenses and tries to pull away, but my arm around her stomach holds firm.

"Yes and no. It was more than jealously. It was fear. Fear you'd get back with Ethan, and that I'd never get my chance to be with you. You should have been my first choice."

Meg shakes her head. "But he dumped me, remember? And he's never insinuated us getting back together. Not once."

I turn her to face me, bending my knees a fraction, so we're eye level.

"Meghan, you have no idea, do you?" I cup her face. "Ethan is still in love with you. He's my twin, I see it, even if he's in denial, which makes me even more of a prick for pursuing you."

She lets out a small rush of air, her eyes widening from my statement, and then the microwave beeps aggressively.

I turn my back on her, pulling out the container, and the steam burns my fingers.

"Shit," I hiss.

"Even if that's true, we've crossed a line now," she says. "And what do you mean, I should have been your first choice?"

"When I chose Clara over you."

"Then why did you?" she asks, and I hear the hurt in her voice. I hate myself, but the truth is that I was only trying to do the right thing.

"It's complicated. There are things you don't know."

I carry the container to the table and spoon a large heap of pasta onto each plate.

"Then tell me," she says, sitting down. I move my placemat and sit opposite.

"The closer I am to her, the more distracted I'll become."

She gives me a wounded look.

"Don't look at me like that. If I sit next to you, there'll be no talking. All I'll want is to have your legs spread eagled for me as I eat your pussy, *again*."

She swallows hard, and her cheeks heat before she focuses on her plate. I watch as she blows on her pasta, moaning as she wraps her mouth around the fork, savouring the taste.

"Not helping," I grunt, adjusting myself.

"Sorry, but your mum's pasta bake is my favourite."

I take a massive bite of mine, burning the roof of my mouth in the process.

"How do you know she cooked it?" I ask, feigning hurt.

Meg points her fork in my direction, raising an eyebrow. "Because you can barely make an omelette," she replies, shaking her head.

I clutch my chest, but she's right, of course.

We both eat in silence, but the conversation I started is heavy in the air.

"Are you sure you want to know about Clara?" I ask, still giving her an out.

Her eyes rise to mine, and she nods.

"It was a drunken one-night stand, the first time we were together… we both knew it too."

Meghan scrunches up her nose and drops her fork, pushing her plate away. I slide it back and raise an eyebrow, and then stab at my pasta, taking a bite before continuing, urging her to do the same.

"And then, about six weeks later, she came to me in a panic. She'd missed her period."

Her jaw drops, and I know what she must be thinking.

"And before you judge me, it wasn't like that. We used protection, but the condom split, and she was on the pill, so we thought she'd be okay." I clear my throat. My palms are clammy. "I couldn't let her deal with it on her own, so I did the only thing I could think to do. I asked her to be my girlfriend."

Meg's sitting up straighter now. "What? She never told me she was pregnant."

I shake my head. "We wanted to wait until she was twelve weeks before we announced it, and then we miscarried. I couldn't leave her, not after that."

She reaches over, surprising me when she takes my hand in hers. "I'm sorry about the baby," she says, and I hear the sincerity in her voice.

I'd be lying if I said it doesn't still hurt, because it does. For a brief moment in time I had envisioned becoming a dad—being the father figure Ethan and I never had growing up.

"I did try to make it work for the most part, but our relationship was toxic. She lashed out, pushed me away. The final straw was when she cheated on me with Emilio. He always wanted what he couldn't have, and I guess in a twisted way, he gave her something I couldn't."

She shakes her head. "It wasn't your fault, Henry."

"No? You don't think it was some sort of twisted karma?"

Meg frowns. "What? Why would you think that?"

"Because it was *you* that I wanted the night I slept with her, but I also saw the way Ethan looked at you."

"Oh," she says, releasing my hand.

I take the last bite of my food but no longer taste it.

"Did Ethan know about the baby?" she asks quietly.

I shake my head and stare back at her. "No. We agreed to wait, and then we lost it."

Her features soften.

"So, you had no one to talk to? Only Clara?"

My throat thickens. "No, and when I did try to talk to her about it, she'd just shut down, so I didn't push." I didn't know what was right from wrong.

She gets up and rounds the table to straddle my lap and cradles my face between her soft palms. Her touch is a heat source all of its own.

"I'm so sorry, Henry. I know how hard it was for you to share that with me."

And then she brushes her lips against mine, the caress slow, sensual, and full of purpose, like she's trying to express herself through this kiss.

Chapter Thirteen

Meghan

Stretching, I let out a contented sigh. I can still feel the aftereffects of having Henry inside me, remembering how he worshipped my body and then fucked me into a state of oblivion. At one point, I wondered if someone could die from such extreme stimulation because I've never had so many orgasms in one night. Maybe it was from all the pent-up sexual frustration, but I'm not complaining.

I woke early hours and went down on him. It was only fair after the number of times he made me come with his deliciously wicked tongue. I wanted to repay the favour.

Something about him waking to find my mouth wrapped around him spurred me on, and he let his pleasure be known.

With the early morning sunlight leaking through the curtains, I take in his room. Other than when they moved in, I've never had reason to be in here. And last night, I was preoccupied.

I love how it's all him, simple and yet bold. He has a pair of boxing gloves hanging on the far wall, beside a shelf full of trophies. The covers on his king-size bed are all dark, even the sheets, but the room is otherwise light, the walls coated in fresh cream paint while all the furniture is solid black oak with silver handles. The colours compliment his space perfectly. And it's all him.

Memories of our conversation last night come back to me of how he believes Ethan is still in love with me. Of Clara and him losing their baby. I can't even begin to imagine how hard that must have been, but it hurts she never confided in me, and yet, she never told me about her affair with Emilio either.

I love her. Of course I do, even if I do disagree with her choice in men. I'm Jacob's godmother, for crying out loud. Emilio didn't give a shit about the christening as long as there was ample alcohol afterwards.

Squeezing my eyes shut, I try to ignore what bothers me the most, and if I'm honest, it's that Clara was ever with Henry in the first place. How two-faced is that? I'm lying naked in Henry's bed; his twin brother is my ex—and my best friend. I'm a hypocrite, because I'll never regret what I had with Ethan, even though he hurt me.

And now, in the light of day, the more complicated it all becomes. I know we can't go back, Henry warned me, and even though we're both single, a sense of foreboding settles over me like hot sticky tar.

What happens now?

Will he act like it never happened? Will he ostracise me because of the guilt he'll no doubt feel?

Everything I'm feeling is a contradiction.

I can't regret last night, but I also feel as though I've done Ethan wrong.

Keeping a kiss or two from him is bad enough, but this sleeping with his brother is something else entirely. In what twisted alternative universe did I genuinely believe that Henry would choose me over his twin brother, even after this?

And I would never ask him to make that choice, but eventually, Ethan will find out.

I know I can't keep this from him. I must tell him the truth.

Will he have thoughts like Henry? Will he wonder if I'm comparing the two?

My feelings for them have never overlapped; they've always been separate—

compartmentalised. Even I know being an emotional cheat is just as bad as cheating. I shut down my attraction for Henry when I gave myself to Ethan.

And if Ethan does still love me, then why did he dump me?

I lean over and give Henry a gentle kiss. When I pull back, he's smiling, but his breathing is still a slow rhythmic staccato, and instinctively, his arm around me tightens.

Being with him is both familiar and brand new. Something I've been longing for, and the thought terrifies me. The last man I gave my heart to wrecked me, and by relinquishing myself to Henry, I'll be giving him the ultimate power to do the same.

Quietly, I slide out of Henry's hold and reach for his discarded T-shirt and my phone. I should have grabbed my clothes when I got my phone to text my dad, but it was the last thing on my mind.

I slip into his bathroom, closing the door softly behind me.

Greeted by my reflection, I see my hair is a mess. I hunt in his bathroom cabinet and find a hairbrush, and I wonder if it was Clara's. The thought makes me uneasy, but I pull it through my hair anyway and then tie it in a long ponytail, leaving an indent of my hairband on my wrist.

After relieving my bladder, I squeeze a pea-size amount of toothpaste on my index finger, scrub it over my teeth and then rinse my mouth out under the tap.

Perching on the edge of the bathtub, I can't help but smile.

It's my favourite feature of the entire house, I always wanted a claw tooth roll-top bath, but my ensuite is too small.

I remember pointing it out to Ethan when we were out shopping, but he had shaken his head. Only the ensuite would accommodate a bath like that, and Henry had lucked out in a game of paper-rock-scissors, earning himself this room.

And then Henry had gone ahead and ordered it, claiming I had good taste.

I swap my phone between my hands and let out a deep breath as I type out a text to Ethan. I know it's early, but he's always been an early riser.

Can we talk? Are you awake?

Bubbles appear, and I know he's typing back. Hairs on my arms rise, and my stomach becomes jittery as I wait for his reply.

I'm awake, what's up?

Cold air rushes down my spine and my mind is a jumbled mess. I have so many unanswered questions about him, about us.

Are you free this morning? Can I see you?

His reply is instant.

Of course x

My stomach drops because I'm not sure I'm ready for this, but the longer I prolong it, the harder it will become.

I open the bathroom door and see Henry hugging the pillow next to him. I need to go before I lose my nerve. I creep over to the bed and lean over.

"Henry, I have to go. I'll speak to you later," I whisper.

The last thing I want is him waking to find me gone, but I'm also not ready to address this—or us—in the light of day, not until I've spoken to Ethan.

"Henry," I say a little louder this time.

"Hmm," he replies.

"I've got to go. I'll speak to you later."

He rolls onto his back, and his eyes open half-mast.

"What time is it?" he asks, stretching before grabbing my arm and pulling me to him.

"Just after five," I say.

"Do you have to?" he asks, closing his eyes, and he's already asleep again. I tiptoe downstairs like a coward and retrieve my clothes. I dress quickly and leave Henry's T-shirt on the back of the kitchen chair, the same one where he fucked me with his mouth. My channel clenches at the thought. Hit with a sudden wave of guilt, I turn and leave.

When I arrive home, I'm grateful my dad is still not up—no doubt he would have shamed me for coming home at this hour, and I would have felt guilty.

I make myself a cup of tea, desperate for the caffeine and a slice of toast before I text Ethan.

Is an hour okay?

Bubbles appear, and I wonder if he is ever without his phone. The one thing about Ethan is that he's always been my constant—always been present.

Yeah x

I take a bite of my toast, but it might as well be sawdust.

Okay, see you soon x

When I hear my dad moving around upstairs, I quickly dash to my room, hoping to avoid him until he leaves for the wholesalers. I lock my door and go straight to my bathroom.

When my mum left, he couldn't bear to stay in their bedroom, so he moved to the third bedroom and said I could have the master with ensuite.

I turn on the shower and let the running water drown out the world around me as I begin washing my hair. Long hair is hard work, it's naturally wavy and coarse, so it pretty much has a life of its own on any given day. I have hair so much like my mum's, and the thought annoys me. Maybe it's why I'm always dying it.

By the time I'm dressed and ready, an hour has already

passed, but I know Ethan won't question my timekeeping. I grab us both a coffee on the way. I know it won't help with my already building anxiety once the caffeine wears off, but we all have our vices.

Walking up the path I know so well, Ethan already has the door open, waiting.

"Curtain twitching, were you?" I ask, trying to cover my unease.

He smiles and pulls me into a side hug as I pass him his coffee. The door clicks closed behind us.

My body tingles with nervous energy as I follow him into the living room and join him on the sofa. His leg brushes against mine, but he doesn't seem to care as he reaches out and grips my knee with a smile.

I think of how tactile he's always been, even after we broke up. I never doubted he cared, but now I'm confused more than ever with what Henry said.

"Are you okay, Meg? Has something happened?" he asks just as I take a sip of my coffee, which goes down the wrong hole. I cough, and he quickly pats my back, but I wave it off and laugh uncomfortably.

He knows something is wrong. I can see it in his eyes. I thought I'd come here to confess about Henry and me, but the truth is… I'm not sure I'm ready, and I realise this is more about us.

"Why did you do it?" I ask, my voice catching as old feelings resurface.

"Do what?" he asks, and I have to resist the urge to smooth out his frown.

"Dump me." My voice wobbles, and I try to breathe through my emotions.

He takes my coffee, places it with his on the table, and turns to face me, reaching for my hand. I'm torn between wanting to pull away or hold on tight.

"Where is this coming from?" he asks, and it's not lost on me how he's redirecting my question.

"You never told me why, and then after the accident, I didn't know how to ask."

He sighs, and I watch his eyes as they search my face. And though he and Henry have the same eye colour, Ethan has a richer brown ring that surrounds his irises.

I study the way he swallows, his Adam's apple bobbing up and down. He always loved it when I kissed his throat. My stomach flutters to life. *What the hell is wrong with me?*

"It was one of the hardest things I've ever done," he admits, completely throwing me off guard.

Now I'm the one frowning. "Then why did you do it?"

He shakes his head, and I hold my breath.

"Because it was the right thing to do. Maybe deep down, I'd hoped you'd fight for us, fight for me."

I want to pull my hand away as his confession slices through me.

Me? Fight for him? For us? He dumped me!

"You always were too good for me, Ethan. Were you with me out of pity?"

His jaw ticks and I see a war of emotions cross his features as his eyes grow dark.

"In the entire time I was with you, did I ever make you feel less than what you deserved?"

I shake my head and try to keep my emotions at bay. No, he didn't. He always treated me like I was his everything.

"No, not until you dumped me."

He licks his lips and holds my stare, his gaze so intense. "When I said I loved you, it was real. When I made love to you, it was real. All the times I kissed you, it was real. Don't ever question my feelings for you."

I don't miss how he uses the present tense.

He leans in, so close our breaths mingle, and I think he might kiss me. I should move away, but I'm frozen in place. I try to digest his words. Ethan has always had the power to make me feel.

But so does Henry. Even though it's different, it doesn't matter, because for the first time, I can't ignore the fact I am now comparing them. I care about both these men, and no matter what happens next, I know without a doubt someone—or all of us—will get hurt.

None of us are getting out of this unscathed.

I stand abruptly. "I'm sorry, I have to go," I say, not even bothering to grab my coffee or even explain myself. All I know is I can't breathe being this close to him. And now I'm even more confused about my feelings towards him and Henry. Ethan says something to my retreating back, but I can't hear him. My ears are ringing from the sudden spike in adrenaline, and I'm grateful he doesn't try to stop me.

Chapter Fourteen

Henry

I wake up and notice Meghan's absence almost immediately. Her scent lingers all over my sheets and pillow. I recall something about her telling me she had to go. I reach for my phone. It's a little after six. What time did she leave?

Sitting up, I stretch my neck, and it clicks. I let out a satisfying groan. I have a training session at seven-thirty this morning. Though I'm pretty sure last night's activities probably equate to an entire session, I can't help but harden even more as I recollect my exploration of her body. And it's something I most definitely need to repeat.

But something about her leaving when she did sets off a niggling sensation in my mind.

I manage to relieve myself without pissing all over the ceiling and then get straight in the shower. It's caffeine most people need to wake up, but it's a cool shower for me.

I lather my body in my shower gel, and as I reach my dick, I recollect her mouth on me, and I hate to have to wash her away. I enjoy sex, but it's never been like it was with her. Just thinking about her has my length thickening. You'd think my body would be sated the number of times I was inside her, but it would seem not. I'm going to need to take care of it. The last thing I need is to be uncomfortable and semi-hard all day while training.

I dry off and change into some workout clothes and make myself a protein shake, making sure to take a stupid arse selfie and upload it to Instagram. If it weren't because they are my sponsors, I wouldn't do it, but needs must.

I stare at my kitchen table, and a flashback hits me. Groaning, I adjust myself, wondering if it's just me feeling this way. I need her again, and I must know if the feeling is mutual. I grab my stuff and send her a message as I walk to my car.

You left early, is everything all right?

I sip my shake on the way to the gym, disappointed that every time a notification comes through on my phone, it's not from Meg.

My good mood from last night begins to turn sour. I need to get a grip. I know she isn't on shift until midday. And yes, I'm aware it might seem a little stalkerish that I know her fucking work rota, but whatever. I'd be lying if I said it was so I could avoid her when I'm training. It's the opposite.

Pulling into the car park, I see her dad unloading stuff from his boot. I grab my gear and walk towards him. I wonder how he'd feel about me being with his daughter, especially after what happened with Ethan. He's always been strict with Meg, and I know he wasn't particularly pleased about Ethan and Meg's relationship. But she's in her early twenties, for crying out loud.

I don't have kids, so maybe it's not my place to question his protective nature where she's concerned, but it's almost overbearing, and that isn't healthy.

With the sound of my feet meeting the gravel as I approach, he pokes his head around the side of the car.

"Morning," he says, ducking his head back in the boot.

"Morning, Ian, do you need a hand?" I ask, putting my gym bag over my shoulder.

"That would be great," he replies, straightening and placing two boxes in my arms.

"Stick another one on top," I say, nodding my head back to the boot.

We manage to get everything unloaded in three trips. I stack the last box in front of the reception area and use a pump of anti-bacterial gel to clean my hands. I might be a bit of a germaphobe.

"Thanks, Henry."

I shrug. "No problem."

He tosses me a cold bottle of water from the fridge, and I drink half of it in one go.

"So, how's Ethan doing?" he asks.

I shove my hands in my pockets. "Yeah, good, he mentioned about coming back soon." He's been working out at Mum's, but she makes it difficult. Not that I can blame her. The accident scared the shit out of us. I'll never be able to erase the image of him lying in a coma in ICU. I'm surprised he hasn't just moved back in with Nathan and me.

"Anyway, you have a big fight coming up. You ready?" he asks.

"Almost," I reply, my eyes glancing around the gym and the few members here for an early session.

"You'll get there. Just make sure to avoid distractions," he says, patting me on the shoulder with maybe a little more force than necessary before walking away.

Was it just me, or was that a warning tone I heard in his voice?

Usually, these sessions consume me, but not today. I'm distracted—yet again. This is why I tried to stay away from

Meg. Everything depends on this fight and me winning. It's not the title I'm after. Emilio thinks he's the better man, but he's not, and everything he's done proves otherwise.

I know Clara and I weren't right for each other long before he got her into his bed. When we weren't arguing, we were fucking. And I know it wasn't healthy, our relationship, and the more she pushed, the more I pulled back emotionally. I couldn't give her what she needed emotionally.

But even so, the most challenging part was finding out she was pregnant with another man's child. All the feelings resurfaced over the miscarriage, and I had no one to turn to, not even Ethan.

I stare at the giant digital clock again and know Meg is due here any moment. She usually arrives early, but the closer it gets to her shift, the more I wonder if she's coming in at all. Maybe she's avoiding me after last night?

And then I see her and let out a breath. My unease dissipates a fraction, but even from here, I can tell she's tired. Her hair is in a plait over her shoulder, but wisps of hair are escaping. When she heads to the staff room, I try to talk myself out of following her, as I wipe my face and drop my towel back on my bench with my water bottle to let anyone else know the equipment is still in use.

Looking around, I make sure no one is paying me any attention before I slip into the room behind her. She turns just as I'm closing the door. Her eyes go round, and I swear her shoulders tense.

"Everything all right?" I ask.

"Yeah, just running late," she replies, looking at her Fitbit and then back to me, but I know it's more than just her timekeeping. I step towards her and she takes one step back.

"I texted you, but you didn't reply," I say, crossing my arms, trying to keep the hurt out of my voice.

She bites the inside of her mouth. "Sorry, I just had a lot

going on. We should go. I don't want anyone walking in on us," she says, glancing over my shoulder.

I step back and rest against the door. "Problem solved," I reply, and stare, trying to gauge her reaction. "Anyone would think you didn't want to be alone with me."

Her eyes soften. "That's not true."

"Then come here," I say.

To my relief, she walks towards me and stops, staring up at me.

"Satisfied?"

"Nope." I reach out and pull her flush against my body. My hands slide down to cup her arse.

"And now?" she says, letting out a breath.

"Hmm, I'd feel better if you let me kiss you," I reply honestly.

"Who's stopping you?" she asks.

I lean in and kiss her softly, with a bit of tongue. Everything in me wants to devour her, but right now, all I want is to give her sweet and tender.

When I pull back, she gives me the most serene smile.

"Now, that's the kind of hello I could get used to," I say and kiss the tip of her nose.

She looks down, and my stomach sinks.

"Are you regretting last night?" I ask.

When she makes eye contact, it's not hard to see she's conflicted.

"It's complicated," she says, biting her lower lip.

"I know, but I meant what I said. There's no going back, not for me."

Her eyes soften, so I continue. "Did you think I'd spend the night exploring your body to then just let you walk away as if nothing happened?"

"I don't know. I was caught up in you, in us." She strokes her fingers across my cheek. Her touch does wicked things to my body.

"I'm a slave to you. Do you honestly not know how affected I am by you?"

I grip her jaw and implore her to see past my unspoken words, wishing I could say more.

"I think I'm beginning to understand."

She goes on her tiptoes and draws me in for a slow kiss, seeking out my tongue. I jerk into her in response. It's so easy to get lost in her touch, but we have things to discuss.

I pull away before talking myself out of it. After all, we're already pushing our luck.

"So, what's going on? And why were you in such a hurry to leave me this morning?"

I'm not trying to sound like an insecure dickhead, but I need transparency. I don't want her to act like we're doing something wrong.

"I had to go home to shower—and then I went to see Ethan," she admits, and now I understand why she had that expression on her face when I came to seek her out.

I loosen my hold. "Are you serious? The first thing you do after fucking me is run to my brother?"

She flinches, drops her arms from me and steps back. I don't stop her. My words taste like acid, but knowing she ran off to him is too much.

Her eyes turn to slits. "Is that what you're calling what we did last night? Fucking?" she demands, her nostrils flaring.

"I don't know, Meghan, you tell me. What about Ethan? What did he say about us fucking?"

I don't see it coming, and it's already too late by the time I do—the echo of her palm connecting with my cheek, followed by the sting. She fucking slapped me.

Chapter Fifteen

Meghan

What the hell? I drop my hand, squeezing my fist closed. I can already feel my palm welting. And the mark on his face is enough for me to know I went too far. His stunned expression mirrors my own. He's about to say something, but the door handle rattles behind him and stops him in his tracks. He presses up against the wall, hidden as I pull open the door.

"Oh, hi, Meg. I think the door is sticking," Natasha says, eying the door jamb. "Anyway, sorry to jump on you the minute you arrive, but I need to make a move. I have a dentist appointment," she says, pointing her thumb over her shoulder.

I shake my head. Of course, I'm already late.

"Of course, go," I say, moving towards her and edging her out of the doorway. Henry's fingers brush the back of my hand as I let go of the door.

I don't dare look back as I walk towards the reception area and see loads of boxes stacked behind the counter.

"Would it kill her to fill up the damn fridge," I grumble under my breath. "Rather than her flirting with gym members?"

Swinging the glass door of the refrigerator open, I slide over a box to prop it open and begin to fill it, pulling the colder ones to the front: my hands shake, and palm throbs. I can't believe I did that. I'm not this person. I wipe my cheek angrily. The last thing I want is to cry at work. I'm a grown arse woman, and if my dad catches me, he's going to start asking questions.

A familiar scent surrounds me. "I'm sorry," Henry says.

I stare blindly at the contents of the fridge and try to control my breathing. Knowing he's behind the counter with me, the heat from his body envelopes me, and his hand cups my elbow for me to look at him. I stare past him, but everyone is busy using the equipment, working out. No one is paying us any attention.

"I'm sorry, Meg, it's more than just fucking, and you know it," he whispers in my ear. "But hearing you went to him, rather than waking up beside me, was a low blow," he admits.

"Yeah, well, how do you think I feel? We had sex, and *then* you tell me you think Ethan still loves me. What was I supposed to do?" I hold his stare. "So, yes, I needed to see him. I'm confused. But it doesn't excuse me slapping you, and for that, I'm sorry."

He nods and looks back over his shoulder before moving closer. "Listen, I don't want to argue, not when we've barely begun."

It's the last thing I want, but I'd be lying if what he told me about Ethan doesn't complicate this whole thing further.

"You're right. We need to talk properly, but not here."

I hear the sound of footsteps approaching, causing my heartbeat to spike. Quickly reaching for a bottle of water, I thrust it into Henry's hand right as my dad rounds the counter.

"Everything okay, Meghan?" he asks, and it's not lost on me how he says my name like an insinuation rather than a question.

"I was just giving Henry a bottle of water," I say, smiling.

Henry nods at me. "Cheers," he says and walks back onto the gym floor, leaving me alone with my dad.

"Must you really flirt while you're at work?" he says loud enough for Henry to hear. His steps falter, but I'm grateful when he carries on walking away.

My cheeks heat with embarrassment. "Is that really what you think of me? I'm nothing like Mum," I shoot back, and straight away, I see the hurt in his eyes, but too bad. I can't keep allowing him to tarnish me with the same brush. I am not my mother.

Without another word, he turns his back on me and walks away.

My dad is a good man, and he took on the role of both parents when she walked out on us. And I know it's hard for him, and he did the best he could, but he needs to stop throwing out hurtful comments my way because of what she did to him, to us. I don't even know if he realises. He uses her indiscretions as a weapon against me. And this is a prime example of why I need to move out and take control of my life.

Thankfully, my day has been busy with clients, so I don't have time to dwell on everything that's transpired. My body feels heavy with fatigue by the time I've finished work, and I'm walking out into the car park. I notice a figure leaning against my car and pause until he turns his face towards me… Henry. I start walking again and sigh as I approach him. "Henry, can we talk tomorrow? I just want to binge on a pizza, have a bath and go to bed."

He uncrosses his ankles and pushes off my car, the gravel crunching under the movement.

"Then come back to mine. Nathan is still at my aunt's.

You can take advantage of my bath while I order us pizza, and then we can talk."

My stomach somersaults.

"Come on, I promise I'll behave," he says, giving me a boy scout salute. I swat his hand.

"You were never a boy scout," I say and peer back over my shoulder, expecting my dad to make an appearance any moment. When I face Henry again, he's pleading with his eyes, pressing his palms together in a praying sign.

I roll my eyes, my resolve weakening, and I do love that bath. "Fine, but I need to go grab some overnight stuff. I'll meet you back at yours."

He smiles, and it's my undoing as I get a twinge in my chest. It warms me to see him happy.

"See you soon," he says and gives me a chaste kiss.

I unlock my car, and it's not until I have the engine running and I look up into my rear-view mirror that Henry gets into his car. He's so protective, and maybe it should annoy me? I am, after all, an independent woman, but I can't deny it warms my insides.

Back at mine, I pack some clothes for tomorrow and grab a wash bag, filling it with some toiletries as I send my dad a quick text. I know he doesn't particularly like it, but I'm an adult and I pay rent. But I know now with certainty I need to start looking at places.

It's not long before I arrive back at Henry's. I pass a pizza delivery guy as I'm walking up the path. Henry is waiting at the open door.

"If you're trying to soften me up, it's working," I say when I enter the house. "I hope you got stuffed crust." The smell of greasy pizza makes my mouth water.

"Of course. I also got garlic bread and that nasty dip you love so much."

He closes the door, and I'm surprised he even remembers

the dip, but then again, I know how he takes his tea and coffee. And his absolute distaste for tomato sauce—he can't stand the stuff. He practically dry heaves when people have it near him, something about the sweet vinaigrette smell or some weird shit.

"Thank you," I say and drop my holdall at the bottom of the stairs.

I follow him into the front room where he already has plates on the table, some kitchen roll, a bottle of wine and two glasses.

"Don't worry. I replaced Nathan's," he says with a wink.

I take a seat on the sofa and watch as he loads our plates. And for the first time today, I begin to relax. My stomach grumbles, and I don't hesitate to take a huge mouthful, the stringy cheese the perfect consistency of gooeyness—my comfort food. I used to feel guilty about eating food I enjoyed, especially as I began putting on weight, but the gym helped me turn some of it into muscle. The only ones who never made me feel self-conscious about my body were Ethan and Henry.

I wanted desperately to be skinny. It ruined my relationship with food so much I started skipping meals altogether. Until the boys noticed and subtly told me about the importance of a balanced diet and exercise. They saw my downward spiral. It was so easy to get consumed by my thoughts, and it still is, but the truth is, I was hurting myself.

Chapter Sixteen

Henry

I don't know what I would have done if she hadn't have agreed to come over. I let my jealousy get the better of me, and I want to put it right.

Watching her eat one of her favourite foods so unapologetically brings me so much satisfaction. For so long, she was at war with her body and had unrealistic expectations of how she should look—her relationship with food was unhealthy, and it hurt us to watch.

She's always been beautiful. Before Clara and I were together, and maybe even during, my eyes would seek her out. It wasn't even a conscious action, and perhaps I was more transparent than I care to admit.

Maybe it's what drove Clara to pursue me. She and Emilio are both very similar in that regard.

"Nice?" I ask her as she reaches for another slice.

"Delicious," she says, licking the string of cheese from her upper lip with her tongue.

"I'm glad I did something right for a change."

Her eyes soften, and she lets out a sigh. "We're going to make mistakes, Henry. Especially with this, and with it being so complicated."

She's not wrong there.

"I know you're right. And I am sorry about earlier. I don't ever want to hurt you." I pour us each a glass and pass one to her, holding mine up in a toast. "To not being an idiot," I say, clinking our glasses.

Once we've both eaten enough, she leans back into the sofa cushions and closes her eyes.

"So, what happened when you went to see Ethan?" I ask, unable to hide my curiosity.

Her eyes spring open. "Nothing, we just talked."

She wrings her hands in her lap, and it takes everything in me to keep from reaching out to her.

"And?"

Sighing, she shrugs. "And nothing."

"He deserves to know about us," I say, and I don't miss how she recoils.

"No, not yet. It's too much too soon." Meg gets up and walks over to the DVD cabinet, her fingers blindly tracing the titles as she moves from one foot to another.

I pinch the bridge of my nose.

"Do you want to be with him?" I ask.

She scoffs at my question. "I've been with you too now, Henry."

I go over to her, and she tilts her head to look at me.

"I'm sorry. I know it's complicated, and I'm not making it any easier. I'm a selfish bastard for wanting you the way I do. I've never been chivalrous. That's Ethan, and I don't know if it's his curse or my downfall."

Her eyes glisten with unshed tears, and I feel even more of a dick.

"And I want you too, and it terrifies me, because ultimately, I'll lose one of you or worse… both."

Guilt engulfs me because she's not wrong. I wish more than anything I could give her guarantees everything will work out.

"You know I loathed myself after kissing you when you were so vulnerable because I had never felt so much in one kiss in my entire life. I kept thinking you wished it were him kissing you instead of me. It's why I fought this for so long, the pull towards you."

Her skin flushes from my admission, and I pull her to my body and hold her close.

"We've made a mess of this, haven't we?" She sniffs on my chest.

I stroke comforting circles over her back. "I don't think there is any right way to do this," I admit. "I know Ethan and you have history, but I believe if we gave us a chance, if we did this, we could be infinite."

Meg chews on her lip. "I don't think I'm worth all this trouble. Maybe the best thing I could do is put distance between us, take some time away."

The thought leaves a lead weight in my gut. I inhale loudly. "Running away isn't going to fix this, and you know it." I kiss her temple. "Besides, I don't want you to leave."

She leans back to stare up at me. "I just want to keep this between us for now."

The thought of hiding makes me feel like we're doing something wrong.

"So, what? We sneak around? Go behind his back?" I ask.

Meg steps out of my hold. "Can't we just take a minute to see where this goes, just the two of us?"

I shake my head but find myself relenting. "For now. But we need to talk to him sooner rather than later."

Meg's posture softens as she places her palms over my chest. "And we will, but not right now." Her tone is full of relief, and a big part of me hates it because I want this all out in the open. But I know once it's out there everything changes, permanently.

I pull her into my arms. "Fine, we'll wait." We stand in silence until she draws back, her eyes rising to meet mine.

"So, when am I getting this bath you promised me?"

Smacking her arse lightly, I reach over to the table for her wine. "Finish this, and I'll go get it ready."

I stack the empty pizza boxes and take them into the kitchen, and glance back in the living room before running upstairs, and fuck me if my steps don't falter. She's sitting on my sofa, legs tucked underneath her, a soft smile ghosting her lips.

Once I have the bath running, I start rummaging through my bathroom cabinets.

"Where is it?" I grunt in frustration.

"Lost something?" Meg sings from behind me, causing me to startle. I turn to face her and try to cover up the fact I didn't hear her approach. "I thought I had some bubble bath, but I'm sorry to say that I don't."

She slides her holdall off her shoulder to the floor and pulls out a ball.

"It's okay. I have a bath bomb," she says, holding it in her hand.

I frown. "I'm not sure I like the sound of a bomb anywhere near my bath."

She laughs, and the sound is refreshing to hear after a day filled with so much tension.

"You'll see, and I have no doubt you'll be begging to join me when you do."

I groan. This side of Meg is hard to ignore—carefree, playful.

"You're not making this easy on me, you know?"

She leans against the door frame. "Maybe things worth having aren't meant to be easy." And with that, she sashays towards me. I can't take my eyes off of her. She goes up on tiptoes, her lips so damn close. I turn my face, and her lips graze my cheek.

"I'm trying to behave," I say, and I meant it.

"Oh, so it's not because I stink of chive and garlic dip?"

I shake my head. "No, I'm sure I ate enough of the garlic bread to outdo your dip."

She runs her soft lips over my jaw. "So, prove it," she says, blowing onto the sensitive patch of skin below my ear.

Fuck me.

I spin her around, backing her up against the sink, stepping between her legs. I hold the back of her head firmly as my tongue dominates her mouth.

Pulling back, I wait until her eyes flutter open and she's staring up at me.

"Satisfied?" I ask, smirking.

"I will be once I get to sample your beautiful bath."

I release her and take a step back, the bath already half full.

"How deep do you want it?" I ask, turning on the cold tap, the bathroom mirror beginning to steam up.

I look over my shoulder and catch her checking out my arse.

Her cheeks heat. "Usually, I'd say as deep as it could go," she says, raising an eyebrow. My dick twitches. "But on this occasion, not too deep, if you're planning on joining me."

She removes her jumper and drops it to the floor.

"You're fucking killing me," I groan.

Her plain, black bra hugs her breasts perfectly. She undoes her jeans and slides them down her toned legs, exposing her matching black knickers, which hug her arse to perfection.

"So, is that a yes?" she asks, reaching behind her to unclasp her bra. She hangs it from her index finger, spinning it once before tossing it at my face. I catch it and drop it to the floor, and then in one stride, I'm in front of her, dropping to my knees. I hook my fingers into the waistband of her knickers, sliding them down to her ankles. I lean into the apex of her thighs and inhale; she smells like sin. If I'm having a bath with her, I will make sure she's well and truly dirty first.

Chapter Seventeen

Meghan

I want his touch everywhere and only between my thighs, all at the same time. Greedy for his touch, I pull his face against my core. The more he does that thing with his tongue, the bigger the build-up to my climax, which I know is imminent.

"Yes." I grip his hair and tug. "More."

He doesn't hold back, giving me what I so desperately crave. I release my hold on his hair and reach for the edge of the sink behind me, barely able to keep my body upright through my climax. Waves of pleasure fill my senses, and I come in his mouth; he laps it up like I'm the best thing he's ever tasted.

"Fucking hell," I say as my body twitches from the aftermath. He rises to his feet and pulls me in for a searing kiss which steals the air from my lungs.

Pulling back, he strokes over my pebbled flesh with the tip of his nose until he reaches my earlobe.

"So, are you going to show me this bath bomb?" he whispers.

"Give a girl a minute," I reply with a giggle. The rippled after-effects are still coursing through my body.

He laughs, a rough baritone, and my nipples harden in response. Is there anything about this man which doesn't turn me on?

"Are you going to join me?" I ask again.

He ponders my question, and I swat his shoulder. Aware of my complete nakedness compared to him, I reach for the hem of his T-shirt and help him undress.

His erection springs free when I rid him of his boxer briefs. But if I touch him, I know it won't stop there, and I don't want to let this bath water go to waste.

Locating my bath bomb, I drop it into the water. It bubbles and spins, dissolving with a golden explosion.

"Shit, will it stain my bath?" he asks.

I laugh and shake my head. "No, it'll be fine."

I love the smell of this one. It's my favourite, lemon and bergamot.

"I don't know. It looks a little glittery to me," he says as he watches me step into the water.

"It's a golden lustre. I promise you won't sparkle like a vampire in sunlight."

He gives me a quizzical look, and I don't bother enlightening him as I step in and sit down, immersing myself in the water with a satisfied sigh.

Henry still doesn't look too keen.

"Come on, just think of it as a sherbet lemon sensation." I hold out my hand to him.

He relents, climbing in. "Sit forward. I'll wash your back," he says, sitting down behind me, his massive thighs either side of my body. His erection floats in the water, tapping my spine.

"Sorry, can't help it," he says without an ounce of remorse, planting a soft kiss on my shoulder. It's a big bath but still a tight fit with the two of us, but I am in no way complaining. He leans over me to grab his body wash, pouring some into his palm, and then begins to wash my back with meticulous precision before massaging my shoulders.

I moan at his touch. "Feels so nice."

He kisses my neck when he's done, and I relax against his chest, savouring the peace and tranquillity of being with him like this.

"You know I fantasised about having you in the shower this morning. I had to take care of myself so that I wasn't a walking hard-on all day."

I chuckle. "I don't think the girls would have minded at the gym," I reply.

It's the truth. Ever since he became single again, he's been a hot topic with the female members.

"Yeah, well, it wasn't them I was thinking about."

I turn around to face him, kneeling between his legs, and I take his hard length in my grasp and begin working him up and down until he's leaning into my touch and breathing heavily.

"Is this what you had to do?" I whisper in his ear. The water laps up towards the edge of the bath. I hear a glug sound as he releases the plug.

"Yes, but it was weak in comparison to your touch," he says—his eyes remain fixated on my hand. There is something very erotic about pleasuring him while he watches.

The water drains with a whirring sound, and with a heavy grunt, he lets go, and I feel his climax as it covers my hand and thighs.

Henry grabs the showerhead, rinsing us both off. This time, I reach for the shower gel and make quick work of washing myself, passing it to him to do the same. Otherwise, we might never get clean.

After he shuts off the water, he grabs a towel and wraps me in it before sorting himself out. Neither of us speaks as we dry off. I don't look away when he slips on a pair of grey tracksuit bottoms, sans underwear, and damn if that doesn't make my baby-makers jump to attention.

Rummaging through my bag, I pull on my oversized lounge sweatshirt and leggings, then release my hair from its bun and tie it into a plait. He walks towards me when I'm done and reaches out, stroking my hair between his thumb and forefinger.

"Your hair feels better than I ever imagined."

I smile up at him. "Oh, and what does it feel like?" I ask, curious.

"Soft like silk, thick like a rope," he says, giving it a slight tug.

"Have a thing for Rapunzel by any chance?" I ask playfully.

"No, I have a thing for you," he says, and my breath hitches. The seriousness of his reply throws me, and just like that, every reason I have not to be with him completely disintegrates.

Chapter Eighteen

Meghan

Henry goes to grab us a bottle each. I sit on the edge of his bed, my face in my hands. Something about staying with him tonight seems more profound since our talk earlier.

"You okay?"

As Henry enters the bedroom, I look up at his large frame filling the doorway, the light behind him giving him an almost ethereal glow.

"I don't know which side you sleep on," I say, my cheeks heating.

He walks over and kneels in front of me.

"Which side do you prefer?" he asks.

"The side furthest from the door."

Leaning down, he turns my palm face up and kisses it. "Then you sleep this side, and I'll spoon you," he says with a boyish grin.

"I never took you for a spooning kind of guy," I reply, my voice coming out raspy.

Winking, he stands up, and I watch as he walks over to his chest of drawers, drops his joggers, and pulls on a pair of boxer briefs. He turns on the lamp before switching off the big light. "Oh, and what kind of guy did you take me for?" he asks, rounding the other side of the bed as I lay down, facing him.

"Love them and leave them," I say but instantly regret it when his smile falls. Clara was the one who left him. The bed dips as he joins me.

"Are you going to come over here?" he asks, laying on his back, lifting his arm for me to tuck myself into his side. I sigh; this is heaven. I love his warmth.

"Can I ask you something?" he says as he strokes a pattern over my shoulder.

"Yes," I reply. My hand rests over his chest, feeling his heartbeat under my palm in a melodic rhythm.

"If Ethan asked you to give you and him another go, would you?"

I squeeze my eyes closed.

"I don't know." My voice cracks. I'm lying here in his arms; surely this should be a sign. I should be able to say an outright no, shouldn't I? "I'm sorry."

He kisses my hair, his hold tightening a fraction. "You don't have to apologise. But you'd tell me if he did, right?"

I hate that he even has to ask, and I don't blame him if he doubts me. This is so fucked up.

"Yes." I wish I could tell him with a resounding no that I won't, that he is all I want, but I won't lie to him.

He sighs. "I'll wait until you're ready."

A cold shiver rolls through me as goosebumps rise on my arms because I don't deserve him. I tilt my face towards his, drawn to him like gravity.

We're only a breath apart.

"Kiss me," I say, unable to hide the vulnerability in my voice.

Stroking my plait over my shoulder, he cups my cheek. His kiss is slow, controlled, before he nips at my chin, his fingers roaming up and down my arm. It's not hard to get lost in his caress. Every stroke of my tongue with his is an apology for the words I wish I could share. He pulls me on top of him, and I rub against his arousal.

The friction between us intensifies. Sitting up, I pull at his boxer briefs and work them down his legs before ridding myself of mine.

He rolls me onto my back, his body framing mine. Knowing we both need this; he reaches over to his drawer and sheaths himself.

"I stole it from Nathan's stash," he says, and I can't hide my laugh.

"I'm beginning to wonder if you're a bit of a kleptomaniac."

I lean up on my elbows, and my mouth waters in anticipation as he strokes himself.

His fingers slide up and down my folds before he takes his time and pushes two inside me, and I let out a groan. He pulls them free and brings them to my lips, sliding them into my mouth.

"Taste."

I hollow my cheeks and suck on his fingers, and he slowly fills me until he's balls deep. And then he's moving. His sole focus on me is both sensual and utterly enthralling.

Wanting to hold onto this moment, all of these titillating sensations vying for my attention, my hands grip his arse to keep him still.

"Don't move, stay just like this." I hum, clenching my channel around him.

He twitches, and sweat forms on his brow. His hand reaches out for my throat, his fingers tightening just a fraction, and I lose it. Arching into him, he rewards me with slow, measured thrusts.

But I crave more. I need more. "Please, Henry," I murmur against his skin. "Please."

I don't know what I'm begging him for, but he continues his ministrations with fervour, one long thrust after the other —each one taking us both higher. I open my mouth on his neck, tasting, licking, nipping. And then his lips find mine when he sucks my tongue into his mouth.

Our movements and gyrations become more feral and out of control. His hands reach for the headboard, using it as an anchor. His thrusts are deeper than before. I clench my teeth; his hips move in uncontrollable bursts. Grunts spill from his mouth until, together, we fall. His entire body goes rigid, a long guttural moan escaping him.

Muffled curses and incoherent words leave my mouth in breathless gasps as I shatter around him. And I feel it from my head to my toes. The air is momentarily sucked out of me as I'm suspended in time. Never have I orgasmed like this, so wet and out of control. My body spasms, rinsing Henry for all his worth. Weak, my legs finally give out and fall open. Both of us entirely spent, he collapses against me, his head resting on my heaving chest, my fingers tangled in his hair.

"I think maybe those bath bombs were laced with something," he says, causing me to laugh. I think he might be right. That was some scorching make-up sex.

Henry moves off me and discards the condom whilst I slip away to the bathroom to relieve myself. When I return, he's laying down with his arm covering his eyes, smiling. My heart skips a beat, knowing I put it there. The bed dips as I climb in beside him, and he pulls me to his side.

"Don't sneak off in the morning. Stay and say goodbye." He sounds vulnerable. There is no way I can refuse him, not after the way I snuck away this morning.

Henry

Something flutters over my skin, tickling me, and I brush it away, but when it happens again, I peek out of one eye, and Meg faces me, her hand trailing over my naked torso, the cover wrapped around my legs.

"What happened there?" I ask, kicking my legs free.

She laughs and pokes me. "I have no idea, but who knew you were a cover hog."

And in one quick move, I roll on top of her. "Is that so?"

Nodding, she hooks her arms around my neck and pulls me closer. "It's okay, though. You kept me warm all night," she says, nipping my bottom lip.

"Did you brush your teeth?"

"Yes."

I breathe into her neck. "You left me," I say, whining.

"Yes, and it wasn't an easy feat freeing myself from the death grip you had on me."

I raise my face to look at her. "Did I hurt you?"

"No, of course not." She runs her palm over my stubble, and I press my face into her touch.

I spring up out of bed. "Don't move," I say and dash to the bathroom.

"Yes, master," she echoes behind me, and I can't help but like how it sounded.

When I come back out, she has the cover pulled up over her, and I shake my head.

"I told you not to move." I kneel on the bed and crawl up her body. Her hands clutch the material.

"I was cold," she says, pouting, and I lean down and bite on her lip softly.

"And are you still cold? Do you need warming up?" I offer.

Her eyes go wide, and she licks her lips.

"You do have a filthy mind, Meghan. I never said how I'd warm you up."

She raises an eyebrow. "No? Then do tell…"

I tug the cover and pull it down until her body is exposed.

"Hmm, someone was sneaky," I say, pinging the elastic waistband of her shorts, slipping my fingers beneath the material before pulling them down. I glance up, her following my movements.

"Henry," she warns but makes no move to stop me.

"What?" I ask and sweep my tongue over her thigh. She slams her head back into the pillow, her eyes still locked on me.

"Do you not want me to warm you up? I bet I can do it without using my hands," I challenge, and use the tip of my tongue to tease between her wet folds.

"Ahh, you think, huh?"

I shake my head. "Believe me, I know."

I nudge her thighs apart with my head and pepper kisses over her flesh until I'm at her entrance, plunging my tongue into her hot channel. She strangles the sheets between her fingers as I lick her out.

A loud door slamming causes her to flinch, and I hold up my finger to my mouth before my tongue slips back inside her. She glances to the closed door and then back to me. I want to touch her so badly, have my fingers join in the fun with my tongue, but instead, I suck her clit hard in my mouth and she bucks into me. Her hands grip my hair forcefully, and fuck me if I don't like it. My erection is beading with pre-cum, desperate for its release, but this isn't about me. If I could make her come every day until the end of days, I'd be a happy fucking man.

I continue to fuck her with my tongue until she has to cover her mouth to stifle her cries. It's not lost on me, the possibility of my bedroom door swinging open at any moment. Not that Nathan has ever barged in before, but there's a first for everything.

When she climaxes, I come up for air, take myself in my hand, and squeeze from base to tip. Crawling to her knees with a wicked grin, Meg pulls my hand away, replacing it with hers.

I throw my head back and close my eyes. "Fucking hell, Meg, your touch is poison."

The mattress dips as she straddles me. Slowly, she lowers herself until sheathing me completely. She rolls her hips, and then she's riding me, her movements salacious and so damn stimulating.

"Meg, I need to pull out—I'm going to come," I grunt, knowing it's imminent and having no way to prolong it.

"I'm on the pill."

And it's all I need to hear as my seed fills her in long hot bursts, and then she's coming again. I reach between us, circling her clit, her teeth bite down on my shoulder, and I hope like hell it leaves a mark.

I am fucking wrecked.

"Henry?" Nathan's voice booms through the door. Meg leans back, her eyes going wide.

"Yes," I say through gritted teeth but hold Meg tight, the aftershocks of her orgasm still pulsing through her.

"We have training in an hour. Wanted to check you were up?"

I eye the ceiling. "Well, as you heard, I'm up," I say and glance down between our entwined bodies. Meg hides her face in the crook of my neck, trying to smother her snigger. I'm still semi-hard, so I give a quick thrust as she gasps.

"Cool, and one other thing…"

I roll my eyes. "What?" I all but yell.

"Morning, Meg."

His heavy footsteps let us know he's retreated downstairs.

I stare at Meg, expecting to see panic or guilt, but instead, she bursts out laughing.

Grabbing her face between my palms, I kiss her with a renewed reverence, hoping it conveys all the ways she makes me feel.

Chapter Nineteen

Meghan

It was hard leaving Henry this morning; everything about being with him last night was intense and heavy. Today it's as though a partial weight has lifted. I know the situation between Ethan and myself is still up in the air, and maybe that should be my priority, but when Henry said we could be infinite, my resolve crumbled, and whether I want to admit it or not, I'm falling for him.

Nathan didn't emerge while I said goodbye to Henry, and for that, I'm grateful. He's a jokester most of the time, but I also know he's not stupid. This has been brewing between Henry and me for a while, and I hate how he's now stuck in the middle.

I promised Clara I'd see her today while Emilio is busy with training. After what Henry shared with me, I know how much worse her betrayal was when she cheated. I love her, of course I do, but I won't defend her actions. She's always been able to manipulate a situation to her advantage. She's a survivor. Her parents gave up on her as soon as she turned sixteen and pissed off abroad. And if I'm honest, if I didn't already know Emilio, and I hadn't seen it for myself, I don't know how much of what she might have said I would have taken as gospel.

Emilio is a sociopath. He wasn't always that way, and he does well to hide it, but we know better for those who grew up with him. He has a location tracker on her phone, and the one time she forgot it at home, he tracked her down using the GPS he had installed in her car. I know he hit her that night. She tried to hide it, make excuses for him.

He keeps her around for appearance's sake, and he only wants her when it suits him. The fact he can't keep it in his pants only proves it. I mean, look at the other night when we went out... I knew it was too good to be true the moment he showed up at Rattlers.

I eye the perfectly mowed green lawn as I walk up the winding path next to the carport driveway to their newly built detached townhouse. Or I should say *his*... it's all in his name; of course, she quit her job after discovering she was pregnant as per his request. I know she didn't want to, she loved hairdressing, and she was good at it too.

Even though I know he's at his gym training, I still feel like he's watching, and I can't stop my shiver. My fingers barely reach for the doorbell when the door swings open.

"Thank God you're here. I was losing my mind," Clara says, gripping my arm and hauling me into the house and checking over my shoulder before closing it behind us.

I shake off her hold and she stumbles into me, the stench of alcohol oozing from her breath.

"Have you been drinking?" I ask in disbelief. "And where's the baby?"

She rolls her eyes. "Oh, calm down. He's with Emilio's bitch of a mother."

I take hold of her elbow and she wobbles as we walk into the open plan kitchen come dining room. Pointing, I direct her to one of the bar stools at the white granite breakfast bar and flick the switch on the kettle. Pulling the coffee container towards me, I scoop a spoonful into a mug.

Turning to her, I cross my arms; her body is limp, her movements lethargic.

"Why are you drinking at eleven o'clock in the morning?" I ask, unable to hide the disappointment in my tone.

She rests her chin in her palm. "I'm cooped up. He stays out for days. I'm like a prisoner." Her speech is slurred. "Apart from with you, its mundane things"—hiccup—"His bloody mum picks up Jacob last minute. I swear he does it on purpose."

The kettle clicks and I fill the mug and add a dash of milk and some sugar.

"Drink this." I set it in front of her and she pokes out her tongue and pushes it away. "Come on. It's better than alcohol."

She rolls her eyes. "Says you."

"Clara, I want to help you, but you're not making it easy. Do you want him to take Jacob away from you?"

Her eyes fill with tears. "No, course not." She chews on her chapped lips.

"Then please, help me help you. Sort yourself out. He'll use anything he can against you."

She hugs her mug between her hands, blowing it before taking a sip and cringing. I pull out a loaf of bread and slot two slices into the toaster. Her eyes are absent as she stares past me, and then she comes back to herself, taking another gulp of coffee. She's quiet for a few minutes, and I wait until she speaks, knowing she's trying to sort out her thoughts.

"Sometimes, when he comes home, it's good with us. Like before, and I find myself falling for him all over again."

I hold up my hand. "You have got to be fucking kidding me. This is the same man who grabbed me by the throat when I turned down his advances."

She flinches. "I know, and I'm sorry." It pisses me off that she apologises for his behaviour. I hiss, burning my fingers as I retrieve the toast and drop it onto a plate. I butter it and pass it over, perching on the stool beside her. "Listen, we've known each other a long time, and there isn't anything I wouldn't do for you, but if you can't help yourself, how am I supposed to help you?"

Her eyes go wide. "So what? You're not going to help? Is that what you're saying?"

I touch her arm. "No, but it's why I talked to Ethan."

She slams her mug down with force, some of the contents spilling over the rim.

"What the fuck, Meghan?" She shakes her head. "Why?"

"Because he saw my bruises, and I trust him."

She throws her arms in the air. "Next, you'll be telling me Olly is getting involved."

I say nothing—I do still need to talk to him.

"Oh, for fuck's sake."

"He knows people. It will mean you and Jacob can start over. But if you're too accustomed to all this," I say, waving my hand around. "Then say so now, and I'll leave you to it."

He's always tried to buy affection; it's always been about material possessions with Emilio. He's frivolous—this house is no different, all for show and nothing more. It's hard to reconcile the monster he is now from the boy we once knew.

"I don't want that," she says, her shoulders slumping. "I just never envisioned this for my life. I don't want this for Jacob. He deserves a father like Henry, not Emilio."

Her comment surprises me. She rarely brings him up.

"Do you regret cheating on Henry?" I ask before I can think better of it.

She ponders my question while sipping her coffee. "No, he was never really with me. Don't get me wrong, I know Henry loved me, but not in the way I wanted to be loved. Emilio made me feel the things Henry didn't." She shrugs. "I guess Emilio stroked my ego."

I give her an incredulous look. Maybe I'd expected her to say no, because if she hadn't, she wouldn't have Jacob.

"Oh, come on, don't look at me like that. Are you telling me it wasn't the same for you with Ethan?"

What the fuck?

"No, we loved each other."

Why is she bringing up *my* relationship?

She laughs, but it's bitter, and I know it's a side effect of the alcohol. "That might be so, but don't deny it. You were devastated when Henry chose me." This is the spiteful side of Clara coming to the surface now. I lean back, her words a low blow. Of course I liked Henry, but the moment I found out about the two of them, it changed everything.

But now I know differently, the real reason he stayed with her, and if I were a lesser person, I'd probably say as much, but I bite my tongue instead. I won't use it as a weapon. I don't want to become that person.

"I won't say it didn't sting. You knew I had a crush on Henry, but I accepted it when you got together, and I moved on. It's what friends do."

Meg picks up the mug and downs the remaining coffee.

"Oh, you moved on all right. Into the arms of his identical twin brother, and you have the cheek to sit on a pedestal, judging me."

How did this escalate so fucking fast?

And the fact I've since been with Henry only adds to my issues and insecurities where these brothers are concerned.

"I'm not. I was here to help you. But I think I should go. We'll talk when you're sober."

"Fine, whatever, I don't need your help or your pity," she says, her voice laced with venom. It's the drink talking, but it still hurts.

I get to my feet and make my way to the front door. Peering over my shoulder, I call out, "Do yourself a favour, eat that toast, have another coffee, and take a damn bath before Jacob comes home."

She says nothing as I let myself out. I wonder if I'm doing the right thing—getting caught up in all of this. This could all backfire so badly, but she's my friend. I'm the closest person she has to family, and I'm not about to let her down when she and Jacob need me the most.

Chapter Twenty

Henry

Nathan hasn't said anything about Meghan being at ours this morning, even though he's dying to. The longer the question lingers unasked, the more agitated he's becoming, and he's starting to get on my nerves. It's radiating off him in waves as we eat lunch at our kitchen table. I finish my omelette and glance up, his eyes boring into me.

"Just ask me already."

He swallows the last bite of his burger and swipes his mouth with the back of his hand. I throw a serviette at him. He rolls his eyes but wipes his hands anyway.

"Fine. What the fuck are you doing, man? It's going to end in disaster."

It's a strong possibility. "I can't help how I feel about her. I've tried."

"Well, you should have tried harder."

I push away from the table and stand up. "You have no idea."

"You're right. I'm just a heartless bastard, right?" He points to his chest, and he continues before I get a chance to counter his comment. "I know what it's like to care about someone and not be able to act on it. But for the sake of hurting others, I let it be. No one is going to come away from this unscathed, and you know it."

His chest heaves, and I wonder who the fuck is important enough to him that he's willing to keep it in his pants. And I know none of this is fair on him. But the longer I kept her at arm's length, the harder it's become to ignore what she means to me. I'm weak when it comes to Meg. She's my guilty pleasure.

"Yeah, you're right, and if I were a better man, maybe I'd be more like you—or Ethan. Do you think I want to hurt anyone?" I sit back down with a heavy thump. "It's become a physical ache, and it's not the matter of it being a choice anymore. It's a need."

His shoulders relax as he lets out a breath. "Then do the right thing. Own up to it and tell Ethan. There have been enough secrets, don't you think?" He gets up and grabs our plates.

"I know, and believe it or not, I'm working on it," I reply to his retreating back.

He peers over his shoulder. "In that case, one piece of advice... stop with the sneaking around. Keep your hands to yourself and your dick in your pants until you come clean," he says, loading the plates into the dishwasher—something he rarely does. Something is up with him too, but I know there's no point asking because he'll deflect. And as much as I'd like to tell him to piss off right now, I know what he's saying is valid.

I decided to ring Meg. If I had my way, we'd do in person, but I'd struggle not to touch her. Getting lost in her could easily be my most favourite pastime.

"Hey," she answers on the first ring.

I slump down on my mattress, the bed slats creaking in protest. I need a new bed.

"You okay?" I ask, staring at my ceiling like it might give me some miracle answers.

Her breathing is heavy, as though she's been running. "Yeah, just been doing housework."

I need to get to the point before I start rambling about the weather and chicken out.

"Meg, I spoke to Nathan today." I pick at the skin around my thumbnail.

She clears her throat. "What did he say?"

"That we shouldn't be sneaking around."

I hear her sigh, and I know that whether she admits it or not, she feels the same. She doesn't want to hurt Ethan, and neither do I, but if we carry on like this, it's precisely what will happen.

"No, we shouldn't, and I wish part of me didn't feel guilty, but I do."

I nod even though she can't see me.

"Going behind his back isn't fair to him. He's my brother, and he's your ex."

"He's not just my ex, Henry. He's my best friend too."

Sighing into the phone, I cover my eyes with my arm. Her coconut scent still lingers on my bedding.

"I know, and I still feel as though the two of you have unfinished business, and I know you're still conflicted; otherwise, I think you would have agreed to tell him already."

I hate that I've voiced it, but I'm indeed fooling myself if I believe otherwise.

"So, what are you saying?" she asks, and I can hear the vulnerability in her question.

Inhaling deeply, I force myself to say the words that go against everything I'm feeling for her, but I know it's the right thing to do.

"We stop being physical and put the brakes on."

There's an awkward pause, and I have to pull my phone away from my ear to see if she's still there. It's so quiet.

"Meg?"

"Sorry, yeah, you're right." Her voice cracks before she continues. "I'll let you go. I'm sure you have lots to do."

I sit up. "Meg, I never said anything about acting like you don't exist. I still want to talk to you, its just holding off on being physical."

If she thinks I'm just going to walk away completely, she's sorely mistaken.

"Oh," she replies, and I swear I can hear the smile in her voice.

"In the meantime, let's get to know each other better," I suggest.

Of course I know the Meg we grew up with, the one who dated my brother, but I want to know her as she is now. Not the woman at the gym who hides behind a façade in front of her dad and her friends.

I relax against my headboard. "So, tell me something about you no-one knows."

"Hmm, like what?" she asks.

I let out a short laugh. "The deep stuff, something you've never spoken about to anyone before."

She's quiet as she ponders my question. The only sound is coming from the TV or radio in the background. I wait in the hopes she opens up to me the way I deeply crave.

"Okay." She clears her throat softly. "I found out where my mum lives, so when I'm feeling low, I drive to her house and sit in my car outside."

That's something I didn't expect her to say.

"You don't go inside?"

"No, we haven't talked since I was thirteen, the day before she walked out. Leaving my dad was one thing, but she left me too, without so much as a goodbye. I lost all respect for her."

Damn, I knew her mum and dad separated, but I never knew this. Now that I come to think about it, she's never talked about her before now.

"I'm sorry, Meg."

She sighs into the phone. "It is what it is. I didn't even realise they were still married until about four years ago when I accidentally saw the divorce papers on my dad's desk. It's the only reason I have her address, and curiosity got the better of me." I can hear Meg moving about, and I wonder if she's pacing up and down like she sometimes does when she's on the phone. "I don't even know why I go. It's weird, right?"

"No, not at all. Maybe you need closure or something?"

Our dad—or should I say sperm donor—left my mum when we were barely one year old. I don't know much, only what I overheard when my mum would talk to my aunty, and I know their relationship wasn't a pleasant one. So, we never pushed or even asked about him. We don't even remember him, so it's probably easier for us.

"Maybe. Who knows? Meh, I don't want to talk about my mum anymore. Your turn, tell me a truth."

I chew on the inside of my cheek. "After Clara left me for Emilio and I heard she was pregnant, I was so angry. Part of me wished it was mine. The other part was grateful. Could you imagine trying to co-parent with her and that arsehole?"

The sound of water running echoes in the background... I wonder if she's running a bath and wish I was there. I shake the thought away.

"If Jacob had been yours, would you have taken her back?"

I close my eyes and pause before answering. "No, I made that mistake once, and I know now it's not a good enough reason to stay in a relationship."

She scoffs. "That's true."

Rolling onto my side, I glance over my trophy shelves.

Until Clara fell pregnant, my only priority was my fighting. That changed when I thought I was going to be a dad.

"Do you want to know the worst part?"

"What?"

"Sometimes, I question if the baby we lost was mine at all."

I hate myself for even thinking it, but any trust I had where she was concerned was broken when I found out about her indiscretions with Emilio. I can't believe I'm even saying this out loud. I scrub my palm over my chin. I need a shave.

"Your feelings are warranted. She gave you a reason to doubt her. But I can't lie, I do feel sorry for her, and I know you probably don't want to hear that after she hurt you."

I smile. "I admire your empathy, Meg."

And it's true, she has a good heart, and she's loyal—all the things Clara isn't.

"I try my best to be. I feel sorry for Clara. She has this twisted fairy tale ideal about Emilio." It's hard to ignore the sadness lacing her voice.

"Have you seen him since he…" I can't finish my sentence. The thought of him touching her makes my blood boil.

I can already feel my blood pressure rising as I imagine that cunt with his hands on Meg.

"No, I made sure he was training before I went to see Clara. She was drunk and said some hurtful things."

Damn. I can't say I'm surprised; she always was a mean drunk. I doubt that's changed.

"I bet that wasn't pleasant."

"No, not particularly. She mentioned you," she admits.

I squeeze my eyes shut. "Oh, right. I'm sure that was enlightening."

"To be fair, I think there may have been some truth to her words. She said some things about us, about Ethan. Is this weird us talking about this?"

Shaking my head, I let out a deep breath. "No. How else

will we work through this? Ethan is your ex and my twin. Clara is my ex and your friend. It's just complicated."

"Do you think Ethan will forgive me when he finds out about us?" Her voice catches ever so slightly, and a stab of guilt pangs tightly in my chest cavity.

"If anyone needs his forgiveness, it will be me. You don't owe him anything, Meg, he dumped you."

"I'm sorry," she whispers.

"Don't be. We'll figure it out. We have to."

Growing up, me and Ethan had an agreement to never go after the same girl. This was only after the one time we did, and it didn't end well. We were thirteen when I wanted to ask Elissa Monroe from our karate class to be my girlfriend. And it turned out, so did he. It was the only time we physically fought outside of training or messing around. I got a busted lip and Ethan a split eyebrow—he still has a faint scar. Our mum was livid. It was the only time she ever grounded us. For two weeks, we had all our privileges removed. No karate, no outside of school clubs. It was torture.

By the time we did return to karate, Elissa was holding hands with some other boy. I felt like it was the end of the world. That night lying in bed, I had an epiphany and knew it would have hurt worse if she had chosen one of us, because then one of us would have been left hurting. And the thought of knowing it's inevitable when this all does come to light—someone will get hurt—makes me feel like a prick, but it's too late to go back now.

Chapter Twenty-One

Meghan

Henry and I stayed on the phone for over an hour yesterday, and as heavy as it was in places, I won't lie, it was freeing to be able to talk with him about anything and everything. His voice was calming, and yet at the same time, it set my skin ablaze. Not being with him physically isn't going to be easy, but it's a sacrifice I'm willing to make until this is all out in the open.

What worries me the most is what I can't control. How do I move forward while Ethan's feelings for me are still up in the air? And I know it's selfish of me, the way I need him. He's my safe place. I don't want to forfeit what we have, but it's cruel of me to expect him to continue allowing me to take from him when I'm not giving him anything in return. This is on me, not Henry. I owe it to Ethan to tell him the truth, he deserves to know, and I want it to come from me.

I've been sitting outside Ethan's mum's house for the past twenty minutes until I find the courage to knock. My stomach recoils with what I'm about to do. Turning up unannounced any other time wouldn't even be an issue. Yet right now, it feels wrong just to show up. I've had texts from Clara apologising about yesterday, but if I'm honest, the entire situation is becoming a little suffocating.

I stare at the newly bloomed tall stem irises with the ruffled flowers. They're the most beautiful wine tone. I think I just found my next hair colour. And then the door swings open.

Ethan is standing there, his face lighting up when he sees me, and I can't help but smile in return. He's always been infectious like that. He pulls me in for a quick hug in greeting and closes the door behind us.

"Couldn't stay away," he says with an easy smile.

I feel a pain in the back of my throat as I try to swallow before answering.

"I need to talk to you," I reply honestly. "Is your mum here?" I ask, my eyes scanning the length of the hallway, expecting to see Janet appear at any moment. She's a social worker but only works part-time now.

"No, she's at the office. Come up," he says, already heading upstairs, taking two at a time, the movement tightening his jeans over his perfect arse. And I hate myself for even making that observation. I take a deep breath and follow him, pausing in the landing at his door. I shake my head and enter. It's weird being in his childhood bedroom—old posters on the walls and trophies on the shelves with a stack of CDs and DVDs.

"When do you think you'll be moving back with Henry and Nathan?" I ask. It made sense for him to come here after the accident, but now he's recovered.

He shakes his head. "I'm not. I need my own space. I spoke to my mum about it and already have a studio flat lined up."

This surprises me. "What? I thought you liked living with Henry and Nathan?" I ask, arching my eyebrows.

"Come, sit." He sits and pats the space beside him on the double bed, but with his size, it might as well be a single.

"Meg, I know you're not here about my living arrangements. Is this about us?"

I kick off my trainers and join him, my thoughts filling with self-loathing as I think about how I will say this.

Nodding, he looks down at his jean-clad legs and begins picking at the frayed lining split over his knee.

I expect him to say more, but when he doesn't and the silence continues, my anxiety kicks in. I speak up before my fear takes over.

"The other day, when you told me not to question your feelings for me, the way you said it in the present tense, it confused me. It took me a long time to get over you, to get over us. And I'd be lying if I said this didn't change things between us."

He lets out a heavy sigh, his eyes locking on to mine. "Believe it or not, it was never my intention to hurt you. I didn't want to let you go. I've only ever wanted you."

My pulse drums heavily in my ears. "None of this makes sense."

"Believe it or not, I thought I was doing the right thing by you. It hurt me more than you know."

His words are sincere, but this still doesn't make any sense.

"I didn't know you were hurting. After the accident, I was consumed with my heartbreak and wanting you to get better... I didn't notice."

How was I supposed to know?

Ethan wraps his arm around my shoulder and pulls me into his warm body. I wrap my arm around his middle and rest my cheek against his chest. Being here like this with Ethan feels right—and yet wrong. It's not just about the two of us anymore.

"I should never have let you go," he admits, and those words have the power to destroy me.

My breathing speeds up, and my pulse throbs wildly. All my emotions surface, and I try my hardest to keep them at bay. And then I'm crying because how do I tell him about Henry and me after his admission?

"Come on, it's not that bad," he says, stroking my back gently.

I shake my head. "I care about you, Ethan, and that's never changed, but I care about Henry too," I choke out.

His chest heaves with a huge sigh.

"I know you do. You always have. It's okay," he says, trying to comfort me.

I pull back, searching his face. "Do you hate me?"

He shakes his head. "I could never hate you, Meg," he says, kissing my forehead.

"You say that now," I say, panicking. "But I need both of you, as selfish as that sounds, and I know that sounds fucked up."

Ethan doesn't say anything, just regards me with a pensive expression. He takes hold of my hand, his thumb rubbing over the palm of my hand in the comforting way I love so much.

The hairs rise on the back of my neck, and I hate how he still has a physical effect on me, even now.

Maybe if he didn't, this would be easier.

Everything he does is natural. It's not second-guessed or pre-empted. He's always been very tactile like this. Even after the breakup and the accident, he'd still pull me into his side and hug me. At first, it messed with my equilibrium, but then I remembered he was that way before we'd even started dating, so I stopped trying to overanalyse it and realised I craved the contact.

I wonder what his mum must think of our friendship? Does she know I have feelings for both her sons? His thumb tops circle my palm, and I glance up to find him watching me. His focus is intense. The way he stares makes my flesh break out in goosebumps, and a warm, familiar flutter comes to life in my stomach. I take a deep breath, needing to fill my lungs with his eyes roaming over my lips. The moment is charged, my body hyper-aware of his presence as he lowers his face, his nose softly brushing against mine.

"Tell me to stop," he says, barely above a whisper—the familiar scent of fresh peppermint skating across my lips. But I can't. Instead, I pull him closer, longing to feel his lips on mine once more, to see if his touch is still as I remember.

His lips meet mine, soft at first, tentative. I cup the back of his neck, drawing him closer as our kiss becomes more demanding—desperate.

And then I'm on my back as he rolls on top of me, his hardness pressed against my centre. I open my legs instinctively, a long-forgotten reaction as I wrap my legs around his waist. My eyes roll to the back of my head as he rocks into me, once, twice, three times. And allowing myself this moment of pleasure, being under him once again, it's all-consuming. So many sensations flood through my body. The way he smells so familiar, soapy, fresh, and radiant. I always loved how my clothes lingered with his scent when we were apart.

But when he groans in my ear, the spell is broken, and it's Henry's face that flashes behind my eyelids. I struggle beneath Ethan, pushing him and untangling my limbs from his. I shove at his chest, recoiling from our kiss.

"Oh my God," I say, breathless, covering my mouth with the rise of bile working its way up my throat.

"Meg…" Ethan's voice is pained when he says my name, and I hate that it's my fault.

But I can't deal with this, not right now. I'm off the bed, shoving my feet into my trainers, my hands shaking uncontrollably.

And then I'm leaping down the stairs.

The echo of him calling my name follows me, but I don't stop. I pull open the front door and sprint down the path. I fumble with my keys, trying to unlock my car.

And then I'm inside, locking my seat belt into place. I've barely turned the ignition when I slam my foot down on the accelerator, the wheels spinning as I pull away too fast. But I don't care; I need to put distance between us.

But it's not long before I pull over in a neighbouring street, braking hard, unable to see shit through my barrage of tears.

What did I just do?

I've well and truly fucked up this time.

Chapter Twenty-Two

Henry

After my recent conversation with both Meg and Nathan, I know now what I need to do. I can't keep pretending this isn't happening—that either way, Meg and I are inevitable. I need to be the one to speak to Ethan. He deserves that much. I talked to my mum earlier, so I know she's at work, and with him working remotely, I decide it's now or never.

How do I explain to him that this isn't a passing affair and the feelings I have for Meg run deep? I want to be free to explore this with her without the guilt afterwards. Even though we're not cheating, part of me feels as though we are.

I almost don't notice the car parked outside and have to double-take—Meg's car. The hairs on the back of my neck prickle, and a sinking feeling swamps my stomach. Using my key, I let myself inside. The sound of movement above my head has me creeping upstairs, making sure to avoid the ones that creak.

My breathing is so loud I wonder if anyone else can hear me coming. I couldn't even tell you why I'm sneaking, but something has my twin senses on high alert. My adrenaline begins to spike as I pause on the landing.

And now there is no denying the familiar sounds coming from Ethan's room—I've heard them myself. I hold my breath and approach the open door. It takes me a moment to understand the scene before me. I blink, but no, my eyes are not playing tricks on me.

Ethan is covering Meg's body, her arms wrapped around his neck, her legs gripping his waist. They're kissing one another so fervently, as though nothing else exists at this moment but the two of them.

I'm suspended in time, unable to pry my gaze away from them. My pulse speeds up, my heartbeat pounding. Red hot heat flushes through my body, and my palms are sweating. I remind myself to breathe.

Struggling to fathom a coherent thought, the illogical part of me wants to rip him away from her and beat the fucking crap out of him before I scream at her and demand she tells me what the fuck she's playing at. The other part of me knows I need to step away and remove myself from the situation.

It takes all my strength and self-control to back away and make my way back downstairs. My head is pounding, and I feel nauseous. Shit, I'm going to vomit. I rush to the downstairs toilet and make it to the sink just in time to lose the contents of my stomach.

I run the tap and rinse my mouth, splashing my face with cold water before slumping down onto the toilet seat. Noises from above grow heavier, feet pounding. Ethan is calling out to Meg to stop.

Forcing myself to my feet, I step out into the hallway to see the front door wide open and Meg sprinting to her car. She's barely situated, slamming the door closed before she's peeling away.

The stairs creak behind me, and I turn to see Ethan mid-step, his hair sticking up all over the place, his T-shirt dishevelled.

And all I can do is try to breathe through my rage.

"Shit," he curses.

His face is pale, his eyes haunted.

I tilt my head as we share a silent exchange.

"What the fuck, Ethan? You just couldn't leave her well enough alone, could you?"

Ethan shakes his head. "It's none of your fucking business," he says, clenching his fists, his knuckles white.

I scoff at that, edging closer. "Isn't it? I care about her, and all you're doing is confusing her even more, giving her mixed fucking signals."

Ethan raises his eyebrows. "Why the fuck do you care so much?" he asks, coming down the stairs the rest of the way.

"Because, unlike you, I won't throw her away as you did."

I can see the way he's grinding his jaw. His pupils dilate, his nostrils flaring.

"And what the fuck is that supposed to mean?"

Shaking my head, I let out a humourless laugh. "It means she deserves better than you."

"Oh, and by that, you mean you?"

"I wouldn't have slept with her otherwise," I grit out.

A sense of both relief and regret fills me simultaneously.

His entire body is tense, and I know it's taking him every effort not to lash out.

"When?" he asks, his voice strained, his eyes dark.

I know what he's asking, and I shake my head. Out of everything, the fact he even has to ask hurts the most. "Never while you were together. It was the other day." I shift uncomfortably, hating this boiling tension and unease between us. "I was coming here to talk to you about her... about us."

A noise behind me catches my attention, and I realise the front door is still wide open and Mrs Ronald is staring at the house while walking her corgi from across the way. I close it.

The last thing I need is her gossiping with the other neighbours or relaying this back to our mum.

"So, what, are you two together?"

I shake my head. "It's complicated."

His reply is full of mirth. "I'd say. She just had her tongue down my fucking throat."

"Watch your mouth," I snap, leaping forward.

I shove him hard, and he falls back against the stairs.

But he rights himself quickly, and before I know what's happening, he slams me into the front door. The entire frame rattles.

I see red and swing for his face. He blocks me and punches me in the stomach, but it's not enough to stop me. I punch him in the kidney.

We start to scuffle, and then the sound of glass smashing causes us both to freeze. I look past him to see the mirror which was hanging on the wall is now shattered, littering the hallway floor.

"Fuck." I push off Ethan and go inspect the damage. This is my mum's house, and this is beyond disrespectful.

I grip my hair. "Why couldn't you just leave her be?" I say through gritted teeth.

"Why couldn't you?" he says from behind me.

I turn back to him. His T-shirt has a slight tear, there's a bruise to his cheek, and his hair is ruffled. If my mum walked in now, I'm pretty sure she'd rip us both a new one.

"You think I wanted this?" I say, pointing to myself, waving my hand over the destruction caused by our altercation. One that should never have happened—there's a reason he's no longer allowed to fight professionally.

"I think if you were any kind of brother, you would have talked to me first. Not fuck her behind my back," he says incredulously.

I take a step toward him but stop myself. My muscles

quiver and I know there'll be no taking this back if I don't walk away.

"I'll let you have that, one time, just one time." I hold up my finger. "But if you say that again, we are no longer brothers. I'm not the one leading her on a year after dumping her. You are. You're the only one who is fucking with her."

He shakes his head, and I know he's at war with himself too. For the first time in my life, I hate that we're twins. I wish we weren't so emphatically attuned to each other.

"Again, you don't know shit. Meg kissed me back."

I nod. "Yeah, I saw, but I also saw her running out of here like her arse was on fire too. What the fuck does that tell you?"

"It tells me she doesn't know what the hell she wants."

His insinuation that she might well choose him makes me feel physically sick again.

"Which is why I was coming here to talk to you."

Ethan turns and pulls open the door under the stairs, retrieving a dustpan and brush.

"Yeah, well, it's too little too late. So much for loyalty. You should have talked to me before you got your dick wet."

Shaking my head, I look him up and down.

"Is that what you think? I was just after some action?"

He raises an eyebrow and shoulder bumps me out of the way as he begins sweeping up the shattered glass.

"What I think is that you should have tried harder and at least spoke to me before you shacked up."

I want to argue with him, tell him he's wrong, but he's right, and it only makes this whole situation worse.

"So, what, you're together now?"

I shake my head. "No, and after today, I think it's clear she doesn't know what she wants."

Ethan leans against the bannister. "Or who."

"You had your chance, E, and you threw her away like she was nothing."

He propels himself towards me, and I stand firm, expecting him to lash out, but he stops right in front of me.

"You don't know what the fuck you're talking about," he says through gritted teeth.

I raise my eyebrows. "No? And who's fault is that?"

We both stand toe to toe, chest to chest, both of us breathing heavily. He never talked to me about what drove him to dump Meg. We'd always been close, but I guess we all have our secrets, don't we?

My phone starts ringing in my pocket, breaking the crackling tension between us. It's Nathan, and I realise before I swipe to answer that I'm late for training. Fucking fantastic.

"I'm on my way, and before you chew me out, I'm sorry," I say, already opening the front door. I don't give Nathan the chance to reply before I hang up.

"I need to go, but when you're ready to talk about this properly, you know where to find me." And with that, I turn and walk away, leaving him to deal with the mess we made.

Chapter Twenty-Three

Meghan

I drove home in a daze as I stewed over what I just did. I kissed Ethan. I went to confess about Henry and me, and instead, I stuck my tongue down his throat. I made out with him like I didn't have a care in the world.

What the actual fuck was I thinking? Oh, that's right, I wasn't, because for a brief moment, I was his and he was mine, and everything was good again. I was right where I wanted to be, safe under his touch.

All my thoughts evaporated until they returned like a hurricane of hailstones. How is it possible to have feelings for them both? What is wrong with me?

I go straight to the fridge, searching for I don't know what and then I see a bottle of Prosecco.

Peeling off the foil, I untwist the wire cage covering the cork and push up with my thumbs. The bottle slips between my palms, and my heart lurches as I almost drop it. Reaching for a tea towel, I wrap it around the neck of the bottle to give me a better purchase as I try again.

"What the fuck is wrong with this damn cork?"

Not willing to give up, I wrap the tea towel around it and wiggle it until it pops, and Prosecco bubbles over my hand and down my wrist.

Of course it does.

I bring my hand to my mouth in an attempt to lick up the mess and then reach for a high ball glass. Do I care it's not a wine glass? Nope. I take myself to my room, locking my door behind me. The last thing I need is to be caught by my dad. No doubt he'll question the wine bottles' disappearance, not that it's any of his business. I'm a grown arse woman for crying out loud.

Grabbing my noise-cancelling headphones, I pull up my Bastille playlist and hit shuffle, turning the volume up as loud as my eardrums can handle.

It's my go-to when things around me become suffocating. I once listened to the same Imagine Dragons album every day without fail for an entire month. It's probably why my dad got me these headphones for Christmas.

This is just one example of why I need to get my own place. I don't want him to think I'm deserting him as my mother did, but I need the freedom to breathe both at home and at work. I know I need to make some drastic changes. All I have to do is wait it out until Henry has his fight with Emilio and get Clara away from him once and for all.

As soon as Henry's fight is over and Clara is away from Emilio, I need to make drastic changes to my own life. The longer I ignore it and allow it to fester, the more of myself I lose.

Filling the glass, I take a huge gulp, and yes, granted, I should sip it, but what-fucking-ever. Surprisingly, it doesn't take long before I'm pouring the remaining dregs into my glass and finishing off the bottle.

I'm not a big drinker, so I'm already feeling the effects of the alcohol as it works its way through my system. Unfortunately, I can still remember what I did, and if anything, the guilt is even more encompassing.

Breathless, I reach for my phone; I don't know if it's my anxiety rising or the alcohol or both, which has my heart racing in my chest. It's as though I've done a workout. Is this what it feels like to have a heart attack? Okay, fine, I know I'm dramatic, but this whole situation is fucked up beyond all recognition.

Henry deserves to know what a weak arse bitch I am.

It takes me typing and deleting six messages before I settle on one.

I'm so sorry, Henry. I kissed Ethan.

I hit send before stopping myself and then break out in a hot flush, sitting up so fast my head spins.

"Oh my God. Oh my God. Oh my God."

Bubbles appear, and I wait, and wait, and wait, but they vanish. I pull up his number. My finger hovers, but I can't do it.

"Shit."

I throw my phone across the room, but the moment it leaves my hand, I regret my outburst. I watch as it hits the wall before smashing to the floor with a thud. I scramble onto my knees, praying it's not damaged. Surveying my phone, I see a crack on the screen protector, but otherwise, it doesn't look too bad.

And that's when a notification banner appears. I slide my thumb to bring up the message from Henry and hold my breath.

I know!

My breathing comes out choppy, my head pounding.

He knows.

I saw you with him.

I cover my mouth as ice-cold shivers break out all over my

flesh. My stomach rolls violently enough for me to know I won't make it to my bathroom, so I stagger to my wastepaper bin and regurgitate an entire bottle of Prosecco. When the dry heaving subsides, I take some deep breaths before pushing to my feet, taking the bin into my bathroom and flushing the contents down the toilet. I'm grateful it was at least free of rubbish—small mercies. I hose it down with the shower and leave it in the bath.

Henry saw Ethan and me kissing.

I rack my brain, trying to figure out how even to respond. How to explain it was a moment of weakness, and how at that moment, a wave of nostalgia took over. To tell him I was confused about us—about Ethan. I want to ask him to forgive me, but if he loathes me as much as I hate myself right now, it's a moot point.

My knees are weak as I force my legs to move, one foot in front of the other, as I drag my—now—shaking body to bed. Shivering, I crawl under the covers, but the moment I lay back, the room starts spinning. I throw a leg off the edge of the bed to ground me and cover my eyes with my arm, willing my heart to calm down.

A guttural moan works its way up my throat, a sob breaking free, knowing I've made this worse, and I have no idea how to begin to make this right.

None of this would have happened if I'd been strong enough to leave Henry alone. I am drawn to him like a magnet. And now I'm alone, with only myself to blame. It's not like I can confide in Clara, not about this, and Nathan is already stuck in the middle. There's Olly, but he's probably still pissed off with me over the incident with Rachel, not that I can blame him.

Until this moment, I've never been bothered about having a small circle of friends, but now that circle is so fractured, I'm questioning if keeping myself cut off from others outside of work is such a good thing.

Fuck my life.

The truth is there is no easy fix. Hell, there might not be a fix at all. Before I do something stupid like sending embarrassing text messages, or worse, drunk dial Henry, I hold my thumb down on the off button and then swipe to power off. I just want to sleep and forget this even happened.

Chapter Twenty-Four

Henry

Meg didn't respond to my text last night, and in a way, I'm glad. I was already too vexed after my altercation with Ethan. I don't know where we go from here or how we can move past this. I want to kick myself. Ethan had been withdrawn, he'd pulled back from me, and I thought it was because of the accident, but now I know it was more than that. He's still in love with Meg.

I still don't understand his reasons for letting her go. She was in love with him. I know she never would have strayed. Our first kiss only happened because she was hurting, confused, and I still worry I took advantage of that situation even though it was never my intent.

And then I caught them in an embrace. So many emotions were vying for my attention—anger, hurt, betrayal—and then there was the dominant part of me that wanted to claim her as my own.

But Meg isn't a damn possession, she isn't a fucking toy, and this isn't a game. I don't know if I'll ever understand what happened or why she kissed him, but seeing it was too much. I wanted to be the one devouring her mouth, touching her, pleasing her.

"H, you aren't going to be any good in this fight if you can't concentrate."

I let out a grunt, lowering the weight to the ground with a heavy thump.

"I'm trying, man, but what can I say? You were right."

He doesn't bother to gloat at my admission. "Sorry, H, it was always going to get messy." It's a resigned statement, not a dig. He knew something was up, so I told him. Hell, I needed to tell someone. The shocked expression would have made me laugh under any other circumstance.

The hairs on the back of my neck stand to attention, and I know it's her. I've always felt her presence even before I gave into my feelings and began to acknowledge them.

Nathan's eyes dart from me to Meg, his eyebrows drawn in, his shoulders now tense as she makes a beeline towards us.

"I'm going to grab a bottle of water. You want one?" he asks. I shake my head and silently thank him as he makes himself scarce while Meg steps up beside me. Her dark hair is plaited over her shoulder, her face free of makeup, and even now, I can't deny my attraction towards her.

She opens her mouth to speak, but nothing comes out. She clears her throat and tries again—still nothing. Her eyes go to mine but quickly look away. They're bloodshot, the opposite of how they usually appear.

I think she's about to bolt as she makes to step away, but she owes me some kind of explanation, at least. So, I reach for her elbow and hate how my body betrays my inner turmoil, and I instantly let go.

The gym is pretty empty except for a few regulars, but none are within earshot, and I know if I don't speak now, I never will.

"Why, Meg? Why did you do it?" It's the one question I

want answers to as much as I don't. Hell, I'm a glutton for punishment.

She shifts on her feet as she takes a deep pained breath and blinks before focusing on me, trying to hold back unshed tears.

"Honestly, I don't know. I wish I did," she replies, her voice cracking before she stares down at her feet. She looks haunted, and I want to comfort her, pull her into my arms, tell her it's okay and that we'll work this out, but it would be a lie.

"I'm sorry," she says, her words so quiet I barely register them over the sound of the music echoing from the sound system.

"It's a little too late for sorry," I reply coldly, and even I don't recognise my voice.

And this time, when she turns to walk away, I don't stop her.

I'm restless, bouncing on the balls of my feet as I watch her retreating shoulders slump, and then she disappears inside one of the training rooms.

When Nathan sees she's gone, he comes back over and hands me a sports drink. With a sympathetic look on his face, he points over his shoulder. "You cool?" he asks, and damn if that isn't a loaded question.

I shrug. "I have to be. I need to focus on this fight," I reply, hoping I sound more confident than I feel. Nothing has changed. Emilio still needs to be put in his place. And this fight is personal.

I've been pounding the training bag for the past hour, so I hardly notice the commotion of excited chitter-chatter until I hear a familiar laugh.

What the fuck?

I pull back from the bag and peer over my shoulder—Ethan's here.

He hasn't been back to the gym since his accident, and even from here, I can tell he's uncomfortable. But I don't miss the way his shoulders relax a fraction when he notices me.

Even though he won't admit it, I know it's a lot for him to show up here. He turned me down a few months back when I asked if he'd be up for helping me with my training. I think it was too soon, a reminder his fighting career had been cut short.

I wipe the sweat from my forehead and nod when he stops in front of me.

He gives me a small smile, and regardless of the Meg situation, there's something nostalgic about him being here.

"E," I say, finally breaking the silence and holding out my wrapped fist to connect with his.

"I never thought I'd see the day," Nathan chimes in, slapping him hard on the back.

Ethan rolls his eyes. "Yeah, well, this one needs my help. No way am I letting my baby brother into the lion's den unless I'm sure he's ready."

I let out a puff of exaggerated air. "Hardly little, brother. You have six minutes on me—*six*—and I'm still an inch taller than you."

He laughs. It's genuine and damn good to hear. "And doesn't your ego know it."

"Burn," says Nathan, laughing, and I'm transported back to a time when this was how things used to be between us.

"Not going to lie, I'm surprised you're here, considering."

"Yeah, well, things got out of hand yesterday, and I'm here to try and make it right."

Nathan glances between the two of us and gives me one curt nod.

"So, you're what? Here to help me train?" I ask.

"Yep," he says, stuffing his hands into his jean pockets.

I smile in response. "Okay then, old man, lead the way."

Nathan relays what we've been doing and where I'm lacking, and Ethan makes some suggestions, all of which are pretty good too.

We all laugh, breaking the tension, when a loud noise catches our attention. Meghan is scrambling to pick up a dumbbell, but her eyes are darting between Ethan and me, a look of utter dismay crossing her features.

Ethan turns to me, clearing his throat. "I should talk to her, especially if I'm going to be spending more time here," he says, pointing his thumb over his shoulder.

I don't say anything in response. A war of emotions crosses her face, and I get an uncomfortable twinge in my gut as she struggles to meet his eyes. He leans in to whisper in her ear. I see the slight nod of her head before she turns, and he follows her into the staff room, where they both disappear behind a closed door.

"Well, that's not fucking awkward," Nathan mutters under his breath.

"It is what it is."

I angle myself back in front of the bag and punch it repeatedly—one, two, three, one, two, three. I try to breathe through every controlled punch, ignoring the unease in my gut, curious about what is being said between them. Is he asking her to give them another chance? I hate everything about this situation. I can't even be self-righteous enough to say I deserve her over him. Maybe its karma coming back to bite me on the arse for pretending what Clara and I had was more than what it was.

If she chooses him, then so be it.

I buried my feelings for her once before. If I have to, I can do it again, right?

Chapter Twenty-Five

Meghan

My entire world tilted on its axis when I saw Ethan and Henry standing around chatting as if nothing had happened—fumbling to pick up the dumbbell, which was centimetres from landing on my foot. All I did was draw attention to both sets of eyes on me. If I could have got up and run, I would have.

Ethan approaches me in confident strides, and I hate him for it. The closer he gets, the more uncomfortable I become. The guilt of kissing him weighs heavy.

"Can we talk somewhere private?"

I nod and lead him to the staff room, where he closes the door behind us. I inhale and exhale before I find the courage to face him. I go to speak, but he silences me by bringing his forefinger to my lips. He drops his hand. "I knew you were conflicted, and I kissed you anyway, and for that, I'm sorry. It was a dick move on my part."

I hate how he's so gracious about all of this. You know that saying about the good ones? Yeah, that's him, he is one of the good ones, the best even, making it so much more difficult.

"I'm just so confused," I reply honestly.

He reaches for my hand and rubs his thumb over my skin. "Because you have feelings for both me and Henry?"

This is it, the time to stop denying all of this. "Yes."

"You slept with him."

Air rushes from my lungs. He knows.

I nod. "But never… not while we were together," I stutter.

"I believe you," he says, leaning closer.

Panic rolls through me, and for a moment, I think he might kiss me again, but his lips land softly on my forehead.

"You don't hate me?" I ask. My voice is weak.

"No, not even a little bit. I should have been honest with you, told you I still had feelings for you."

He squeezes my hand, giving me the anchor I need to brave asking him my question.

"Then why didn't you?"

Ethan sighs and a faint scent of peppermint washes over me; I swear he's never without a roll of polos.

"Because it wouldn't have changed anything, and besides, my feelings aren't your issue, Meg, they're mine." He lets go of my hand and steps back.

I'm losing him all over again.

"I wanted you to know that you'll likely see me hanging around again. I want to make sure H is ready for this fight."

I bite my lip, unsure how to respond, my nose tingling as tears threaten to escape.

"Isn't it awkward with everything?" I ask, pointing back and forth between us.

He shrugs, and I know he's trying to appear indifferent, but he's tense. "A little, but we'll work through it. He's my brother." He's trying to spare my feelings. Even when he dumped me, he wasn't horrible about it, and even now, after I kissed him and slept with Henry, he's still gracious about it—something I don't deserve.

"Maybe you and I can talk soon?"

I give him a weak nod, and he leaves me alone, standing in the middle of the staff room, wondering how everything around me imploded. I wish I could be anywhere but here right now, but I have a training session in less than fifteen minutes. The last thing I need is my dad giving me grief.

After a few deep breaths, I get back out there and set the equipment up ready. To say the next hour is horrendous would be an understatement. It's unavoidable, this invisible fucking pull, and anytime I subconsciously seek out Henry, I find his eyes on me when he's not focused on Ethan.

It's as though I'm silently being scrutinised, and I feel exposed for the woman I never wanted to be and yet I'm quickly becoming. We agreed not to be physical, even though we were never together, not really. And yet, I can't justify my behaviour no matter how I try to spin this. What I did was wrong. I betrayed my best friend, and in turn, I betrayed Henry.

I lose track of my client's number of sit-ups and immediately suggest cardio on the rowing machine for ten minutes instead. My emotions are haywire, and everything is so up in the air. I'm no good to anyone like this. I chew on the inside of my cheek. The best thing I can do for myself is take some time away from Henry, the gym, and the drama. I'm due some annual leave, and it's about time I took it.

When my dad turns up towards closing, he spots Ethan as soon as he enters. I snort under my breath as they chat it up like they're old buddies. *Yeah, right.* He couldn't stand him when we were together. I shake my head and scan through the computer, pulling up the diary for my appointment schedules. If I jiggle some around, I can take the entire week off—starting this Monday.

I make the calls necessary and block out my appointments for next week and update the diary.

"Shit!" I startle, my hand flying to my chest when a shadow falls over me. Henry stands beside me at the reception counter.

"Sorry, I thought you heard me," he says.

"No, I was preoccupied," I admit, trying to cover my unease.

His lips pull into a firm line, his usual smile vacant.

"I just wanted to see if I can get some time in the upstairs training room booked out for the next few weeks."

I clear my throat. "Of course." Moving the cursor to the diary, I see what's available. "Wednesday afternoon, Thursday morning and Sunday afternoon are all free."

I peek up as he mulls it over. "Can you put me down for Wednesday and Sunday?"

"Yep." My voice sounds shaky, but I try to ignore it as I type in his name and highlight the days. "I've blocked them out for the month, and then you can re-access if you need them after that."

"Thank you."

This is all very formal, and I try not to allow it to sting. Is this how we'll be now? Amicable? If I thought things were stunted after our initial kiss, what would they be like now we've had sex?

I notice my dad approaching, along with Ethan and Nathan, and I wish I could flee.

"Of course, just get her to sign up with Meg," my dad says, and I feel a twinge of annoyance. I'm a trainer first and foremost, not a fucking receptionist.

"What's that?" I ask, hoping I don't sound how I feel, staring over Henry's shoulder as Nathan comes to stand next to him.

"My sister needs some guidance, and your dad suggested you."

I nod, my cheeks heating. He was recommending me. "Of course, no problem," I reply.

"Do you have anything free for next week?" he asks, leaning on his elbows, trying to peer at the screen. I turn it away from him, and he holds his hands up in surrender.

"No, I'm off next week, but I can do the week after."

I feel all eyes on me as I glance back down to the keyboard.

"What? Since when?" asks my dad. And this is why working for my father has got to change.

"Since I need some time off and I have annual leave. All my appointments have been re-arranged, so it's all good."

Dad grunts in response, but thankfully doesn't challenge me any further.

"The following Tuesday good?" I ask Nathan, plastering on my best fake smile.

He nods and gives me her details, and I hand him one of my appointment cards to pass on to her.

When everyone disperses, I can breathe a little lighter. And I get busy closing down the computer and turning off the sound system. Finished, I head up to my dad's office, tapping on the open door as I enter.

"I'm off. You finished?" I ask.

He shakes his head. "No, I'm going to stay a while, finish off these accounts," he says without so much as a glance in my direction.

Grabbing my bag, I dig out my keys and make my way outside and through the car park. I swear the lights are getting worse out here. It's creepy as fuck.

So when I see a dark figure leaning against my car, I pause mid-step, my heart racing.

"Meg," Henry says, and I let out a relieved sigh and continue walking.

"What are you doing lurking in a dark car park?" I ask, only half-joking.

"I wouldn't be if your gym had better lighting installed out here," he says, uncrossing his arms and holding them out for emphasis.

I shake my head. "We would if it wasn't a private car park. My dad is working on it," I say defensively.

"Sorry," he replies, rubbing his palm over his chin.

I pull my bag closer to my body. "Did you need something?"

He pushes away from my car. "I wanted to know if you're taking time off because of me—and the situation?"

The situation. I'm a fucking situation now?

"No," I reply—probably too sharply.

He steps closer. "You're lying. I could talk to my sponsor, ask about moving my training to another gym."

I shake my head. "Please don't. It's not fair and my dad shouldn't have to suffer, not because of me," I reply.

Not when I was the one who fucked up.

Henry doesn't counter my comment about me insinuating it's my fault, and I'd be lying if I said it didn't hurt.

Instead, he looks over my shoulder, stuffing his hands into the front pocket of his hoody.

"Anyway, it will probably do us some good if I have some time away, so we can move past this," I say, waving my hand between us.

"Yeah, you're probably right."

And fuck if that doesn't feel like a slap to the face.

Unable to form a reply, I step around him and focus on going through the motions of getting in my car.

"Bye, Meghan," he says, right before I pull my door shut.

I only nod, knowing if I try to speak, all that will come out is a stifled sob. It takes everything in me not to let him see how much this affects me, especially when he is so indifferent. Instead, I focus on my drive home, biting the inside of my cheek until I draw blood, enough to make my eyes water.

Understanding dawns on me that no matter what happens, things will never be the same again, and I've never hated myself more than I do at this moment.

Chapter Twenty-Six

Henry

This week has been the longest I've ever gone without seeing Meg, and to say it feels wrong is an understatement. Before, I took her presence for granted because she's always been there, up until now. The longer she's away and radio silent, the bigger this emptiness grows.

Training has been challenging but going better than I would've expected. It's helped with Ethan having my back, and between him and Nathan, we have a good routine going.

But it's bittersweet and nostalgic. I can see how much it hurts him, no longer fighting, and even though he acts indifferent, I know better. I'd be lying if I said I wasn't grateful to be spending time with him like this again, though.

We're as similar as twins can be to look at, and other than having MMA in common, we couldn't be more different. He's super intelligent. It's why he's doing so well as a computer programmer. I'm probably the only person I know who can mess up my TV just trying to use a remote controller.

And then there's Meg—and no denying we've both fallen for the same woman. The selfish part of me wants her all to myself, but I have no idea where we stand, or if there's even an us. I thought about reaching out to her, sending a text or calling, yet I couldn't find my nerve. What would I even say?

I know I had my tongue in your pussy, and then you kissed my brother, but I still want you.

It sounds sick and twisted even in my head, but I can't help my feelings any more than Ethan can help his.

"So, you heard from her?" Ethan asks. I hate how we do this—pick up on each other's thoughts.

"Nope."

He nods. "Me neither. It's unlike her. Even after everything, we've always spoken to each other. I'm worried about her." His admission causes me to stop what I'm doing and face him.

"Are we doing this? Are we going to talk about it?" I ask, a little taken back.

Picking up a towel, he tosses it to me, and I wipe my face.

"Yes. It's not like this is going to sort itself out," he says, taking a seat on the empty bench.

I hate how he's right.

"So, what do you think we should do? Invite her for dinner and get it all out in the open?"

His eyebrows rise as though he's contemplating my suggestion.

I shake my head. "I was being sarcastic."

"It's not the worst idea. And I want to make sure she's not doing anything stupid where Clara and Emilio are concerned."

My muscles tense. "What do you mean?"

He lets out a heavy sigh. "You know she wants to help Clara leave him?"

I shake my head, because no, I didn't know.

"And how exactly does she plan to do that?" I ask, trying to keep the bite from my tone.

Ethan wipes his palms over his jean-clad thighs. "I think

she has an idea, but it's sketchy at best, and I think we should try to talk her out of it."

I let out a grunt. "Like she'd listen to us. You know better than anyone what she's like when she has something in her head, there's no talking her out of it."

I use the towel to wipe down the handles of the leg press bench I've been using.

He shrugs. "I don't know, but I think she'll listen to you."

I scoff at him. "I doubt it." He's beginning to irritate me. "I think it's best I keep my distance."

Not that I want to, but what choice do I have without Ethan's blessing?

He looks up, his elbows on his knees, his hands gripped together. "I think you're wrong. There's always been something between you two, whether you want to admit it or not. Contrary to what you might think, I do understand. I ended things with her. I was the one who planted the seed."

So, what, was it some kind of test? Because if it was, I failed in epic proportions.

"But it never would have happened if you'd stayed with her, and you know it."

His jaw ticks. "Yeah, but I didn't want to be with someone who was settling. She didn't feel the same way I felt about her."

Is he serious?

"Right, so then why did you have to go and kiss her?"

I watch as he clenches and unclenches his fists. "Because I needed to know."

"Know what?"

"If we still had something."

I shake my head. "So you what… want to rekindle your relationship, is that it?" I ask, raising my voice. A few heads turn our way.

"You're twisting my words."

"Okay, so what do we do now?" I ask and reach for my gloves, wondering if Olly is here yet.

"We let her decide what she wants to do."

So what is he saying? If she chooses me, what? He'll give us his blessing?

"Let's spar," he says, nodding to the gloves in my hand.

I recoil. "What?"

"I said, let's spar," he replies, rummaging in my bag for Nathan's gloves.

I snatch them off him and drop them on top of my bag, but he bends down and swipes them up again.

"Don't be a dick. I can still spar and probably wipe the floor with you while I'm at it."

I can't hide the twitch of my lip. He probably could even without the conditioning training. He always was the better fighter, even I can admit to that.

He can see me wavering, and he pouts.

"Come on, a little light sparring," he says. His eyes sparkle with something I haven't seen in such a long time, and it's impossible to hide my smile.

"Okay, fine. But we're wearing headgear."

He shrugs like it's no big deal, which is good because I won't take the risk otherwise.

Once we're ready and in the ring, he crowds me, hopping from one foot to the other, baiting me, punching the air, and I can't help but laugh.

"You ready, little brother?"

I take my stance and let him come at me. I'm a little surprised when his punch causes me to lurch backwards, not expecting him to go so hard so fast.

I swing at him, but he dodges my attack, and my fist meets air with a loud whoosh.

"What the fuck, man? Have you been training on the sly?"

His smirk is enough of an answer, but I'm surprised he

managed to do it under our mum's watch. If she had her way, he'd be dressed in bubble wrap.

"I guess it's game on then."

We go at it for a good twenty minutes when we're interrupted by a loud wolf whistle.

"Never thought I'd see this again," Nathan says as he approaches the ring.

"It's in the blood," Ethan replies, hardly even out of breath.

I can't imagine what it was like to have his dreams ripped right out from under him. But he's never been the same. For a long time, he wouldn't even talk about it. I never thought he would get back in a ring again, even if only to spar. But I'd also never want him to fight again, not professionally, not when I know one blow to the head could leave him dead.

It's not long before we have a crowd, Olly and Nathan making backhanded comments, trying to throw me off, but it's all good-natured, and it feels fucking good. The human body, although fragile and delicate, can be strong and resilient too. Ethan is a prime example.

And for the first time since all this started with Meg, I feel better. The tension between Ethan and me, though it's not gone entirely, is now lighter. Granted, he didn't come out right and say he was cool with it, but he didn't say he wasn't either.

Chapter Twenty-Seven

Meghan

Laying on the sun lounger, I stare up at the passing clouds. Listening to the cars in the distance on the dual carriageway, it's about a ten-minute walk from my house, but the sound is comforting, familiar.

My time off has hardly been a vacation, and to be honest, I'm exhausted. I reached out to some old acquaintances, looking to see if anyone was hiring a personal trainer. I was a little surprised when one came through almost instantly and invited me to go for an interview at a gym in Glasgow.

So, I agreed, got myself a ticket and took the—almost—six-hour train ride to Glasgow. I booked a hotel and stayed a few extra days to take advantage of the beautiful city and did some sight-seeing.

The gym is on the banks of the River Kelvin. The building has history, and that in itself is appealing. My dad's gym sits on an industrial estate. Apart from a small café up the road, there isn't much else other than warehouses. I returned on an early train this morning and arrived home a few hours ago.

And to my surprise, I received a call offering me the job. It's a great opportunity, but something made me pause rather than outright accept. They understood I needed some time to think about it, with me needing to relocate. And their current trainer is still under contract for another month. The money is good, and I can't deny it's a great opportunity, but I know what's holding me back. I still have unfinished business to sort out first. I want to help Clara and try and clear the air between Henry, Ethan and me.

I was, however, able to catch up on some reading which was a much-needed escape from reality. I didn't realise how much I needed it for my mental health.

Closing my eyes, I rest my book on my stomach and soak in the warm heat from the afternoon sun. The birds nearby chatter wildly, the scent of freshly mown lawns hit my senses, and I relish this moment.

I saw Clara before I left for Glasgow, but it was awkward. Emilio turned up, made his presence know. The way he talked to her was enough to make me lose my shit, but Jacob was there, so I made sure to give him as much attention as possible. He's started walking more confidently now, even running in short bursts too. One minute he's a new-born, and now he's a toddler—sixteen months old already. His curiosity knows no bounds. Anything he can get involved in, he will. It concerns me how he has no sense of danger. You can't take your eyes off him for even a moment. Oh, and his favourite word is 'no.' Constantly testing boundaries, something Emilio hates, being a control freak.

Emilio is so obtuse in the way he is with Clara. He has unreasonable expectations, wanting things done a certain way but refusing to do anything he deems beneath him. It's clear he only tolerates Clara for his benefit, to have her at his beck and call when he is home. And as long as she's pandering to his every whim, he keeps the verbal abuse to a minimum. He also verbally abuses her when Jacob throws a temper tantrum, and I worry how long will it be before he hits him. If he's capable of doing it to a woman, I'm sure he's capable of hitting a child.

He watches Clara when I'm around, waiting for her to slip up and say something to me she shouldn't. I'm not stupid. I know he's involved in drugs, to what extent, I'm not too sure, but I am pretty confident he uses something from his erratic mood swings alone. I have no idea how he evades getting caught when he's drug tested.

The sooner we have a solid plan of action, the better. I need to speak to Olly about arranging somewhere safe to go until she's back on her feet. She's never been to the police or filed a report, even though I've told her she should.

Groaning, I sit up and dog-ear the page of my book. Ethan hates it when I do this, and I smile until reality kicks in. Things will never be the same again.

My dad was suspicious about me booking time off work last-minute, and then me running off to Glasgow. I just told him I was going to stay with some friends for a few days.

I know we need to talk, and what better way than over dinner, so I messaged and asked if he could be home by seven and spent the past hour and a half cooking his favourite meal.

He walks in just as the timer on the oven goes off.

"Just in time." I wave at the table.

He smiles. "Someone's been busy," he says, taking a seat.

"It'll be about another fifteen minutes if you want to freshen up," I say as I reach for the cutlery.

He nods, his eyes scanning the table.

I raise an eyebrow. "What are you looking for?" I ask, pausing with a fork in my hand.

"Are we expecting company? Just wondering, what's the occasion?"

I grimace. "No, no one is coming. I just wanted to do something nice. We haven't had a proper meal together in weeks." And it's mostly true with our shifts. He tends to heat up whatever I made, or vice versa.

"I'll be quick," he says, already exiting the kitchen.

It makes a nice change to share a meal, and it makes me more anxious about discussing my plans with my dad. He rubs his stomach exaggeratedly as he reclines back in his chair. And I notice the grey speckles in his otherwise dark hair.

"That was delicious," he praises. "And as nice as this has been, I guess it was a lead up to something, so have at it," he says.

Pushing my plate away, I drop my hands into my lap, hoping it keeps me from fidgeting.

"Okay, so the reason I went to Glasgow was that I had a job interview." There, straight to the point.

He sits forward, a frown forming. "What do you mean, a job interview? And since when are you moving out?"

I let out a sigh. "Staying here and working at the gym was never meant to be long term. Come on, Dad, you know that."

He looks wounded, and I hate that it's because of me.

"Yeah, but things haven't been that bad. I mean, I know I can be a little overbearing at times, but I still see you as my baby girl."

I open my mouth to interrupt him, but he holds up his palm, signalling he's not finished.

"I know you're a grown woman now and an invaluable trainer, and I'll work harder to remember that at the gym."

It's nice to hear him say that, but I worry about everything going on. This is all too little, too late.

"And I appreciate it, I really do, but lately, I feel suffocated. I think this will be good for me, a fresh start somewhere else."

He crosses his arms and tilts his head, staring down at me, and I feel like a teenager all over again.

"A fresh start... is it to do with those boys? The twins?"

I push away from the table and stack the plates, albeit roughly, and I cringe internally.

"Really, Dad?"

He reaches out for my free hand. "Listen, I know I didn't make it easy while you dated Ethan, and I know he hurt you, but I also see how you look at his brother. Anyone would think you're interested in that boy now too," he says with indignation.

I can barely swallow the lump forming in my throat, and my palms grow sweaty. Pulling my hand free, I grab the stack of dishes and turn away.

My face burns, and I wonder if my mum were here, would this conversation still be as humiliating?

"He isn't a boy, Dad," I throw over my shoulder. "And so what if I was interested in him? We're both free and single."

My dad gets to his feet and brings the empty glasses as I rinse the plates and load them in the dishwasher.

"Listen, I know I'm hardly an expert in relationships, but I know enough to know you need to make better choices."

I pause what I'm doing. "And what is that even supposed to mean? Why do you have such a low opinion of me?"

Leaving the dishes, I straighten and cross my arms.

"Meghan, don't be like that."

Is he even listening to himself right now?

"Be like what? Please enlighten me."

His brows furrow, and I know he's not impressed with my attitude, but I'm not impressed with his either. It's not like he rebutted my comment about his opinion of me.

"So defensive," he replies, his jaw working overtime.

I throw my arms up into the air. "Do you know what...

forget it. I thought we could have a normal fucking conversation, but clearly, we can't."

"Meghan," he scolds as I brush past him, done with this shit. I storm up to my room, slamming the door so hard the structure rattles.

"Fuck this bullshit," I grumble through gritted teeth as I change into a pair of workout leggings and then slip on a hoody. I'm fucking over this crap. Grabbing my workout bag and crossover handbag, holding my keys, I swing the door open with exaggerating force, the door handle banging into the wall. I know it's probably caused a dent, but right now, I'm past caring.

I take the stairs two at a time. "I'm going out," I shout, not waiting for a response as I storm out the front door and to my car. I need to let off some steam. I try to keep from speeding, aware that the last thing I need is to get a ticket, or worse, cause an accident. And it takes a concerted effort not to put my foot down on the accelerator.

Chapter Twenty-Eight

Henry

It's quiet here on a Friday night. Most people are getting ready for a night out or went out straight from work rather than going to the gym. They'll try and make up for it tomorrow or Sunday, of course, sweat off the excess alcohol, but they don't tend to last long. I wear my headphones when I am training on my own, otherwise people take it as an opportunity to talk, and I don't want to seem like a dick when I cut them short.

Ethan was only here for a few hours, but he had a deadline, something to do with finalising some programme. Honestly, it all goes over my head. And Nathan left over an hour ago, he's helping a friend, and it's not lost on me he's holding back some things going on with him—I just don't know what.

After a thirty-minute run on the treadmill, I slow it to a walk, reach for my water, take a huge chug, and pull out my ear pods. They lost power about ten minutes ago. I turn the machine off and hunt through my bag for the case to charge them, and that's when I hear a familiar voice, one I've missed. Over my shoulder, I see a red-faced Meg, muttering to herself.

"All I wanted to do was spar, for fuck's sake."

She doesn't usually openly swear, not at work at least, but I'm aware she's not here to work. Natalie looks up from the computer and raises her eyebrows, and Meg quickly apologises, and then with her eyes cast down, she's walking in my direction.

As she gets closer, she glances up and jerks to a stop.

"Perfect," she says under her breath, and I can't help but feel slightly wounded by her reaction towards me. Granted, things are... well, fucked up, but still.

"Nice to see you too, Meghan," I say, trying to keep my tone light. I can't help but notice her freckles across her nose are more prominent, like she's been in the sun.

"Sorry, it's just... ignore me. Do you know if Olly is about?" she asks, her eyes scanning upstairs in the direction of his office.

I tilt my head to the side. "He's on a date."

Her shoulders slump, but she's antsy, rolling on the balls of her feet.

"Anything I can help with?"

She shakes her head, her long plait whipping back and forth.

"Nope, not unless you're up for sparring with me," she says, causing me to almost drop my water bottle.

"Yeah, no. I don't think so."

Her eyes turn into dark slits. "Then no, you can't." She surveys the rest of the gym and sets her sights on Phil, turns on her heels, ready to head in his direction, but I lurch forward and grab her shoulder to still her.

"If you're thinking of asking him, I'd rather you didn't."

She turns to face me so fast I have to take a step back.

"What the fuck, Henry? I'm a trainer, in case you hadn't noticed. I know how to bloody well spar."

I hold up my palms in surrender. "I never said otherwise, but Phil is a loose cannon. Come on, you know he self-medicates." And it's true, plus I don't want him touching her at all.

Her eyes glance to him and then back to me. Resignation settles over her face, frown lines still taught.

"I can't get a fucking break," she says, biting her lip. She moves past me and makes her way upstairs.

Every logical part of my brain warns me to leave her be, but it's impossible. I need her like oxygen, am drawn to her like gravity. I can't stay away. I quickly grab my bag, stuffing my water bottle and towel on top, then make my way upstairs before I can think better of it.

I hear her grunt as she drags a mat into the centre of the room. Her eyes glance up to mine, but she says nothing. Moving her head from side to side with a crack, she turns her back to me before reaching for her leg and pulling it up behind her, stretching. Wound up and tense, she's still the most beautiful woman I've ever seen, but she's so much more than that—she's tenacious and smart.

She's vexed and in need of an outlet, and I can at least help her with that. Dropping my bag, I clear my throat as I approach. "Okay, I'll spar with you," I say.

She drops her leg, focusing on my reflection in the mirror.

"Fine, but no going easy on me, Henry. I don't need easy right now."

I peer down at myself and back to her reflection, waving a hand towards my torso. "Meg, I'm triple your weight, of course I'll fucking go easy on you. It's sparring, not a damn death match," I reply.

Rolling her eyes, she shakes her head. "Fine, whatever."

But I know she is anything but fine. She has a determined look on her face. Either way, she needs a fight.

Unzipping her hoody, she tosses it to the bench. My eyes lower to her chest, and I have to adjust myself in my shorts. I've seen her in a training top plenty of times, but being alone up here, just the two of us, it feels more intimate, and besides,

I now know what she looks like naked. She's oblivious to me openly ogling her and kicks off her shoes and pulls off her socks. Pink catches my attention. Her toenails, and damn, even her feet are attractive.

I kick off my own, followed by my socks and drop them over by the bench, then join her in the middle of the mat.

I'm tempted to suggest headgear but don't want to give her too much of a green light. I'm only sparring with her because she needs this, not because I want to.

"You ready?" I ask. Her stance tells me she is, and before I can even utter another word, she kicks her leg out towards me, earning a grunt from me.

"I'll take that as a yes."

I circle her and deflect her jabs which she continues to throw, going in fast and hard. I'm glad she didn't go near Phil, he would have taken this as a challenge, and he would give as good as he got.

Her reactions are quick, and there's no denying her form is on point, and a strange sense of pride fills me.

Twenty minutes or so into sparring, her chest is heaving from the exertion, but it's clear she's not done or easing off any time soon. So, we keep going, but each blow I counterattack only pisses her off more and drives her on harder. She's relentless.

"Easy, calm down," I say, grunting.

"Why is everyone always telling me what to do?" she heaves. I've never seen her so enraged with anger, and I worry if she keeps going, she's going to hurt herself. I need to stop this. When she focuses on her uppercut, I sweep my foot behind her leg, and she goes down. I reach out to try and control her fall, but she takes me with her, sending me off balance too. We both land in a tangled heap, me half on top of her. I'm hit with a wave of apples, mixed sweat and the rubber padding from the mats, and damn if my dick doesn't stir to life.

"Are you okay?" I ask, lifting my weight from her body.

"Yes, I'm fine," she grits out but winces as she moves to sit up and falls back to the mat with a grunt.

I shake my head. Why does she have to be so stubborn?

"No, you're not," I say, and before I can stop myself, I'm sweeping the loose hair away from her forehead which is beading with sweat.

She bites her lip, her chest rising and falling in quick succession as she tries to catch her breath.

"What's going on, Meg? Talk to me," I plead quietly.

"I'm just so fucking angry," she admits.

"With what?" I ask, my eyes scanning her face.

"Everything, always being told what to do, everyone thinking they know what's best for me," she replies, her fingertips wiping at a trail of sweat on my temple. And then her other hand moves to the back of my neck, and she pulls my face towards hers roughly. Her eyes dart between mine and my mouth.

"I need you to fuck me," she says, her voice wanton.

"What?" I double-take at her boldness. Don't get me wrong, I love a confident woman, but she's never been so forward, and it's thrown me.

Rejection fills her eyes, and her skin flushes a deeper shade of red.

"Forget it," she spits out and pushes herself to her feet, making a beeline for Olly's office, typing in a code. It unlocks with a loud click as she turns the handle and enters.

"For fuck's sake, Meghan," I growl, following her, stopping the door before it slams shut in my face, and I step inside close behind her. The only source of light is coming from a desk lamp. Olly must have forgotten to switch off.

I can hear her ragged breaths as she tries to control her breathing, her shoulders rising and falling.

"Meghan?" I question.

"Why is it so wrong for me to have what I want for a

change? Without having to explain or worry about everyone else. Why can't I do what I want to and fuck the consequences?"

Gripping her shoulder, I spin her to face me and tilt her chin up with my thumb and forefinger. Her eyes are so dark.

"And that's what you want? For me to fuck you?" I ask.

"Yes," she says, glaring back at me, a vein pulsing in her temple.

Unable to deny her, I step back and drop my shorts and briefs, my erection springing free. I drop to my knees, tearing down her leggings and knickers in one swift move, causing her to let out a loud gasp. Her hands go to my shoulders as she steps out of them.

Rising to my feet until I'm to my full height, I lean in close, and her breathing hitches.

"Turn around, bend over the desk and spread your legs." I barely recognise my voice.

Meg is quick to obey, which only turns me on more. I stare at the shape of her arse and hold back a groan, biting my lip. The head of my dick grows even more engorged, leaking pre-cum in anticipation.

She peers over her shoulder. "Are you going to fuck me or what?" she challenges. Watching me spit on my palm and stroke myself up and down, she swallows hard, her tongue darting out to lick her lips. I step forward, and she faces forward when I wrap my arm around her stomach, angling her hips right where I want them.

I inhale her scent, and even sweaty from our sparring, she's sweet and fruity—a heady mix. I bite down lightly on her shoulder.

"Don't move," I grunt into her neck, my fingers digging into her hips as I align myself. Then without even checking to see if she's ready for me, I impale her with a deep hard thrust.

She lurches forward, a surprised squawk escaping her

throat, and I freeze, my dick fully sheathed and pulsing inside her, eager to move.

"Don't stop," she croaks out, pushing back against me roughly.

Without a word, I pull almost all the way out before thrusting back inside her like a man possessed. Grabbing her plait, I wrap it around my fist and tug hard. She lets out a loud gasp as I pull her closer to my chest.

"Is this what you wanted?" I growl, nipping the flesh of her ear lobe.

She grinds into me. "Yes," she breathes out.

I run my hand down her spine and push her forward until her chest is flat against the desk and pin her at the back of her neck, my other hand digging into her hip as I pound into her. Her knuckles turn white as she clings to the edge of the desk. The sound of my balls slapping mercilessly against her arse has me growing even harder. It's filthy, and I love how she takes everything I have to give.

I stroke the length of her spine. Watching myself move in and out of her is enough to make me shoot my load. Gritting my teeth, I reach my hand between her and the desk, teasing her clit, desperate to find our release together.

The words spilling from her lips are sinful, and all it does is spur me on harder, faster—damp flesh on flesh. I pummel into her over and over until I can't hold back anymore, and I careen over the edge with a feral groan.

Chapter Twenty-Nine

Meghan

I arch my back and shudder. The moment Henry teased my clit, I was a goner. My orgasm explodes, and I spasm around him. His release fills me, and it's so intense I see white spots scatter behind my eyelids—on the verge of blacking out as my channel pulses without mercy. Gasping to catch my breath, I rest my forehead on the desk. The scent of furniture polish, coupled with sex, engulfs my senses.

Henry just fucked me over Olly's desk. I begin to come back to earth, and there's an awkward silence, except for our laboured breathing. He draws back, cold air licking at my spine as he slides out of me with a wet sound, and I feel the aftermath of his release as it runs down the inside of my thighs.

I want to say something, but when I open my mouth, I can't form any words, and the reality of what we just did, how I asked him to fuck me, hits me full force.

The air around us crackles with tension as I swallow back the onslaught of emotions and scramble for my discarded clothes, using my knickers as a makeshift cloth in an attempt to clean myself up before dragging on my leggings and clutching my soiled underwear in my fist.

Out of my peripheral, Henry is just pulling on his shorts as I reach for the door, but he rushes forward and intercepts me, blocking my path. I square my shoulders, raising my chin.

"Henry, let me the fuck out," I ground out.

His brow creases, his face marred with confusion, and something akin to not knowing what the hell just happened either.

"Meg, what the…"

Without waiting for him to articulate himself further, I shove him to the side as hard as possible.

"Just drop it, Henry."

I'm almost through the doorway when he pulls me back inside, slamming the door and crowding me.

"Meghan, what is wrong with you?" he asks, his nostrils flaring.

"We fucked, end of story," I say, crossing my arms, tucking my hands to my sides, so he doesn't see them shaking.

His eyes go wide, his jaw tight, and I find myself shrinking under his glare.

"Hold up. You wanted me to fuck you." He takes a step back and rubs his palm over his jaw, but something in his expression hardens. "And now you're acting cold and indifferent. I thought you needed a release, an outlet. But this"—he points between the two of us—"Hell, no, Meghan. I've done the whole toxic thing before with Clara, and I'll be damned if I do it again."

It's as though he's slapped me; a gut-wrenching sinking feeling swarms my stomach like a hoard of wasps.

"Do not compare me to Clara," I bite back, more than aware it wasn't so long ago I was comparing him to Ethan.

"No, Meg, don't you dare try and turn this back on me. I love a good fuck as much as the next guy, but I won't be used to appease your anger issues or whatever shit you're choosing to suppress rather than deal with."

I drop my arms and point to myself. "I used you—as I recall, you were the one happy to take on the task, telling me exactly where you wanted me. No one bloody forced you, Henry." I'm not being fair to him, but I don't need his judgement right now.

He shakes his head, disappointment dripping off him in waves. And I know he has every right to be pissed. He steps away from the door, pinching the bridge of his nose, turning his back on me. He can't even look at me, and honestly, I don't blame him.

Mortified, I twist the door handle, swinging the door open. Henry makes no move to stop me. I collect my belongings, dragging my handbag over my head and shoulder while stuffing my feet into my trainers. I grab my hoody, stuffing it into my holdall with my socks before rushing down the stairs. I keep my face cast down as the torrent of tears free fall.

It took me a good ten minutes for my sobbing to abate before I could bring myself to drive home. My phone has been pinging relentlessly, and I wonder if it is Henry. A small wave of hope engulfs me at the possibility. I pull up on my drive and reach inside my bag for my phone. My hope is squashed when I see messages from Clara. I scroll through them to see incoherent gibberish texts. They are frantic, asking me to come to hers, and as much as she's the last person I want to see right now, guilt ensues. She's still my best friend.

Reversing back off the drive, I turn around and make my way to her house.

I let out a heavy sigh of relief when I don't see Emilio's car when I arrive. He is the last person I want to see right now. I knock and wait, rubbing my arms, staring back at my car, wishing I'd put my hoody back on. The adrenaline from the past couple of hours is waning. I'm cold, tired and just want to climb into bed and sleep for a decade.

As soon as Clara peeks through the opening and confirms it's me, she slings it all the way open and pulls me inside before slamming it closed behind me.

"You came," she yells out, hugging me and letting go just as quickly.

"Clara, what is wrong with you?" I ask.

Her makeup is half done; her movements exaggerated as she flails her arms in front of me.

"Nothing," she singsongs, laughing to herself.

"Really? Because you sent me loads of garbled messages," I reply when she grips my wrist and tows me into the living room. I look around. Apart from some toys in the corner, the room is otherwise immaculate, just how her control freak boyfriend likes it.

She slumps onto the couch and pulls me down with her so suddenly that I land in an awkward position.

"Easy," I say, pushing myself into a sitting position.

She leans in closer, and it's only now I see how dilated her pupils are. I glance to the glass coffee table and spot a small clear bag with tiny pink and blue pills. I grab it and eye them suspiciously.

"What are these? Have you taken any of them?" I ask, examining them.

She scoffs at my question but nods in answer.

"For fuck's sake, Clara. What are they?"

"Oh, don't get all preachy, just a little ecstasy."

She makes a grab for the bag, but I hold it out of her reach, and when she tries again, I stuff it into my bag.

"You need to give me those back," she says, trying to reach for my bag, but I swat her hand away.

"Please, they're from Emilio's stash," she whines.

I lean back so I can see her face more clearly.

"What flipping stash?" I ask.

She giggles, covers her mouth, and mocks pretending to zip her mouth closed.

"Clara, I'm serious. Is he bloody well dealing from here?" I ask incredulously as I move to my feet and start pacing. What does she think will happen if the police find out?

"This isn't a fucking joke, Clara. What about Jacob?"

She at least has the dignity to appear slightly remorseful when I mention her son.

"He's fine. I would never let him get his hands on it," she says, crossing her arms in defiance, her cleavage pushing up higher.

"Really? Because it was openly laying around on your coffee table when I walked in."

Flicking her hair over her shoulder, she begins bouncing her knee up and down, gnawing on her thumbnail.

"Whatever, Meghan. I don't need you being all holy. It's not why I messaged you."

"Then why did you? I've already had the day from hell, and now I find you high."

She continues biting her nails, and I shake my head. She'll regret it come morning when Emilio makes her get a fresh manicure. Because it's all about appearances. I don't know how she does shit with those talons.

"I'm worried about this whole leaving Emilio," she whispers, her eyes darting over the room. "He's getting suspicious, and he's acting weird."

I sit down beside her and place my hand on her knee to still the shaking. "What do you mean?"

She hisses through her teeth when she nicks at the skin of her fingernail, causing it to bleed, and I pull her hand away from her mouth.

"He's been asking me questions."

Clutching her hands in mine, I squeeze them. Her palms

are sweaty, and instinctively, I have the urge to pull away, but I need to keep her grounded somehow.

"What did you say?" I ask, studying her face, and her eyes keep losing focus and looking past me.

"Nothing... said he was being paranoid... it's how I got this," she says, lifting her top, flashing a fresh bruise on her side.

"Fuck. He can't keep hitting you," I say through gritted teeth.

She shakes her head. "He shoved me into the worktop."

Like that makes it any less wrong. I glance around the room.

"It doesn't matter how he causes you injury, Clara. It's wrong. Where is he now?"

Her leg starts bouncing up and down again. She can barely keep still.

"I overheard him talking about picking something up. He didn't tell me where he was going," she scoffs.

"But I doubt he'll be gone long. He only took one of his phones," she says, nodding toward the kitchen counter where one has been left on charge.

I stand abruptly. "What the fuck, Clara? And your first thought upon him leaving was to drop a pill and then get me to come over?" What is wrong with her?

Her eyes well with tears as she sniffs. "No, I'm sorry, I didn't think."

"Listen, Clara, you need to stay away from whatever shit he's bringing into this house. What about Jacob? What do you think would happen if the police found out?"

I see it then, fear. I know she loves her son, and isn't that the whole reason she's determined to leave Emilio? I turn and walk towards the front door. The thought of being here with Emilio at this time at night gives me the willies.

"I'm sorry," she says remorsefully.

I stop and face her. "Clara, you're an adult. You're responsible for the choices you make. If you can't help yourself, how am I meant to help you? Do you want me to report you to social services? Have Jacob taken away?"

Her mouth gapes open, her eyes wide. "You wouldn't."

I let out a humourless laugh. "That's where you're wrong. You asked me to be Jacob's godparent for a reason. If I have to choose you or him, it will be him."

She's already at my side, her nails digging into my forearm. "I love Jacob, please, I'm sorry. I was stupid to take a pill; I just wanted to take the edge off."

"That's not the answer, Clara. The other day you were drunk before eleven, and now this," I reply.

"I'll sort myself out, I promise."

"You better," I say, pulling the door open, and I hear the tell-tale roar of a Mercedes SLS—Emilio.

"Shit, quick, go," she says, her eyes darting past me. I falter, worried about leaving her, especially in this state.

She notices my hesitation and gently pushes my arm, her eyes more focused.

"I'll be fine, I promise, now go."

I sprint to my car, fumbling for the door handle before I climb inside, just as Emilio pulls onto their driveway. The motion light comes on, surrounding him as he exits his car. He waves at me with an arrogant expression across his face. I can't get away fast enough. As much as I hate to admit it to myself, he intimidates me.

Chapter Thirty

Henry

After Meg walked away, leaving the smell of sex and crisp apples in her wake, it took everything in me not to go after her and almost as much strength not to lash out and break something.

Breathing through my anger, I try to calm myself. I focus on the room, my eyes scanning the office, the small sofa, and the desk where she was so amenable. And then the cork board full of photos.

A familiar one catches my eye, and I move closer, my fists clenched into enough to leave moon crescent marks on my palms. I, Ethan, Nathan, Olly, Emilio, Clara and Meg, huddled together in one of our favourite bars in London's West End—Jewell. Less than a five-minute walk from Piccadilly Circus tube station.

Memories of that night and many after flash through my mind. All our voices hoarse from having to shout over the music just to be heard. A celebrity hotspot and a crowd magnet, the perfect party atmosphere. The low hanging chandeliers giving it a luxurious feel in the cool and chic themed rooms. Lined with dark oak bars, padded benches and bar stools, and wooden flooring that—by the end of the night—was sticky from the copious number of sloppy drunks spilling their drinks. It wasn't a Saturday night unless we were out somewhere getting drunk on too many cocktails and making bad choices. Back when we thought we were invincible.

The nostalgia of it all threatens to suffocate me. I check my wrist and walk out of Olly's office. I still have time to grab a shower. And then I need to talk to someone, and I can't think of anyone more qualified than my mum. And as much as I'd happily leave the scent of Meg on my skin, I don't fancy rocking up at my mum's smelling like sex.

I smell fresh-cut grass as I walk up the path, the motion light blinking on as I approach the front door. Flipping through my keys, I let myself inside.

"Mum," I call out. The house is quiet, and I didn't see her car, but it could be in the garage.

I walk down the hallway to the kitchen and drop my keys and phone on the counter. My stomach grumbles as soon as I smell one of my mum's favourite pasta dishes.

"She's at Aunt Silvia's," Ethan says from behind.

I turn and nod in greeting as he walks over to the oven.

"You hungry?" he asks, reaching into the cupboard, already pulling out two pasta bowls.

"When am I not?" I reply, grabbing us some cutlery from the drawer.

As he sets them on the table mats, we work in silence, and I lay out the forks. He places the oven dish on the heatproof mat in the middle of the table, and I fill our bowls while he grabs us a bottle of water each.

"Thanks," I say, sitting opposite him, trying in vain not to burn the roof of my mouth as I tuck into the delicious bowl of carbs.

I stare at familiar floral design bowls, the same ones we had growing up, and I wonder how they survived all these years. We've been through two dinner sets since moving out.

"I'm going to miss Mum's cooking," Ethan says as he inhales the tomato basil and cheese pasta into his mouth, hardly even swallowing.

"You're moving back?" I ask, my fork paused at my lips.

He shakes his head. "Nah, I was going to tell you and Nathan, but I've found a place. I move in a couple of weeks."

My stomach sinks, and I chew on my mouthful of food before speaking.

"I was hoping you'd come back, but I'm also not surprised. I had a feeling you might not want to."

Ethan glances up, his eyes meeting mine. "I think after everything this past year, I just want to go solo for a while, and you know, find myself again."

The selfish part of me thinks it's a stupid idea, but I know he's right. He needs this.

"Not going to lie, I'm gutted, but I can support your decision."

He licks the sauce from the corner of his mouth. "Anyway, what's going on with you? My stomach was going crazy earlier."

I begin stabbing at my pasta as though it has done me an injustice.

"It's Meg." I look up, and his brow furrows.

His fork pauses mid-air. "You've heard from her?" he asks, tilting his head.

I cough. "Yeah, she came by the gym and we sparred," I say, hating how my voice cracks. I glance up, and he's watching me. I try not to fidget under his stare.

"I see," he says, grabbing his water and raising his eyebrows.

"And what's that exactly?" I push my bowl away, no longer hungry.

He crinkles the plastic bottle between his fingers, the sound grating.

"That things between you are getting messy."

I snort out a huff. "Well, that's hardly a new development, is it?" I groan.

He drags my bowl towards him and finishes off my pasta.

I cross my arms. "Seriously though, E, something is going on with Meg... so much more than you and me."

He is polishing off the last of the pasta as he taps fingers on the tabletop—one of his ticks.

"Probably the whole Clara and Emilio situation," he says, his shoulders visibly tensing.

Sitting up in my chair, the hairs on my arms rise. "What situation?"

Ethan studies me. I can see him warring with himself over what to say.

"Spit it out, man. What situation?" I ask again, grinding my jaw.

He licks his lips and swallows. "Fine, but I'm only telling you this because I'm worried about her." He points his finger in my direction. "But don't go all caveman, all right?"

I hold my hand and create the shape of a halo above my head. He just rolls his eyes and continues.

"So, Meg wants to help Clara leave Emilio." His eyes grow dark at just the mention of him.

"What the hell?"

He holds up his hands as if that will placate me. "I know. I was hoping she'd let it go. But you know Meg, she's worried about Clara and Jacob."

Sometimes it's easy for me to ignore the fact she has a son, but then I get an ache in my chest, knowing there was a time that could have been us. I can't help but feel concerned for that little boy. Using the pad of my thumb, I trace the wood-stained dining table.

"Do you think he hurts him?" It's the question I could never bring myself to ask before. Maybe I never had a reason. Until Meg and I spoke about Clara and the miscarriage, it was never a topic of conversation. But Emilio is a live wire now. The worst part is, he wasn't always that way—it's like he never grew out of the teenage angst and angry phase, and once he got in with the wrong crowd and drugs, it was too late.

"I don't think so, but we both know he's unhinged."

Forcing the chair backwards, it scrapes across the tiled floor angrily when I push to my feet and snatch up the empty bowls—passing the fridge, which still has embarrassing photographs of Ethan and me as awkward teenagers. Pulling open the dishwasher, a wave of heat hits me, where it's not since finished, and I unload everything before adding our dirty dishes and start putting everything else away. I peer over my shoulder. Ethan is rubbing his jaw, lost in thought.

"E?"

His eyes snap to mine. "I'm going to help Meg, and she'll do it with or without me anyway." I see the determination etched across his face.

Sighing, I concede. "Looks like I am too then."

Ethan scrunches his face. "Hmm, you'll be a little too busy kicking his arse."

I lean back against the granite counter, crossing my ankles.

"What, you're planning it on the night of the fight?" I ask, feeling a mix of emotion. I wanted them both there for this fight, and I hate them doing this without me, together.

Ethan walks over and stands beside me. "Don't, man. I can see the wheels turning. But this isn't about Meg and me. It's about Clara and Jacob."

Of course, I know he's right, but it's easier said than done. Along with Nathan, he's been a massive motivator with my training lately, and it felt good.

"Meg didn't want you to know. She wants you to just worry about the fight. I think it's the best day to do it. But we'll need Olly's help. We need to know if he can find out about a women's refuge. Do you fancy talking to him? I don't think Meg has yet, and I'd rather it was one of us."

I nod. Of course, Olly is closest with me after all.

"And then you just stay focused and concentrate on the upcoming fight. I'll make sure Meg is okay."

That's easier said than done though. It's no lie that before I'd been with Meg, I thought my attraction to her was a distraction, and it still is to a degree, but not in the same sense as before.

"What happens after with Meg? Are you going to pursue her?" I ask. My chest tightens, and the thought of it alone is enough to make me sick to my stomach. But I don't have some moronic claim over her, and if I'm honest, maybe she's past that point now anyway.

The sound of the extractor fan above the oven fills the silence before he answers and shakes his head. "No, it's up to her now."

His bare feet pad against the floor as he walks back to the dining table and takes his seat. I follow and sit opposite.

"I know I fucked up, going behind your back. And for that, I'm sorry. But I'm weak when it comes to her. If she said she wanted me, I don't think I'd have the strength to walk away. And yet, I couldn't watch the two of you if you got back together either." I shake my head, aware of how selfish I sound, and it's why deep down, I don't think I'll ever deserve Meg.

He cracks his knuckles as he leans his elbows on the table.

"I very much doubt it will be the latter," he replies.

I raise my eyes to his. "Maybe it would be best for everyone if she chose to walk away from both of us."

With a grimace and a slight shake of his head, he replies, "No, I don't think so."

His response surprises me, and then we're interrupted by his phone ringing.

"And I thought being self-employed would be fun," he says jokingly. We push to our feet simultaneously, and he pulls out his phone from his jeans pocket.

"Sorry, man, I have to take this," he says, looking up from the screen.

I point over my shoulder with my thumb. "It's cool. I'm going to go see Olly," I reply, holding out my fist. Nodding, he bumps his with mine and answers his call. I grab my keys, and he follows behind me, ready to go upstairs when I pull open the front door and pause when I hear the sound of a running engine. It's Meg's car.

Chapter Thirty-One

Meghan

After leaving Clara, my phone was buzzing excessively. I know I shouldn't be checking my phone whilst driving, but what if it's Clara? What if he's hurt her? Stopping at a red light, I reach into my bag for my phone.
Glancing down, I see it's from Emilio.
You have something of mine.
The pills. *Shit.* I forgot I took those from Clara.
Scrolling, there's about ten texts all saying I need to return what I took from him, or I'll be sorry.
I look up and notice the light turn green and pull away. The last place I want to be right now is my house, and before I can think better of it, I pull up alongside Ethan's.
There's easily about five hundred pills or so in the small zip lock bag. How much they're worth, I have no idea. I chew on the inside of my cheek and quickly stuff the bag into my glove box.
I sit outside, trying to calm myself. Maybe this is a bad idea. I shouldn't have come. And the fact I had sex with Henry less than a few hours ago makes me feel even worse

about being here. Contemplating what to do next, the front door opens, and at first, I think it's Ethan, but then the porch light comes on, lighting up his face—Henry.

He pauses in his tracks when he notices me, and at the exact same moment, Ethan's head pops out through the open front door, his phone to his ear. Henry turns back to him and says something before walking towards me. Ethan ends his call, and then he comes jogging outside, barefoot. He stands beside Henry, and they both just stare at me.

"Fuck," I curse under my breath.

I'm tempted to start the engine and drive away, but I think better of it, pull the key out of the ignition and get out. Ethan doesn't hesitate to make his way toward me.

"What's wrong?" he asks, cupping my cheek. Such a natural action for him, but I can't help but see from my peripheral vision the way Henry's face hardens. I ease out of his touch, knowing I don't deserve his comfort, and I try to still the trembling in my hands.

"I need to talk to you. Have you got a minute?" I ask.

He tilts his head toward his house. "Of course, come on."

Placing his palm on my lower back, he leads me up the path, closer to Henry, who is still standing there. I keep my eyes trained on the pathway, it's impossible to ignore the overwhelming urge to reach out and touch him, but I resist. A shallow breath escapes me, a sigh of relief, but it's gone too quickly when his fingers graze over the back of my hand, causing me to halt my steps.

I can smell him now, his scent so strong and masculine, but it's disjointed somehow, and that's when I realise it's coupled with Ethan's familiar fragrance too.

"Meg?" My name falls from Henry's lips, filled with concern.

And against my better judgement, I look back over my shoulder and into his eyes. I try to speak. I want to apologise about earlier, about everything, but I'm flooded with an onslaught of emotions. All that comes out is an ugly choked sound.

I shake my head, covering my mouth with my hand, and then sprint into the house, straight into the downstairs bathroom, locking the door behind me.

I can't hear anything above the manic beating of my heartbeat. I slump on the toilet seat and take deep breaths until knocking comes from the other side of the door.

"Meg, it's me. Open the door."

Breathing in deep, my hands tremble as I unlock the door and gingerly pull it open. Standing on the other side is a very worried looking Ethan. He knows what I need at this moment without a single word as he opens his arms and I fling myself at him.

He holds me close, my cheek pressed against his chest. I don't know how long we've been standing here before he finally shifts me and leads me into the living room, ushering me to sit on the sofa beside him.

I look ahead and double take when I notice the brand-new TV mounted to the wall above the fireplace, and built-in bookshelves on either side.

"When did your mum decorate?" I ask, my eyes surveying the rest of the room.

"I did it over the weekend. Forget about the décor, Meg, what's going on? Why are you so upset?" he asks, taking hold of my hands in his.

"Everything is so messed up. You, me, Clara—Henry…" I get a frog in my throat, and more tears spring to my eyes.

My heart bleeds for things to be back to the way they used to be—when things were less complicated. I long to feel loved again without all this doubt and confusion. And worse of all, I hate how I feel so conflicted.

Freeing my hand, I reach up and cup his cheek. His stubble grazes my palm, and my skin tingles, the sensation familiar.

"Do you miss us? What we used to have?" I ask as I stare into his eyes.

But before he can answer, I respond to my question. "Because I do, even now, even after everything," I admit.

I notice the change in his breathing as his thumb wipes away a stray tear from my cheek. His touch is so tender and full of warmth. For such a strong man, he's always been so gentle. Closing my eyes, I relish the sensation as I tilt my face towards his.

"Meg..." He says my name as both a plea and a warning.

But I don't care, and I'm drowning in the anergia of losing him all over again. I need to remember what it's like not to loathe myself. I close the distance between us. My lips trace his, seeking permission, and he obliges, his tongue connecting with mine. We go through the physical motion of the kiss, but it's not like any of the other kisses we've shared before. It's all wrong.

And I know he feels it too when he pulls back, resting his forehead against mine.

"I'm sorry, Ethan. I shouldn't have done that. I don't know what's wrong with me."

His soft breath warms my face when he replies. "I do," he says.

"You do?" I ask, drawing back, confused.

He nods, his eyes sad but also full of understanding. "You're in love with Henry."

My heart pulses in rapid succession. I want to deny it, tell him he's wrong, but I'm done with lying.

"And yet I just kissed you," I say, my fingers tracing the contours of my lips.

Ethan stares at me with something akin to pity. "It's because you're afraid, Meg. Me and you, we have history, and it's safe and familiar with me."

And it's that word right there... *history*... and I finally understand—we have a past but not a future.

"I'm so sorry, Ethan. I never meant for any of this to happen," I admit.

His Adam's apple moves as he swallows. "Meg, it's not your fault. I let you go first, remember?"

He's trying to take some of the burden from me. Even now, he's protecting me.

"You need to talk to him. Tell him how you feel."

I shake my head. "That's easier said than done. He already accused me of being toxic, just like how Clara was with him, and I think after this," I say, pointing between us. "I might have just proved him right."

Ethan gives my hand a firm squeeze. His palms are still hard and calloused from years of training.

"She hurt him, and not just because of what she did with Emilio. Something else happened before that. He tried to hide it, but I felt it, his pain, and something in him broke. I tried to talk to him, but he told me everything was fine. I guess some things are better left buried."

I can't hide my small gasp from his revelation. I always knew they were intuitive to one another's feelings, but it still blows my mind the empathy they feel for one another.

Is this his way of giving me his blessing, to talk to Henry about my feelings?

"Do you think I used you when we were together?"

A V-shape forms between his eyes as he frowns.

"No, not at all. Why would you think that?"

Casting my eyes down, I pick at the lint from my leggings.

"Something Clara said to me," I admit. "When we were together, it was only ever the two of us," I say sincerely.

His features soften when I bring my gaze back to his.

"I know, Meg, and as much as I wish things were different, I know we can't go back."

It's gut-wrenching to hear.

"But you're my best friend. Where does that leave us now?" I ask, my voice hoarse from my emotions.

He bites his lip, pondering my question, his eyes drowning in sadness.

"I don't know."

Panic rolls through me. "I don't want to lose you, Ethan."

His free arm wraps over the back of the couch. His fingers play with the end of my plait.

"I don't want that either, but I don't think things will be the same, not now."

My chest constricts, and I breathe through the urge to cry again.

"Can we at least try?" I ask, knowing it's selfish of me.

Ethan's at war with himself, it's evident in his expression.

"Meg, I'll always be here if you need me, always. But if and when you and Henry move forward, I have to take a step back."

My lip trembles because I know he's right, and the thought terrifies me. I can't even bring myself to form a response.

"Come here," he says, pulling me into his arms. I go willingly.

As he holds me close, I know deep down this is our goodbye.

He deserves better, and so does Henry.

Chapter Thirty-Two

Henry

I knew something was wrong with Meg. She was pale, and not just from what happened with the two of us. I wanted to be the one to comfort her, for her to confide in me, tell me what was wrong, but it was Ethan she needed. It was him she sought out. He told me he'd look after her, and I believe him. Even though everything in me protested as I left, this wasn't about me. It was about Meg.

It's crowded here tonight. Loud chatter echoes over the sound system, and as I weave through people, standing at high top tables whiles others sit in booths, I'm hit by the fragrance of stale beer and cloying perfume.

Olly is busy behind the bar, but as soon as his eyes land on me, he nods his head towards a free wooden stool, butting up against the brass foot rail at the end of the bar. I take a seat and watch Olly, the sleeves of his white shirt rolled up, showing off his ink, as he fills customer orders.

"Sorry about that, man. What's your poison?" he asks when there's a break in the rush.

"Just a coke, thanks."

The mirror behind him reflects beer dispensers on tap, the shelves holding multiple brands of spirits. He adds a slice of lemon before placing it on the beer mat and pushing it towards me.

I pat at my pockets, and except for my keys, they're empty.

"I forgot my wallet," I say. I left it at my mum's. *Shit.*

Olly just waves it off. "Like I'd make you pay."

"Whatever, I'll sort you out. I left my wallet at E's."

He flips me off. "It's a glass of coke, man."

"It's not the point," I retort.

He shrugs. I know he'll pay for it, that's not what I'm worried about, but Olly always has been too generous for his own good. He's training for a charity fight, raising money and awareness for domestic violence. He doesn't talk much about his parents. All I know is they both died and didn't treat him or his sister well. He was left with scars. I remember him getting shit for them at school. He's since had most of them covered by intricate tattoo designs, but they're still there, beneath the ink.

Fortunately for him, he was fostered by a fantastic family. But the worst part for him, though, was being separated from his baby sister, Lottie. He tried searching for her, but the information was sealed because they were minors and became wards of the state.

I think it's why he gives self-defence classes and takes part in charity fights, a way of helping those who can't always help themselves. It's why it pisses me off when he's judged for his tattoos. Or stereotyped because he works at a bar. He's a qualified architect for crying out loud—he designed our mum's kitchen.

He still dabbles in his degree from time to time, but he thinks his time is better spent elsewhere. He made quite a lot of money out of it early on. He's a clever bastard like that.

The truth is, the man is a damn unicorn.

Not to mention he's a walking wet dream with the dark hair, the violet eyes, and even I admit he's a good-looking son of a bitch. But he's smitten with a beautiful single mum at present.

A loud ping dings from his pocket, and he pulls out his phone, a smile appearing on his face as he reads a message.

"Rachel?" I ask.

He nods, glancing back down and typing a reply before stuffing it back in his pocket.

"Things good?" I ask.

Leaning on his elbow at the edge of the bar, he gives me a toothy grin. "Yeah, but they'll be even better when my fight is over. It's a struggle trying to fit in time to see her and Molly. It doesn't help that her dad is a flaky arsehole."

Olly knows Rachel through Charlie and his fiancé, Sophie. Charlie is the manager and owner of this bar; it's how we became friends with him and his best mate Nate. They both come to the gym and work out regularly. They're good guys, unlike Molly's dad, from the sound of it.

"Some men aren't meant to be fathers," I reply, taking a sip of my drink. And it's true. Mine is proof of that. But fortunately for Ethan and me, we had our mum.

"Anything new on the Smeggy front?" he asks.

His question gives me a moment of pause, but then I catch on.

"Oh, yeah, it turns out she has some hair-brained idea to help Clara leave Emilio."

Olly's eyes grow darker.

"Are you shitting me?"

I shake my head. "I shit you not."

"For fuck's sake."

A customer waves him over, and he holds up a finger to me to wait until he's seen to them. Mavis and some other girl behind the bar work seamlessly together, laughing and joking with the patrons as they serve them.

I check my phone but find no new messages, so I send Meg a text.

I'm here if you need to talk.

And then, I scroll through my social media as I wait on Olly, liking and replying to random comments on my recent posts. It gets tedious after a while, but they support me, and I want to show my gratitude, even if it's only in a small way. There are some posts from Emilio and his PR team, no doubt bad mouthing me, and I scroll past.

Intermittently, Olly and I try and discuss the situation with Clara, but it's too busy. In the end, I give up and tell him we'll talk properly another time. He nods in understanding and holds out his fist for mine.

Outside, the pink neon bar sign has Jase glowing in a shade of pink as he stands outside the main door, arms crossed, stepping closer. I notice he's also adorning some new ink; the guy is running out of skin. He has a bored expression on his face. If anything, he looks indifferent, but I know he's watching and listening to everything going on around him. He's not letting any new patrons enter due to capacity and overcrowding. Some hang around a bit in case anyone leaves. I can't help but laugh as he holds a tiny stamp and pushes it to the back of the hands of the smokers, allowing them back inside.

"You do that so well, man. Did you used to play post office?"

"Fuck off, man," he says, laughing. "I'm surprised to see you here on a Friday night."

I nod. He's not wrong. With my training schedule increasing, I barely get out. "Just needed to speak to Olly, but it was getting too busy."

We chat until two inebriated patrons start swearing and

yelling at one another. Gaining his attention, he rolls his eyes, and I leave him to deal with them. Seriously, he must have the patience of a saint. I know I fight for a living, but I couldn't deal with drunken brawls regularly.

I didn't sleep for shit. Meg consumed every other thought. She never replied to me, and I never heard from Ethan either. Hopefully, he's already up, and I can ask him what happened and grab myself a quick coffee. But as I turn off my engine, I see her car, in the same place as last night. Maybe he drove her home, or she got a cab?

Using my key, I let myself in. The house is quiet except for the sound of running water coming from upstairs. The last time I was up there, I saw them kissing. My pulse increases, and then I take the stairs two at a time.

Ethan's bedroom door is ajar. I peer inside.

My eyes zone in on the bed. Meg's hair is flayed over the pillow, her body wrapped beneath the covers. The air in my lungs freezes, and I struggle to catch my breath.

At that exact moment, the door to his bathroom opens.

"Meg, wake up," he says, a towel wrapped around his waist as he stands at the foot of the bed.

She groans, sitting up and rubbing her eyes.

My gaze lowers to her chest. She's only wearing her sports bra.

I ball my fists and shift on my feet, causing the floorboard underneath me to creak. Her eyes dart to mine, and her mouth falls open.

Blinking rapidly, she leaps out of bed like her arse is on fire, grabbing hold of the oversized shorts so they don't fall.

"Henry," she squeaks.

Ethan steps toward me, about to speak, but I hold up my hand, my eyes scanning between the two of them. And then I turn on my heels and head back downstairs, through the hallway and kitchen and straight out into the conservatory, needing air.

Pacing back and forth, I pinch the bridge of my nose, trying to keep my anger in check, trying to find any semblance of rational thought.

"H, it's not what it looked like."

I turn to face him, and without time to think of the consequences, I draw my arm back, clench my fist, and punch him square on the jaw. My knuckles catch his upper lip, and it instantly splits, blood seeping out from the gash.

He staggers back, shocked, and wipes his mouth with the back of his hand, noticing the claret. His eyes spring to mine, and then he lunges, the force knocking me into the sofa so hard it topples backwards. I manage to stay on my feet when he swings at me. I dodge him the first time, but the second time, I'm not fast enough.

Motherfucker.

"Stop it!" Meg pulls on Ethan's shoulders. He rears back to knock her off and narrowly misses her face before he's swinging at me again, and I'm on the floor. I buck him off me and roll him onto his back, his head knocking against the surface. He flinches, and I freeze.

"Henry, don't…" Meg's voice is hysterical as she slides down next to us, shoving me away from my brother.

"Ethan, are you okay?" she asks, her eyes glistening with tears while she's searching his face and head for injury.

I recoil. "Shit, Ethan. I'm sorry, I don't know what… Shit." I clench my jaw.

He pushes himself up into a sitting position, and Meg staggers to her feet and holds out her hands for him, but he swats her away.

She steps back, wrapping her arms around her middle.

And I see the regret register on his face. "Sorry, Meg. I'm fine," he says, and this time, I'm the one holding out a hand to him, a peace offering if you will. He takes it and stands.

I use the back of my hand to wipe my nose, and it comes back with a bit of blood.

"Sorry about that," he says, with a slight smirk.

"No, you're not, but I am. I shouldn't have hit you," I reply, nodding towards his face.

He raises his eyebrows. "Mum's going to kick our arses if she finds out we fought in the house."

"Technically, it's the conservatory," I say, straightening the sofa. We both let out a laugh.

"I don't find this particularly funny," Meg says, her features hardening. "If you two are done with the testosterone bullshit, I need to go."

I notice she's now dressed in her clothes from yesterday, her hair pulled into a top knot on top of her head. Damn, if she isn't a vision.

Her phone begins to shrill with Harry Styles, *'Watermelon Sugar.'* I only know this because it's practically on repeat back at the gym. The girls have gone crazy over that poor lad.

She fumbles with it, the sound cutting off, her cheeks glowing crimson.

"Great," she mumbles under her breath.

"Come on, I'll walk you out," Ethan says, leading her back into the kitchen and to the front door.

"Bye," I say but don't wait for a reply. Instead, I go to the bathroom to clean up my nose. I wiggle it, causing my eyes to water, but it's not broken. Ethan appears behind me, his reflection in the mirror as he leans against the door jamb.

"So, tell me, this fat lip…" he asks, his tongue sweeping over the slit. "Was it for me when you caught me kissing Meg or finding her in my bed?"

Drawing in a long breath, I lift an eyebrow. "Both," I admit, staring back at him.

He bows his head, lifting his hands. "It's not what you think," he says.

I turn to face him head-on.

"And what's that?" I ask.

He shakes his head and smirks, hissing when his lip begins bleeding again.

"You think we slept together."

I signal for him to move to take this somewhere other than the confines of the downstairs toilet, and he steps back.

"Could have fooled me. What I saw kind of speaks for itself."

I brush past him and into the kitchen, going to the fridge and grabbing two bottles of water. I toss him one, and he catches it with one hand—reflexes like a damn ninja.

"She slept in my bed, yes, but nothing happened. I stayed in your old room." He unscrews the lid of his bottle. I have no reason not to trust him.

"Well, it doesn't matter. I'm not the best version of myself when I'm around her."

He sighs. The bottle crinkles as he rolls it between his palms.

"H, your feelings are heightened when you're around her because you're holding back, refusing to be honest with yourself, with her."

I sit down at the table and lean back in the chair.

"Yeah, and that excuses me lashing out at you, does it?"

He smirks. "Well, no, but maybe we needed to hash it out."

I shake my head. "You're a dick. I could have hurt you."

"H, I might not be able to fight professionally, but I can still hold my own."

Touching my nose, my eyes water again. "Yeah, don't I know it."

"And don't you forget it." He slaps me on the shoulder.

"Come on, if Nathan gets to the gym before you, we won't hear the last of it."

I know Ethan is deflecting, but after the way I acted, I'm grateful. I need to take some time to seriously think about what to do going forward about Meg and me. The first chance I get, I think worst of her. It's not like she owes me anything. We're not even together. And yet, the only bed I want her sleeping in is mine.

Chapter Thirty-Three

Meghan

If it wasn't for the fact Olly is my friend and this fight is for charity, I'd be anywhere else but here right now. Ever since my conversation with my dad about moving out, we've hardly spoken. And how I've managed to avoid seeing Henry this past week since he walked in and found me in Ethan's bed is a miracle.

But it's all beginning to take a toll on me. I've never been an outwardly emotional person, and yet lately, I can't seem to suppress my feelings.

I pull my shoulders back and lift my chin as I walk through the crowd. Mixed voices ring out in high decimals to overcompensate from the music spilling from the large speakers. Round tables and chairs with crisp white linen are laid out all around the ring, lit in a halo of light. All the guests are in black tie and dressed to impress.

I falter when I see Henry, already seated at our table. Greeting my dad with a half-smile, I take my seat beside him.

"You're late," he says under his breath.

Sighing, I rub my palms on the top of my thighs, straightening out my dress. "Wardrobe malfunction," I reply to hide the irritation in my voice.

The dress I'd intended on wearing... the seam split when I was trying it on last night to make sure it would go with my shoes. So reluctantly, I had to buy another, which was a mission with only an hour to spare before the retail park closed for the day.

I pour myself a glass of water. My eyes keep straying towards Henry. He's yet to acknowledge me, and it only makes me more uncomfortable. But what makes it even worse is when he excuses himself and drags his chair to the table opposite, joining Rachel, Charlie, his fiancé Sophie, and their other friends, Nate and Felicity.

A sense of sadness fills me. It wasn't so long ago I would have been on a table amongst my friends, and now everything is so fractured. I miss the way things used to be. I watch as Henry falls into an easy conversation. His smile is genuine, and I find myself again jealous of how at ease he is with another woman. And it's no reflection of Rachel. She seems lovely, and Olly is more than obsessed.

But I hate this awkwardness between us. It's never been like this with us before, and I know now that it's him I want. It's about time I suck it up and find the courage to tell him, lay all my cards on the table. A new wave of determination settles over me. I take a deep breath in through my nose and then out through my mouth, and then push myself to my feet. I grip my clutch like a lifeline as I gravitate towards Henry. I need to fix this.

He looks so devastatingly handsome in a black suit and a pink shirt. I think he's attractive in whatever he's wearing, but dressed up like this, he has my pulse racing and my body tingling in appreciation.

He barely acknowledges my presence as I approach their table and hover in front of him.

"Henry?" My voice comes out weak, and I hate that

others are witness to my vulnerability. A brief bout of panic assaults me when I think he's going to ignore me. His body visibly stiffens when he turns his face to me with a grimace.

"Meghan." The way he uses my full name in greeting in response stings.

"Can we talk?" I ask. Everyone tries their hardest to appear polite, giving me sidelong glances as I wait awkwardly for his response.

"Not now, no. I'm talking to Rachel."

My heart feels like it's shrinking, his rejection like a physical blow. I retreat inside myself a little more.

"Oh, okay, sorry… maybe later?" I ask.

He nods once and turns his attention back to Rachel; his silent dismissal is all the deterrent I need to go, and yet, I'm frozen.

Rachel stares between us, and I sense her confusion, but she surprises me when she compliments my dress, and I can't help but like her a little bit more. Unlike most girls I know, she's genuine, and it's refreshing to be perfectly honest. I find my voice and thank her, returning the compliment. My unease abates enough for me to walk away, and I make my retreat to the ladies.

Once I'm settled back at my table, my dad gives me the side-eye, but I try my hardest to ignore him. I was surprised when Rachel came into the toilets moments after me, asking if I was okay. She even put a couple of girls in their place when they were catty about me, like I wasn't even there. It took all my self-control not to lose my shit, but I'm here to represent my dad and the gym, and tonight is for a good cause. Before we exited, she gave me her number, which made my heart squeeze. I sure as hell could do with another friend right about now.

I've been so caught up in my head, I don't even notice Emilio towering over me until it's too late. He bends down close—too close. I'm hypersensitive to his proximity, which makes me shrink back in my chair. It doesn't matter that I'm on a table with my dad and surrounded by men. My heartbeat is racing.

"You have something of mine," he says under his breath, leaning in as if he's about to kiss my cheek, causing my scalp to prickle with unease.

When he brings his hand to my face, I cringe uncontrollably and instinctively swat it away. His laugh is callous as he grabs my arm firmly. His pupils dilate as his dark eyes bore into mine, and he licks his lips in a way that makes me feel unclean.

And then he's torn away. Henry is now in his space, their faces inches from each other. Emilio has always been quick to anger, and he shoves his chest to Henry's.

My dad intervenes and manages to put distance between them. All the while, I'm still rooted to my seat as there are some whispered threats thrown at Henry, followed by the summoning of one of the events bouncers, and then Emilio is being escorted out.

I try to remain calm, but it's no easy feat when my dad looks at me with disapproval written all over his face. Though this was all my doing, I never asked Emilio to manhandle me.

Henry crouches down in front of me, drawing my attention back to him. His presence is both reassuring and calming. He cups my cheek. "Are you okay?" he asks, his eyes searching my face.

"I'm fine," I reply, my eyes skimming to my dad, who glances at us before continuing to appease one of the other event sponsors in conversation.

"Thank you," I say quietly. I am trying to keep my overwhelming feelings at bay.

His eyes soften, and for a brief moment, I'm captivated by him and no one else exists. I want to wrap my arms around him and never let go. The spell breaks when he nods and drops his hand. Cool air licks my skin. All I want is for him to give me a chance to explain myself. It wounds me, knowing he was gracious enough to allow Ethan to tell him nothing happened between us. He could at least give me the same courtesy.

Chapter Thirty-Four

Henry

If I thought seeing Meg in Ethan's bed was bad, it had nothing on Emilio touching her, and at a charity fight of all places. How his PR company haven't dropped him is beyond me. But of course, it wasn't pictures of him grabbing her that ended up all over social media. It was of our altercation.

This has spurred me to train even harder. No matter what happens, there will be only one winner, and it will be me. Training has been gruelling with early starts and late night finishes. Then there's keeping up with ads for my sponsors—a good way of keeping up my social media presence.

Today is a rest day, which in adult language translates to catching up on housework and laundry. Nathan keeps going on about getting a cleaner to come in every other week to do a deep clean. The only problem with that is he'd use it as an excuse not to do anything. I can put up with a lot, but lack of cleanliness isn't one of them.

I'm just throwing my last load into the washing machine when my phone starts ringing. Grabbing it from the charger, I glance at the caller ID to see a number I don't recognise.

"Hello?"

"Henry, is that you? It's Lily."

Olly's mum.

"Hi, Lily. Is everything okay?" I ask, knowing it's a stupid question, she wouldn't be calling me if it was, and a heavy weight settles in my gut. I know this can't be good.

"It's Olly. He was involved in an accident and had to have surgery, but the doctors assure us he'll be fine. I just wanted to let you know."

"Shi… sorry." I sit down and run my hand through my hair. "Where is he? Which hospital?"

Lily tells me he's at Lister hospital Stevenage and which ward he's on. I reach for the dry marker and scribble it on the whiteboard adorning the fridge door.

"When is he allowed to have visitors?"

"Tomorrow should be fine, but he'll likely be in for about a week."

I nod. "No worries. If there's anything you need, let me know."

I sit down at the kitchen table.

"Thank you, Henry. I've spoken to Charlie, but I haven't managed to speak to Ian at the gym yet."

Bouncing my knee up and down, I tap my fingers on the top of the table. "I can speak to Ian."

"Thank you, love."

Once I've hung up, I pull up Meg's contact. My thumb hovers and I wonder if I should ring the gym and ask for Ian direct, but she's his friend too, and I'd rather she found out from me anyway. Rolling my neck, I dial.

"Hello?" she says, her voice hesitant.

"Hi, Meg, it's me. Can you talk for a minute? It's important."

A muffled sound comes through the phone, and then I listen to the sound of her breathing as if she's moving.

I rub the back of my neck while I wait.

"Okay, yeah, what is it?" she asks.

"It's about Olly. He's been in an accident—" She interrupts me before I can continue.

"What do you mean, an accident? Oh my God. Is he okay?" Without being there, I'd bet she's pacing.

"Yes, but he had to have surgery—"

Again, she interrupts in a rush of air as she repeats my last word.

"Surgery?" She gasps, her voice rising to a shrill. When she's calmed down enough to listen, I repeat to her what Lily told me.

"Can you let Ian know, or do you want me to talk to him?" I ask, running my hand through my hair.

"I'll tell him, it's fine. I still can't believe it," she says with a quiver in her voice.

It puts everything into perspective.

"If you can cancel whatever he has on his schedule for the next couple of days, I can cover his classes over the next few weeks between training."

I hear her sigh. "Are you sure?"

"Of course." He offers the classes around his shift work anyway, so I can take some on if it eases his worry, at least until he's back on his feet and can find someone.

The sound of clicking comes through the speaker, and I know she's already on the computer.

"He has two classes tomorrow morning; I'll call once I get off the phone to cancel."

Chewing on my thumbnail, I pause to speak. "Okay, cool."

"Do you want me to email you over his schedule for you to look over?"

I nod. "Yeah, please. That would be great."

"Okay, that's been sent," she says.

"Thanks."

There is an awkward pause as silence fills the line, and I

wonder if I should see if she wants to come with me to see him when I go, but I think better of it, Olly doesn't need us bringing tension with us.

"Well, I'll let you go," she says, but there's hesitation in her voice. I wait for her to say more but only hear static. I even check the screen to make sure she hasn't hung up already.

"Meg, is everything okay?"

I hear her clear her throat before she answers. "Of course, just worried about Olly."

But I don't believe her. She won't come right out and say it, but her reaction to Emilio was one of fear, and this girl can hold her own when it comes to most guys. It's different when the guy in question thinks he's bloody invincible though.

"Meg, he's going to be all right. He was really lucky," I say, but honestly, until I see him for myself, it's up for debate, not that I'll tell her as much.

A static muffled sound comes down the line and then clears. "Sorry, my client has arrived. I have to go."

We say our goodbyes and hang up. I remain seated, just staring at my phone in a daze, until I remember that I have stuff in the dryer which has probably shrunk two sizes.

Walking past the upstairs toilet, Nathan comes out at the exact moment I inhale.

I almost drop the armful of clothes I'm holding as I try to cover my mouth and nose.

"Dude, close the damn door," I scold.

He laughs and pulls the door shut, and I've never been more grateful for my own bathroom. I cough, blinking back tears as my eyes water from the attack that is his rear end.

"It's not funny. Your arse is like germ warfare."

Nathan rolls his eyes but is not bothered in the least. "Listen, it's not my fault I have IBS."

"No, you just don't know how to shut a door or a toilet lid."

I drop my clothes on my bed, and he follows, leaning against the door frame.

"Dude, who took the jam out of your doughnut?"

Turning back to him, I shake my head. "Sorry, man, it's Olly, he's in hospital."

Nathan's expression turns serious as I relay—yet again—what Lily told me.

"Fuck." He runs his hands through his hair. "Sounds like it was lucky he was there."

I nod because it's true.

"I did ask a few friends over later, but I'm going to cancel. Fancy sharing a Thai with me instead?" he asks as he pushes away from the door.

"Yeah, sounds good," I admit, grateful even if things are different. The last thing I want right now is a group of girls hanging all over me. Don't get me wrong, as flattering as the attention is, some just keep pushing, and it's not an attractive quality. I love a woman who knows what she wants, but not at the cost of pushing herself onto a guy.

When I think of a confident woman, it's Meg who I conjure in my mind. None of these women even hold a flame to her, and that right there is the problem.

Rolling down my window, I grab myself a token, raising the barrier for the multi-storey car park and manage to find a space on level six. I don't mind, it's an excuse to use the stairs.

Entering the main entrance, the first thing to hit me is a bitter antiseptic yet artificial fragrance. I look for the reception desk and where I can find Gloucester ward.

A man passes me in a long gown, shuffling along as he pushes his IV drip along with him. And I notice his arse is on full display for anyone in eyeshot. I'm about to tell him his gown has come undone when an orderly takes him aside and quickly helps him cover back up, so he's no longer mooning everyone.

Harsh fluorescent hallway lighting flickers angrily along the length of the corridor before I enter the ward. Alarms beep from various machines, dissonant but constant. Instead of a sterile crisp white, the walls are layered in beige, and it screams artificial.

I approach a petite but stern-looking nurse, who informs me which room I can find Olly in.

Tapping the door with the back of my knuckles, I walk in, smiling at Olly when he looks up. The room is ventilated well enough, but the air is stale.

"Shit, man, talk about milking some attention."

He rolls his eyes and flips me off, a drip attached to the back of his hand.

"H, what the hell are you doing here, man?" he asks, his forehead furrowed.

"Apart from checking out the nurses, just coming to check you're all right."

Holding up his fist, I tap it with mine and notice the road rash up the length of his arm and let out a hiss through my teeth.

"I bet that stings like a mofo," I say, raising my chin towards his arm.

"It could've been worse," he admits, shifting to get comfortable.

Dragging the chair closer, I sit down. The cushioned seat lets out an angry puff of air.

"What the fuck?" I say and lift myself off the chair before sinking back down again.

Olly gives me a strained look. "Shit, man, if you've come here to make me laugh, you need to piss off."

Now it's my turn to flip him off. "It's not my fault this chair sounds like a damn Whoopee cushion."

He shakes his head, smiling as he takes a sip of water from

the tray table over his bed.

"Nah, seriously, man, you've looked better. But you've got balls of steel. I'll give you that."

The fact he risked his life to save his girlfriend's daughter from being run over is proof enough.

Olly's eyes dart to mine. "It's not anything anyone else wouldn't have done, and I'd do it again in a heartbeat."

I nod. "Well, Molly-Mae is a damn lucky girl that Rachel chose you as her boyfriend. Especially when she could have me," I say deadpan.

He shakes his head. "In your dreams, man." Wincing, he lets out a small groan.

I'm about to ask if he's in pain when a woman stops just outside, wheeling along a trolley. She picks up a plate covered by what looks like a cake lid and places it on his table, along with a child-size carton of apple juice and a small fruit pot.

I watch as he lifts the lid and sizes up his lunch, the smell alone makes me sink back into the chair—along with an angry puff.

He quickly covers it and grabs for the carton. I watch him fiddling with the straw, clearly struggling, and I take it from him.

"Are they trying to torture you, man?" I say under my breath.

Olly lets out a harsh noise. "Breakfast wasn't so bad, two Weetabix and almost two centimetres of watery milk."

I manage to pierce the hole with the straw and pass it to him.

"Cheers, man," he says before bringing the straw to his mouth.

Eying the tray, I shudder at the thought of him having to eat that or go hungry.

"Seriously, do you want me to go grab you something from the cafeteria or the machine? It's got to be better than that," I say, pointing to his plate.

"Nah, it's cool. Mum or Rachel will probably bring me something later."

I tell him not to stress about work, I have his self-defence classes covered at the gym, and I know Charlie already has his shifts covered at the bar for the foreseeable future. He's going to be out of action for at least a month, if not more.

It's obvious he's tired and uncomfortable, even though he's trying to hide it. I remember how Ethan was when he was in the hospital. Glancing to my wrist, I make my excuses and leave him to rest.

Knowing that now I'll also be covering Olly, there'll be no more avoiding Meg—even if I denied it, it's what I've been doing. I just hope like hell we can start moving past this awkwardness between us. It's never been this fractured before, and I wonder if we'll ever get back on track.

Chapter Thirty-Five

Meghan

Henry has been at the gym almost as much as me whilst covering for Olly and continuing his training. We acknowledge each other for the most part, say hello, and he'll ask about clients, but other than that, we haven't spoken, not about us.

The longer it continues, the more miserable I'm becoming. Days feel longer, and I have this unfulfilled desire to be with Henry again. How can someone be so close and yet so emotionally distant in the same breath? I've never felt a longing like this, not even after my breakup with Ethan. All I want is to fix this so we can be together and explore each other again.

I messaged Rachel to check on how she and little Molly-Mae were doing after the accident with Olly. It could have been so much worse, and it just proves how life is so unpredictable. I'm in awe of her, not only as a mum but as a woman. If I could aspire to be half of the woman she is, I'd be proud of myself. And of course, I've text Olly, but his replies are short, consisting of a couple of emojis or a few words, but he's never been big on texting.

On the other hand, Emilio has been relentless, sending threatening messages. Yes, I could block his number, but then what? Phoning my place of work, or worse, turning up here isn't beneath him. There's no avoiding him, and my main fear is he's taking this out on Clara. I've managed to see her, but only briefly when he's not there, and I don't stay long for fear of him coming back, and his mum is always turning up unexpectedly between her beauty appointments. The woman goes to the hairdressers twice a week for a wash and blow dry, which I'm sure Emilio funds, and without sounding cruel, it's probably the only reason she does through fear he'll stop.

I'm disrupted from my thoughts when I glance up to see Olly walking towards me. I double-take, and then I'm rounding the reception desk to intercept him. "Olly, what are you doing here?" I ask, wrapping my arms around his neck and hugging him whether he wanted me to or not. This is non-negotiable. I soak in his warm, familiar scent, earthy and yet sweet.

"Hey, Smeggy, I just wanted to check the rota," he says like it's no big deal.

I pull back. "Olly, it's under control," I chastise.

"Maybe so, but just let me do this. I won't stay long." His violet eyes plead for me not to give him a hard time, and as usual, I'm weak where he's concerned and concede.

"Fine, as long as you promise."

"Of course." He kisses my cheek and turns to walk away.

"And Olly," I say to his retreating back.

He peers back over his shoulder.

"I'm glad you're okay."

"Thanks, Smeg," he says with a wink.

I watch him as he takes the stairs slowly, and it's obvious he's still in a lot of pain, but like everything else, he does well to hide it. I wonder if Rachel knows.

The hairs on the back of my neck rise when I see Henry.

He hasn't seen me yet, and I take full advantage, scanning

the length of his body and the angle of his jaw. His smile is one of the things I love the most about him—so inviting and honest. It's why it hurts my heart, knowing I've been the one to take it away from him.

Just like now, as he looks up and catches me staring, I'm momentarily caught in his snare but force myself to glance away and get back to the workout programme for my client. When I find the courage to peer back, he's making his way upstairs.

My phone buzzes, and I pull it from my pocket—Emilio.

You can't keep avoiding me forever. Give me back what you stole!

I continue to act as though I have no idea what he's talking about, but I know it's futile. The temperature drops and I rub my arms, and it has nothing to do with the air conditioning.

Henry

She can hardly even look at me now, not that I can blame her. The talk between us is long overdue, and I know that's my fault.

I make my way to Olly's office to check the schedule and frown when I find him sitting behind his desk. And just like every time I've been in this damn room since, I can't ignore the memory of being balls deep inside Meg while she was bent over it.

Clearing my throat, I swallow down my wayward thoughts.

"Man, what are you doing here?" I ask, interrupting him.

Olly glances up and gives me a lop-sided grin. "Just wanted to check the rota."

I walk towards him and hold out my fist. "It's good to see

you, but I told you, I got this." I slump down in the chair opposite.

"I know, but I still think it's too much with your fight coming up."

I wave him off. "It's months away, and it's not like the days are booked out solid—it's a couple of classes a week." Less than two, to be exact, but I keep that to myself.

He relaxes a little, dropping his pen and leaning back. "Fair enough. Thanks, man, I appreciate it."

"So, where's your girl at?" I ask, knowing Rachel likely has no idea he's here when he should be at home, resting.

His face contorts slightly. "Work, I think."

I sit up straight. "What did you do?"

He defensively crosses his arms. "Why do you assume I did anything?"

"Because you are a self-saboteur. I've known you long enough."

And it's true. He never really gets past the point of no retreat with women, but she's different, and I know this for a fact. He would never have gotten involved, risking hurting her or her little girl in the process.

"We had a disagreement when I came out of the hospital, but I intend to make it right."

I frown and hold my hand out to the room. "And yet you're here?"

He grabs his discarded pen and launches it at me, but my reflexes are sharp, and I catch it quickly.

"For now, yes. Anyway, what the fuck is going on with you and Meg? I heard about Emilio showing up at the fight and getting in her face."

I can't hide my discomfort. "I don't know, but I plan on getting to the bottom of it." I ball my fists. "Has she said anything to you?" I ask.

It's not lost on me how she's distant with everyone around her lately.

He shakes his head. "Not a damn thing. You two ever going to accept that you like each other?"

Damn him for being so perceptive. I laugh, attempting to cover my unease, but it's forced. "I think that ship has sailed. Besides, I can't do that to my brother, you know?" Lies, all lies. I already have done it to my brother, and I'm the one who set sail like a damned fool, not Meg.

"Talk to him. He might surprise you."

Olly might be *my* best friend, but he's friends with Ethan too, and I know what he's doing. He's trying to make sure I don't do anything stupid—too little, too late.

There's a knock at the open door, and when Olly stares past me, his face lights up.

"Well, damn, look what the cat dragged in."

He gets up to greet them—Charlie, with another guy I don't recognise.

"Heard you had a fight with a car and lost," says the guy, smiling and pulling him in for a hug.

"Henry, this is Simon, Selene's godfather."

Selene is Charlie and Sophie's daughter.

"Hey, man." I nod and get to my feet. "I need to get back downstairs," I say, smiling and leaving them to it.

Back on the ground floor, I glance around until I find her. She's in a daze until someone drops a dumbbell, startling her. She tries to recover quickly, but even from here, I can see the worry etched on her face while her eyes search the gym before landing on me. Quickly she glances away. This time, I'm not backing down. Something is wrong, and I'm determined to find out what.

I take a deep breath before exhaling, nodding in greeting to a few of the other regular members while making my way over.

"You're jumpy," I say, and I notice the dark circles under her eyes.

"Just tired, not been sleeping," she responds, her tone flat.

Even tired, she's stunning. "Well, maybe if you told me what was going on, it would be a problem halved, and you'd be able to rest easier?" It goes against every instinct I have not to pull her into my arms and tell her whatever it is, I'm there for her, and that she's not alone.

She crosses her arms. "It's just stuff with Clara," she replies. "Not to mention we still haven't spoken about us. I at least deserve the chance to explain about me sleeping in Ethan's bed."

She deserves that at least, and maybe she'll lower her guard and tell me what else is going on?

"You're right. We should talk. When are you free?"

Her eyes glance to her wrist, then back to me. "I'm free now. I can grab an early lunch."

And for the first time in what seems like forever, she looks hopeful.

"That works," I reply.

When her eyes light up, my chest squeezes in satisfaction.

"Café?" I ask. It's the only place on the industrial park and local to the gym within walking distance, and you can't go wrong with the food either.

This time she rewards me with a shy smile. "Okay, I'll just go grab my bag."

I stare after her as she disappears into the kitchen to grab her bag, and I notice I'm not the only one. Some guys pause the sets they were doing to watch her as she passes them, and the possessive arsehole in me makes me want to pound my chest while screaming, "Mine."

Meghan

It's early, but the café is always a buzzing hive of activity. Finding a free table over in the corner, I grab one of the laminated menus from between the condiments as we sit down. It's slightly sticky, and it's seen better days, but this place has a food hygiene rating of five which is a win in my book. I glance over the options even though I already know what I want.

My eyes scan over the wall behind Henry, lined with beautiful black and white framed prints of London hot spots, from Regents Park and Primrose Hill to London Zoo and Parliament Hill.

There's the sound of cutlery clinking, scratching plates amidst conversations, and the smell of fresh coffee is strong in the air.

Nadia comes over to take our order and disappears quickly. I watch Henry's hands as he rolls the sugar pourer between his palms.

His eyes meet mine, probing. "So, are you ready to tell me what's going on with you?" he asks.

I shake my head. "No." I let out a shaky breath. "But I do want to talk about you seeing me in Ethan's bed."

He grinds his jaw. "We don't need to. Ethan told me what happened," he says, placing the sugar back in the middle of the table, straightening the salt and pepper shakers.

"And I don't deserve the same courtesy, is that it?" I shake my head.

He raises an eyebrow, but before he can answer, Nadia places our plates in front of us with a thump, followed by our drinks.

We both thank her as Henry passes me two sachets of brown sugar. My heart skips a beat, he knows what sugar I take in my coffee, and I wonder if he's even conscious of what he just did and how stupid I feel that such a small gesture has the power to give me butterflies.

"Thanks," I say, clearing my throat before adding the contents and stirring my coffee.

I push my panini to the side, waiting to continue our conversation, but he moves it back in front of me.

"Let's eat first," he says.

And as if for emphasis, he takes a huge bite of his bacon, lettuce and tomato sandwich.

To appease him, I begin eating mine but can't bring myself to finish it, the knot growing in my stomach, desperate for us to have this conversation.

He wipes his mouth with a serviette before crushing it into a ball and dropping it on his—now—empty plate.

"For the record, it's not that I didn't think you deserved to tell me your side. It's that you don't owe me an explanation."

I swallow down the lump in my throat. "So what? Me and you, we didn't mean anything?" I ask, waving my hand between us.

He looks around the room before his eyes stop on mine and he lets out a sigh.

"Meg, I didn't say that, you're putting words into my mouth." Fidgeting in his seat, he scrubs his palm across his jaw.

"It's what you don't say which screams the loudest."

His nostrils flare ever so slightly as he sits forward, but I don't move, refusing to back down, his face inches from mine.

"I care, Meghan, and that's the problem." He points between us. "But we've already hurt Ethan, and we still are. He's my brother, my twin. You wouldn't understand."

"Of course I do. Give me some credit, Henry." I grip the edge of the table. "He's my best friend, or should I say *was*. I risked it all for *you*. We can't go back. It's why I had to let him go." It takes everything in me not to cry. Ethan will always be special to me. I clench my fists, my nails digging into my palms.

"Maybe after some time, we can move past this."

I shake my head, mocking him scornfully. "So we stay away from each other until you move past your guilt to be with me, is that it?"

Does he not get it? I want him to want me, the same way I want him.

His shoulders sag. "Honestly, I don't know."

And it's like a physical blow, his admission, but at least he's honest.

"Henry, I don't believe in giving someone an ultimatum, and I sure as hell won't emotionally blackmail you to make a decision, so I'll save you the trouble. There isn't going to be a maybe."

I stand abruptly, rifling through my purse, pulling out a ten-pound note and dropping it to the table. He can pay for his own. "Thank you for being honest," I say, my chair scraping on the floor as I shuffle out from behind the table, turning away from him.

"Meg, wait." I hear the sound of Henry scuffling behind me as he calls out "bye" to Nadia, and he's hot on my heels as I exit the café.

Henry's hurried footsteps approach me from behind. His hand wraps around my shoulder as he pulls me to a stop, stepping in front of me.

"This isn't how I wanted things to turn out. You have to believe me," he pleads.

I bite the inside of my cheek and give a slight nod—a lump forms in my throat.

"But can you promise me one thing?"

Crossing my arms, I raise my eyebrows. Is he kidding me right now?

"If you need me for anything, promise you'll call me."

It's impossible to stay angry when he acts like he gives a shit.

"Meghan, if you care about me at all, you will."

I hate him for using my feelings as a weapon.

"Fine," I recede. He steps beside me as we make our way back towards the gym and then go our separate ways.

Once alone, I retrieve my phone. It's vibrating relentlessly. I already know it's Emilio—text after text.

Don't ignore me, bitch!
You have something of mine.
You'll be sorry!

I shiver and drop it back into my bag. I'd considered confiding in Olly, but since he's recovering from his accident, I don't want to burden him, and with Henry's upcoming fight, I don't want him involved if things turn ugly and he gets caught up in all of this… it could jeopardise his career.

Chapter Thirty-Six

Henry

Ethan continues to give me the evil eye, and it's beginning to grate on me. He's always done that ever since we were kids. It's like a silent form of torture, and he knows how much I hate it.

"What, man? For fuck's sake." I ask, dropping my arms at my sides.

He grabs the bag to stop it from swinging and steps in front of it. "You're a fool, bro, playing the martyr. Maybe I was wrong and you never deserved a chance with Meg."

I grind my teeth. "Whatever, man, I'm just trying to do the right thing."

Nathan keeps unusually quiet, and I look at him and raise my eyebrows.

He holds up his palms. "Don't fucking look at me. I'm Switzerland."

The one time I could do with his advice is the one time he's abstaining.

"Well, that's convenient."

"What is?" Olly says, approaching us.

I shake my head and let out a frustrated groan.

"Girl trouble," Nathan says in response.

"And when you say girl, you mean Meg?" He looks between the three of us. Ethan nods, and Olly frowns. "Why, what's going on?"

I snort out a huff. "You sure you want to know?"

Before he has a chance to answer, his phone ringing interrupts us. He smiles wide before swiping the screen. "Hey, you here? Yeah, come on up."

And damn if his expression isn't a force to be reckoned with, it's hard to keep my smile at bay.

"What has you smiling like that, bro?" I ask.

"You'll see. Two secs, and make sure when I come back, you all fucking behave."

Nathan clutches his chest in mock offence, and Ethan does the shape of a halo over his head. Maybe Rachel is here with little Molly-Mae.

Olly practically skips over to the main entrance. A young woman enters, and he pulls her into a hug before grabbing her hand, heading in our direction.

Nathan lets out a soft whistle, and Ethan elbows him in the ribs just before they come to a stop in front of us.

"Guys, this is Lottie, my little sister."

She glows with embarrassment at his term of endearment, but the affection in her eyes is hard to ignore.

"This is Henry, my best mate, and this is Ethan and Nathan," Olly says, pointing to us each in turn.

Nathan pretty much shoves me aside to grab her hand in greeting, but he doesn't let go until Olly punches his arm.

I pull her hand in mine, shaking it once before letting go and moving aside for Ethan. I can't help but notice how she blushes.

"Twins?" she asks, pointing between us with almost a look of surprise on her face.

"Guilty," I reply with a smirk. "But I got all the looks."

She laughs and her eyes sparkle, so much like Olly's.

Olly has been searching for her for years, but it's Lottie who found him after reading an article online after he won his last charity fight. Fate if you ask me.

"Well, it's good to finally meet you. He never shuts up about you," I say.

"Looks like you have me at a disadvantage," she replies, her eyes darting between us.

"Hardly, we have a lot of time to make up for," Olly says affectionately. "It's why I asked her here. I wanted to show her around the place," he says, waving his hand out in front of him. "Lottie said she might even take up some classes. If I'm not about, they'll watch out for you," he says, focusing on his sister.

She rolls her eyes. "Olly, I'm a big girl. I can take care of myself," she says.

I can't help but laugh. "Yeah, good luck with that." Olly is protective through and through. I don't hear what Nathan says next, but whatever it is causes Ethan to slap him around the back of the head.

"Dude," he exclaims, rubbing the spot with a shocked expression.

"Yeah, well, you deserved it. She's not a damn toy," Ethan says in a low voice.

I don't think he realises he said it out loud until I clear my throat, and his eyes spring to mine and then back to Olly and Lottie.

"Olly, where's the ladies room?" Lottie asks.

He nods and points her towards the toilets.

"Damn, your sister is hot," Nathan says when she's out of hearing distance.

Olly tenses and frowns. "Do. Not. Even. Think. About it," he says in a warning.

Nathan holds up his palms and tries to laugh it off, but it's obvious Olly isn't fucking about. Ethan says nothing, too busy typing on his phone.

I can't argue with Nathan. She is attractive, but with eyes so much like Olly's, he doesn't have to worry about her with me.

"I'm so glad she found you, man," I say.

"Thanks, H. We have so much to catch up on. I just want her to feel relaxed around me," he says.

"I can help with that," Nathan says.

This time Ethan punches him in the arm.

"What the fuck, E?"

"What the fuck exactly. I can't believe we're related sometimes. She's not a damn object."

Olly doesn't have a chance to add anything more when Lottie comes back to join us just as Ethan stops talking.

"And by she, I assume you mean me?" Her eyes dart between the four of us.

Nathan rubs the back of his neck. Good, at least he has the good grace to look contrived.

"Yeah, and FYI, be sure to avoid him," Olly says, pointing at Nathan. "But these two are fine."

"Duly noted," she replies and glances to Ethan, whose upper lip curves just a fraction whilst he busies himself with his phone.

"Right, well, I'll catch up with you guys later. I want to show Lottie my office while she's here."

"It was nice meeting you," she says to us as Olly takes her by the elbow to guide her away.

I don't miss the way she looks back over her shoulder.

"Looks like someone likes you," Nathan says, pulling Ethan's attention back to us.

"Whatever, man, just don't be a dick around her, okay?"

Nathan would usually continue playing the fool, but instead, he surprises us both when he replies, "Yeah, you're right, man. I didn't mean to be disrespectful."

I nearly choke on my spit, and Ethan puts the back of his hand against Nathan's forehead. "Are you feeling all right?"

"Fuck off," he says, pushing his hand away and grabbing for the pads. "Are we training or what?"

Adjusting my feet, I take a stance, and then in quick succession, punch the pads.

"I have some friends coming over tomorrow tonight, if you're up for it?" Nathan says to both me and Ethan with a grunt.

"Dude, I live there. Do I get a say?"

I punch the pad harder, and he stumbles.

"Nope," he says, blowing me a kiss.

Ethan laughs. "I might pop over for a bit," he says with a non-committal shrug.

I hope it's not the same group of girls who keep trying to sneak into my bedroom. I'm not in the mood to be having to dodge their advances politely, and I'm not beneath locking my door and hiding in my room either.

The truth is, there is only one woman at the forefront of my mind, and it's Meg. The more I think about my attitude towards her, the more I'm beginning to think Ethan is right. I'm such a fool. He might not have come right out and said I have his blessing, but it was close enough.

She risked losing my brother's friendship to be with me, and I threw it back in her face. I'm a goddamn idiot. I need to talk to her, tell her I'm sorry, and that I want to work this out. I just hope I'm not already too late.

Chapter Thirty-Seven

Meghan

A constant vibration pulls me from my sleep. I slap around, searching for my phone. The screen lights up like firework night, and my eyes instantly water from the assault. I blink past the harshness to see Clara is calling.

"What the fuck?" I grumble.

Swiping the screen, I clear my throat and answer. "Clara?" I say, my voice unable to hide my annoyance at being woken.

"Meg," she drawls.

I sit up, a little more alert, knowing something isn't right. "Clara, are you okay?"

"Mmm, okay, tired. I don't want to do this anymore."

I can't control my shiver when the duvet falls around my waist. "Clara, do what?"

She lets out a heavy sigh but doesn't answer. I switch on my bedside lamp. "Are you drunk?" I keep the phone pressed to my ear and shoulder as I pull on my jogging bottoms, putting my phone on speaker so that I can pull my hoody over my head.

"Nooo, just pills," she replies.

A sudden sensation of fear shoots through me. "Where are you?" I ask.

"Home," she slurs.

"Where's Jacob?" When she doesn't reply, my anxiety begins to increase, and my stomach knots uncomfortably. Grabbing my keys and bag, I shove them over my head and shoulder.

"Clara," I say more forcefully when she still hasn't answered.

"Sleeping." She sounds drowsy.

"And Emilio?"

A brittle laugh escapes her. "Who knows," she says, and I can hear the defeat in her voice.

I skip the stairs two at a time, and it takes me two attempts to type in the alarm code to turn it off before I'm out the front door. Inside my car, I don't bother to remove my bag, I just pull my seatbelt over it, fasten it, and drop my phone in the drink holder. My hands are shaking as I start the engine.

"Clara," I say, but the speaker cuts out right before it connects automatically to the Bluetooth.

"He looks so much like Henry."

The hair lifts on the nape of my neck and arms." Who? Ethan?" I ask. She's not making any sense.

"Tired," she slurs.

"Clara, I'm coming to you. Just stay on the phone with me, okay?" I ask again, unable to keep the quiver from my voice.

"Jacob's dad… he looks his… eyes…"

She is beginning to freak me out. "Clara… Clara?"

Images of the unthinkable flash through my mind as my adrenaline spikes.

I flick the indicator, and my clammy hands grip the steering wheel tightly as I turn onto the dual carriageway.

The call cuts off, and I fumble to pull up her number,

using my hand control, but it rings and rings and rings until it goes to voicemail.

"Fuck." I slam my palm against my steering wheel, accidentally hitting the horn, causing me to flinch.

"Think Meghan, think," I say into the emptiness of my car.

I bite my lip, my throat dry as I swallow. I eye the road and glance back to my call log, and before I can stop myself, I hit dial.

"Hello?"

Confusion assails me at the unfamiliar female voice on the other end of the phone.

"Helllooo," she sings.

I disconnect the call, shake my head, and try ringing Clara again.

But the same thing happens. It rings until it automatically diverts to voicemail.

"Shit!"

I blink back my tears to keep focused on the road. I startle when my phone rings, and without checking the caller ID, I answer in a rush.

"Clara?"

"Meg?" Henry asks.

His voice has the power to destroy me.

"I didn't mean to, um, interrupt you, sorry, I have to go," I say, hardly making any sense—even to my ears. I hover over the end call button.

"No, you didn't. It's Nathan's friend. She grabbed my phone," he says in a rush, and I find myself letting out a small sigh of relief. "Why did you call me Clara? What's wrong?"

My voice cracks. "She's taken something. I was on the phone with her, but we got cut off, and now she won't answer."

I flick the indicator and stop at the traffic lights, my knee bouncing as I will them to turn green. *Come on, come on.*

"What the fuck? Are you driving?"

It goes quiet in the background, like he's moved rooms or something.

"Yes, and I need your help, please?"

"Where are you?" he asks, the sound of him shuffling and the rattle of keys echoing through the speakers.

"I'm on my way to Clara's," I say, frustrated.

He lets out a heavy sigh. "I'll meet you there," he says.

"But I don't know if Emilio is there," I admit, and my voice rises in panic.

"All the more reason for me to meet you there," he says. His voice has an edge to it, one I've never heard before, and I think he might be angry with me, but right now, I can't even think about that.

"I need to go, so I can try and call her again."

"I'll be at hers in about ten minutes. Wait for me if you get there first and drive safely."

"Okay, you too," I reply and hang up. Repeatedly, I dial Clara's number over and over again.

"Come on," I say, frustrated, my foot pushing down on the accelerator. The drive to Clara is distorted but feels like it takes forever. I pull up onto her driveway, next to her Range Rover. I come to a stop, switch off the engine, swing my door open, and climb out, but I'm yanked back into the seat. I look down, still strapped in by my seat belt.

"For fuck's sake." Pressing the button, I unclasp it and disentangle myself.

Heart pounding in my ears, I rush over up the steps, knock on the front door and wait, but nothing. My stomach is swarming with nerves.

"Shit. Come on, Clara, let me in," I plead, trying to peek through the window, but it's no use. The blinds are closed.

Real fear, the kind I have never felt, begins to consume me, threatening to drown me whole. I start pounding on the door even harder.

I palm my forehead. The spare key. I drop to my knees and begin hunting through the flower bed when the sound of a car engine, followed by the flash of headlights, shines from behind me.

I freeze. The engine shuts off, the lights dim, and a car door slams, followed by heavy footsteps pounding the gravel.

"Meg?"

I let out a sigh—Henry.

"What are you doing?" he asks, perplexed.

"I'm looking for the rock," I reply, as if it isn't already obvious.

"What?" he asks, crouching down beside me. His familiar scent washes over me.

"Clara has one with a spare key inside."

My hand skims over something which feels out of place amongst the others.

"Bingo." I grab it and turn it over, sliding open the bottom. Inside is a key.

Clara used to joke about having 'mum brain' after having Jacob and kept locking herself out of the house. And when she saw this on the shopping channel, she knew she had to have one.

Pushing to my feet, I stumble back to the door, but my hands won't stop shaking, and I keep missing the keyhole.

"Fucking hell," I curse.

A hard chest brushes against my back as firm hands still mine, taking the key from me. Henry unlocks the door and pushes it open. I don't wait as I barrel into the hallway and rush into the living room, calling out Clara's name.

Chapter Thirty-Eight

Meghan

My steps falter when I see her lying face down on the living room carpet, unmoving.

"Clara, can you hear me?" I say, my voice rising in panic as I fall to my knees and grip her shoulder to roll her over. I'm not weak by any means, but I struggle to get her onto her back.

Her flesh is ghostly white, her lips blue, and white foam is leaking from the edge of her mouth. Grabbing her hand, I squeeze it in mine and shake her shoulder. But she's unresponsive and cold—too cold.

Henry kneels beside me and leans over, putting his ear to her mouth. Time stops still, and I hold my breath, unable to look away. Worried eyes shoot to mine, his face takes on a pale hue, and suddenly I feel sick.

"She's not breathing. Call nine-nine-nine," Henry orders, placing the heel of his hand on the centre of her chest as he starts chest compressions.

I cover my mouth with my hand, my eyes wide.

"Now, Meg," he grunts out and then continues counting under his breath.

My hand digs around in my bag. Shit, where's my phone?

"It's in my car," I say out loud.

"Use mine," Henry says, tossing me his phone.

An operator asks which service.

"Ambulance," I reply.

Immediately transferred, I'm asked questions, but it's a struggle to focus as I take in the scene before me.

Because in my gut, I know, it's already too late—she's gone. She's cold to the touch, when she's usually so warm.

Oh my God, this can't be happening.

She was speaking to me less than half an hour ago. Everything about this is all wrong.

Inhaling heavily, I force air into my lungs. It's as though my body has forgotten how to breathe, but I wish I hadn't as soon as I do. I don't know if death has a smell, but right now, in this room, there's a distinct smell that has never been here before—which I can only describe as death. Everything about it is foreign.

Bile rises, and I have to do everything I can to push it away.

I quickly put the phone on speaker as Henry's strong arms continue chest compressions. He's so determined in his task, and I wonder if he knows.

I give the address and try to answer as many questions as possible, and then a cry echoes through the baby monitor—Jacob.

"Shit." I run up the stairs, tripping halfway with a loud oomph. I push myself up and rush into Jacob's room. He's standing up in his cot, arms outstretched—crying.

Not that I'm surprised, with all the commotion going on downstairs. I reach down and swoop him into my arms, pressing him to my shoulder, rubbing his back gently.

As I take the stairs as carefully as possible and keep his

back to the scene in front of me, his crying mellows somewhat, turning into small whimpers.

Henry is still performing CPR, and he glances up, his eyes darting between Jacob and me. His face has a look of defeat, and I know he knows it's no use, she's gone, but he doesn't stop.

I move from side to side until Jacob's tears cease. The room is deathly quiet, apart from the sound of Henry working tirelessly in a futile attempt to pump life back into Clara's body.

Though he keeps moving, it's as though time stands still and doesn't move again until I hear the sirens wailing in the distance. The louder they become, the smaller the room feels, until it's almost suffocating.

When two paramedics walk through the front door, which is still wide open, they ask Henry some questions and quickly and methodically take over from him.

His arms hang limply on either side of his thighs as he watches on, his chest rising and falling rapidly.

Jumbled words attack my ears. When they cease their efforts and stop what they're doing, one calls through on the radio.

The other comes over with a sombre expression, saying they could do nothing and they are sorry.

But it's not their fault. It's mine.

She's my best friend, and now she's dead.

I was too late.

The signs were all there, and I ignored them.

Why didn't I get to her sooner?

Clara needed me, and I let her down.

I tighten my hold on Jacob as his soft breath tickles my neck. Goosebumps break out all over my body, and I shiver. He has no idea, but he's half an orphan now. His mum won't get to see him grow up, and the one parent he has left is a narcissist.

"I didn't save her in time," I say, turning my back on the scene in front of me and retreating to Jacob's room.

Sitting in the rocker by his cot, I rock back and forth, holding onto him for comfort. This is the closest I'll ever be to my best friend again, and the thought alone sends my heart into turmoil.

"Meg?"

Henry is crowding the doorway, his eyes darting around the room.

He clears his throat and enters slowly, approaching me and dropping to his haunches.

"I am so sorry," he says. His hand rises over Jacob's sleeping body to wipe away my tears before cupping my cheek. His eyes are glassy, full of unshed tears, and I cup the back of his hand. A war of emotions plays across his face. This is a woman he once loved too.

"The paramedic has to call the police... because it's an unexpected death." His voice cracks on the last word, and my heart breaks even more. "They'll need to speak to us both," he says.

I nod and gently pull his hand away, and he rises to his feet.

"I just want to get Jacob settled," I say, shifting him in my arms.

Henry stares at his sleeping form, studying him, an odd expression on his face. I never share pictures of Jacob on social media, and neither did Clara, so I wonder if it's because this is the first time he's seeing him?

"Okay," he says, his eyes rising to mine as he turns and leaves me alone.

I push to my feet and lay Jacob in his cot. He has no idea his whole world is about to change irrevocably. And the thought that Emilio is all he has left is terrifying.

Chapter Thirty-Nine

Henry

Everything about this situation is surreal—fucked up beyond all recognition. I'm sitting in my ex-girlfriend's house after finding her unresponsive on her living room floor. Now I'm talking to the police, trying my best to answer their questions.

I tried so damn hard to save her.

And then, when I saw Jacob's face, I couldn't look away. It's almost uncanny how much he resembles Ethan and me from when we were toddlers.

I'm clearly in shock. That's the most logical explanation, right?

But trying to push it from my mind is an impossible feat. There is a very strong possibility that the sleeping boy upstairs is my son.

I continue to bounce my knee up and down, my entire body on high alert. Every time the door opens, I tense, expecting it to be Emilio, but it never is. The police haven't been able to reach him yet, so they're trying to contact his mum.

Meg comes down, and I immediately go to her, wrapping

her in my arms, grateful when she lets me, but all too soon, I have to let go so that she can speak to the police.

They were confused about my relationship with Clara, and I said she was my ex-girlfriend, which received some raised eyebrows.

While Meg is asked questions, I sit beside her, clutching her hand in mine. I want her to know I'm here for her, and I'm not going anywhere.

When they're finished, she excuses herself to use the toilet, and I busy myself making us both some tea, not sure if the caffeine will be a blessing or a curse. It's strange. Clara's kitchen is the same layout as to how she organised mine back when we were together.

And it hits me more profoundly. She was someone I once loved. Hell, I'm pretty sure we have a child together. Everything about this situation hurts.

Meg is throwing open all the windows when I turn back to face the living room, and I carry over a cup of tea for her. She scrunches her nose, and I know why. The smell is becoming harder to ignore.

We sit together on the sofa, as far away from the body as possible… the body… it's Clara, for fuck's sake.

"I can't believe this is happening," Meg whispers, her voice hoarse. I pull her to my side.

"I'm sorry, Meg, I really tried. Honestly, I did."

She stares up at me, her lips parting, surprised by my admission.

"Henry, this is my fault. This happened because I didn't see the signs. She was already gone when we got here," she says, no longer able to look me in the eye.

I grip her chin gently and angle her face, holding her eyes captive.

"No, this is no more your fault than it is mine," I say.

A soft knock on the door interrupts us when the police officer shows in a coroner, here to collect Clara.

She's not long gone, when there's a woman's nasally voice from outside, and in barges Gloria—Emilio's mum.

It doesn't matter how much work she's had done to stay looking younger, not when her soul is dark.

"Where's Emilio?" she asks as her eyes scan the living room.

Meg stands, needing to be on level footing with the woman. "Your guess is as good as ours," Meg says, crossing her arms.

She sticks her nose in the air. "Hmm," she says.

I clench my fists. Isn't she even going to ask after her grandson's mother? Or even her grandson?

"Have you tried contacting him?" Meg asks, trying to be polite, but it's not without effort. It's been a long couple of hours, and it's beginning to show.

"He's a grown man, but this is all very inconvenient," she says with indifference.

Meg's entire body goes rigid.

"Inconvenient?" Meg says incredulously. "Jacob has just lost his mother—my best friend."

I'd expect for her to at least look a little contrite, but clearly not.

"Yes, well, drugs will do that." Her response is callous at best, and fuck me if I can't see where Emilio gets his bad traits.

"The drugs your son dabbles in, you mean?" Meg says, her voice rising an octave.

His mum shakes her head. "What he does is none of my business," she retorts.

Meg takes a step forward, her eyes wide, her nostrils flaring. "Well, it should be. It's partly his fault your grandson no longer has a mother."

Gloria stares down at her nails. "You're being ridiculous, and as I said, it's none of my business," she replies.

Does this woman not have any empathy whatsoever?

Clara was my ex, and even with the revelation that little boy might be mine, I'm still cut up by her death.

"Your grandson is going to grow up without his mother. I think that makes it your business," Meg whisper-shouts, the vein in her temple prominent.

I can feel the anger rolling off Meg—she's ready to explode.

"He'll be better off without a drug addict," she says.

Meg lunges forward, and as much as the woman deserves whatever Meg is about to unleash, I wrap my arm around her waist and pull her to my side. She's shaking from the adrenaline.

"Do you have no shame?" I ask.

She sticks her nose in the air, poking out her fake boobs like a ruffled peacock.

"Who are you again?" she asks, knowing full well who I am. I did grow up with her son, after all.

"Gloria, just go. Jacob's my godson. I'll look after him. You clearly don't want to be here anyway."

I'd half expect her to argue with Meg, but instead, she shrugs like it's no big deal.

"I have a spa day today anyway. I'd hate to have to cancel."

I swear I hear Meg grind her teeth, and this time, I'm the one who steps forward, but Meg grabs my hand, pulling me back to her side.

Gloria storms out, slamming the front door in her wake, and I hold my breath, half expecting Jacob to wake up crying, but nothing comes through on the monitor. I turn to Meg.

Her eyes are heavy. How she's still standing is beyond me.

"Can you fucking believe that woman?" she says, her teeth chattering.

"Forget her. She's not worth it," I say and lead her to sit back down.

I'd rather be anywhere but here, and not just because

Clara was lying dead on the floor less than half an hour ago, but because this is Emilio's house, and the thought makes my skin crawl with rage that is vying to be set free. Even with the police outside, there is no way I'm leaving Meg alone.

"Do you want another cup of tea?" I ask, at a loss as to what else to do.

Meg nods, and I retrieve our cups from the coffee table, making us both a fresh cup. I'm both wired and overtired, a weird combo.

"Did you know I caught her using a few weeks ago?" she says when I hand over a steaming hot tea. "I could have prevented all of this."

I put my arm over her shoulder. "This isn't your fault. Clara always had her vices, even when I was with her."

"Maybe, but how do I explain to a sixteen-month-old baby his mum isn't coming back?"

I shake my head, because honestly, I have absolutely no idea. All I do know is that she won't be alone. I'll be here for her no matter what. She sags into my body, and I take the tea from her, placing it on the table.

Eventually, I manage to get her to drink her tea, but she's still trembling. I unzip my hoody and wrap it around her shoulders. She doesn't even argue, her body becomes heavier against my side, and it's not long before she falls into an exhausted sleep.

A small cry comes through the monitor, and I hold my breath to see if I'll hear it again. Sure enough, crying comes through. I'm torn between waking Meg or going to Jacob myself.

Before I give it too much thought, I gently lay Meg's head back against the couch and go upstairs to his room. The plaque on the door spells 'Jacob,' surrounded by different zoo animals—totally something Clara would buy.

I push the door open to see him holding himself up by the cot railings. When he sees me, his crying ceases, and we stare at each other for a moment, checking each other out. The spell is broken when he throws out a blue comforter and begins crying again, holding his hands out to me.

Bending down, I reach and pick him up. The first thing I notice is how heavy his nappy is under my hand. I open the curtains to allow some light to filter in the room—painted in pale blue. He's stopped crying now, but he's studying my face, and before I have a chance to stop him, he pokes me in the eye.

"Shit," I curse, taking his chubby hand and moving it away from my face.

Meg speaks from behind me, and I startle, turning to face her. "Sorry, I didn't mean to fall asleep," she says, holding out her hands for Jacob. He goes to her without any fuss, clutching my hoody she's now wearing in his small hands.

"Henry?"

"Sorry, what?"

"I said, are you okay?"

I scrub my hand over my face as she moves past me and lays him on a mat, on top of a changing table, cabinet thingy, and pulls out a fresh nappy from somewhere underneath. Jacob laughs, trying to roll away, but she holds him in place.

"It's Jacob," I say, clearing my throat.

She removes his soiled nappy and he attempts to grab himself, but Meg is fast as she fastens the fresh nappy. She makes it looks so easy, even with him wriggling around like a worm.

"What about him?" she asks.

"He looks exactly like Ethan and me when we were babies."

She turns her face towards me before glancing back to Jacob as he kicks his chubby little legs in the air.

"What do you mean?" She lays a clean baby-grow underneath him, putting his feet into the legs—and then his arms—before buttoning it up.

"I'm pretty sure I'm his dad, and Jacob is my son."

Her eyes go wide as she stares between the two of us, her face even paler than before.

"Mum-ma," Jacob says when she lifts him into her arms, balancing him on her hip.

"How about we get you some breakfast?" Meg says to Jacob, trying to keep her tone soft, but I can hear her heartbreak.

Meg keeps glancing at me and then back to Jacob, as though she's only just now seeing him for the first time. Clara was her best friend. She would have told me if she *knew* he was mine, *right?*

And as weird as this thought might be, if he is mine—and I'm almost certain he is—I want him… and I want Meg too. Regardless of what's happened, I'm done fighting. I want them both to be my family.

Chapter Forty

Meghan

As ridiculous as it might sound, part of me is still expecting to wake to find this has all been a sick nightmare. But it's a foolish notion. We now know Emilio has heard about the overdose, but he's refusing to come home while there's a police presence.

Which screams implicit and guilty if you ask me, but more importantly, what about Jacob? Even with the revelation that Henry believes Jacob to be his son, Emilio is still his dad and should be here regardless.

And now this. If I thought things couldn't getting any worse, I was sorely mistaken. I wonder if I'm hearing things. Can that happen from exhaustion?

"What do you mean you're taking Jacob?" I ask. The ringing in my ears is deafening, and my heart racing.

With a sympathetic look as though she's used to this, she says, "I'm sorry, but we have to. We have a duty of care to adhere." Like that will placate me, but if anything, it only distresses me more.

"But he's my godson. I already told you that. I can look after him," I say.

My eyes are frantically darting between the social worker and Henry.

"I'm sorry, Meghan, but we have protocols to follow," she says, her tone empathetic but also resigned.

"Surely, you can't just take him?" Henry says, sidling up beside me and taking hold of my hand in his—a show of unity.

Her eyes soften. "Unfortunately, until I can reach his father, who is his legal guardian, Jacob is a temporary ward of the state."

"A ward of the state? He's not a building or a car, he's a baby, and he just lost his mum," I croak out.

"What if he's mine?" Henry asks, interrupting.

Now the social worker looks completely perplexed. "I'm sorry, Emilio Hansen is his father, no?"

Henry nods. "Yes, but only on paper. There's a possibility I'm his biological father," he says, hoping this will swing it in our favour.

She shakes her head. "Listen, even if that was the case, as I said, we have protocols. Emilio Hansen is his legal guardian."

Everything else happens so quickly as she gathers him some clothes and nappies, packing them all into his changing bag—the stupid designer one Emilio insisted Clara used, a pristine white one, impossible to keep clean.

I cuddle Jacob, kissing his head. "We'll sort this out, little man, I promise."

Everything in me is reluctant to hand him over, but I don't want to distress him. Things are going to be hard enough for Jacob. I watch at a complete loss, feeling bereft as I watch strangers take him away, helpless to stop them.

Numb, I feel numb.

After a long silence, Henry looks around the room. "Come on, let's get out of here," he says, gently tugging on my hand.

I nod and follow Henry out to my car—the sunlight harsh.

"Are you going to be okay driving?" he asks.

"Yeah, I'm not leaving my car here." The thought of Emilio coming back and my car still being here doesn't sit well with me. He'll probably have it towed, just to spite me.

"Will you come back to mine?"

I nod. If anyone knows how I feel right now, it's Henry.

"As long as you don't mind?"

He holds my face between his palms and kisses my forehead. "Of course not."

Henry follows me back to his, but I don't remember driving, and it's not until I pull up outside his that I snap out of my haze and turn off the engine. My door opens, and I startle, clutching my chest, trying to calm my racing heart, but it's just Henry.

He holds out his hand, and with trembling fingers, I try to unclip my seat belt. Without a word, Henry leans over and does it for me, his scent refreshing in the confines of my car.

Stepping back, he gives me room to get out, closing the door behind me. Taking my hand as we navigate the path, he unlocks his front door.

"Do you want anything to drink or eat?" he asks, his voice echoing in the quiet of the house.

I shake my head. "No, I'm just exhausted," I admit.

"Do you want to try and rest for a while?"

I think I might nod, because without another word, he eases me upstairs, his palm on the small of my back, and we enter his room. The curtains are drawn, and the room, although dark, isn't pitch black. He pulls back the duvet and I toe-off my trainers before getting on the bed and sliding under the covers, still fully dressed. I curl into a ball, wanting to disappear. The sound around me is amplified as he shuffles, no doubt removing his trainers before the bed dips and he joins me, pulling me against his chest until we're spooning.

"I'm so sorry about Clara," he whispers.

The reality of everything which has transpired grips my chest hard. So many different thoughts and emotions are vying for my attention. I tried to be strong while caring for Jacob, but here, wrapped in the safety of his arms, the floodgates open, and all my pent-up emotions are set free.

"Let it out," he says, his voice filled with tears. "I got you," he says, and his empathy turns my silent tears into heart-wrenching sobs. Henry continues to hold me, whispering words of comfort, telling me I'm not alone and he's here for me, always.

My eyes are sore when I wake, the room dark. I stretch my body, aching all over, like I spent a night out clubbing on a dance floor or a hard session at the gym, but then my memories come flooding back, and it hits me all at once, sucking the air from my lungs—Clara is dead.

I sit upright, my head pounding like I'm punch drunk or hungover.

"Hey, are you okay?" Henry asks, his voice rough from sleep as his fingers gently wrap over my shoulder.

"I feel awful," I admit, rubbing my temples.

Scooting out of bed, he shuffles, and my eyes can just about make out his shape.

"What time is it?" I ask, swallowing, my throat dry.

His phone alights his features. "Just after nine," he says.

I'm surprised I even slept at all, but I guess shock and exhaustion will do that to you.

"I'll go get us a drink. Are you hungry?" he asks, and in answer to his question, my stomach grumbles a strange hollow sound, even though eating is the last thing on my mind.

Once he leaves me alone, I use his bathroom and splash my face with cold water. Heavy dark circles under my eyes are staring back at me, my face pale and hollow. I quickly finger comb my hair and plait it over my shoulder.

Clara taught me how to plait my hair. After my mum left, I tried to do it myself, but I was useless. I smile at the memory, and my eyes water, but I sniff back my tears and go downstairs in search of Henry.

I find him in the kitchen, and he ushers me to the table, where he sets down a mug of tea and a small plate of toast and jam. It's such a simple act, but it has me welling up again.

Whenever I'm not feeling well or I'm hungover, I always have tea and toast. And the fact he knows this makes my chest squeeze in a way that makes me feel selfish.

He joins me, and we eat in silence. Only the crunching of the toast can be heard.

I brush off the crumbs from my fingers and push the plate aside.

"Thanks," I croak out, sipping my tea.

"No worries," he says, his gaze fixed on the table. And I can only imagine the whirlwind of thoughts running through his mind right now.

"Listen—" I begin, but he cuts me off.

"Did you know?" he asks, looking up. "About Jacob?"

I lean back and cross my arms. "Do you think I would have kept it from you?" I ask quietly.

He shakes his head, but his silence is deafening. I let out a sigh. "No, I didn't know… until you said you thought he was yours, and then it all made sense."

"What?"

"I thought there was something, but I could never work it out. I put it down to his resemblance to Clara, but he doesn't look anything like Emilio. I just thought he was lucky in that aspect. But when she rang me this morning, she said something, but she wasn't making any sense."

He straightens in his seat, watching me intently. "What did she say?"

I finger the rim of the cup. "She said he looked so much like you. I thought she meant Ethan, but then she said Jacob and how he looked like his dad… she wasn't making any sense, and then you know the rest, I got cut off."

I look at his features now, his eyes, his nose. "And it wasn't until you were both in the same room, I saw the resemblance. He has your eyes."

Reaching over the table, I take hold of his hand. "I didn't know, and if I had, I would have made her tell you, I promise."

He studies my face. "It's just hard to process. She should have told me. I've missed out on so much," he says.

"She must have fallen pregnant right before you caught her cheating with Emilio. Honestly, if she would have told you she was pregnant and there was a chance he was yours, would you have listened?"

He shrugs. "Maybe, I don't know, and it's a moot point now, seeing as I was never given the opportunity."

I bite at the dry skin on my chapped lip. "What will you do now… about Jacob?" I ask.

His jaw ticks. "I'll prove he's mine, and then I'm getting full custody."

Nothing surprises me about his answer.

"I'll do everything in my power to help you," I say, and I mean it.

"Thank you. We'll get him back together. I can't imagine Emilio making this easy. All I know is, there is no way I'm leaving my son in the hands of that arsehole."

I squeeze his hand in silent understanding.

"I should probably go. I need to speak to my dad, sort out work and figure out what needs to be done now regarding the arrangements for Clara." My voice cracks, but I swallow the lump in my throat, determined to keep my shit together.

"Do you want me to come with you?"

His question surprises me but sends a warm, comforting pulse through my chest.

"What... to stay?"

He nods. "Unless you need space. I just thought... I mean..." He runs his hand through his hair.

I shake my head. "Yes, no... I mean, I'd like that, thank you."

The thought of doing any of this alone is not something I'm mentally or emotionally prepared for, and to know he's offering after everything means so much.

Chapter Forty-One

Henry

When I asked Meg about coming back to hers, I'd expected her to say no, but after everything that's happened, the last thing I wanted to do was leave her alone. So, the fact I'm here with her, under her dad's roof, speaks volumes.

By the time we arrived, he had pizza waiting for us, concerned we hadn't eaten. He sat with us. His concern for his daughter and her losing her best friend brought out a side of him I'd never seen before. And I think I have a newfound respect for him being a single father, which I hadn't considered before now.

In Meg's room, I find myself studying a wall, sprinkled in fairy lights and covered in photographs, hanging on pegs. I've never been in her space before.

There is one photograph that catches my attention of Meg with Jacob. I reach out to take a better look when Meg unclips it from the peg and hands it to me.

"You can have it," she says.

"Thanks," I say.

I sit down on the edge of the bed and wonder if I had

been here with Meg before any of this happened, would I have noticed Jacob in the photograph?

"Thank you for being here," Meg says from across the room.

Walking over to her, I bend my knees and cup her cheek.

"I wouldn't want to be anywhere else." I am all in where she is concerned. This has solidified this for me.

Her eyes soften from my admission. I lower my face to hers, our lips meet for a soft and gentle kiss, her eyes flutter closed as she wraps her arms around me, and I pull her to my chest. When she pulls away, it's hard not to miss the worry etched on her face. I tip her chin up with my forefinger.

"Don't overthink this, Meg. I want to be here with you."

I hate that I've put the doubt there, for all the times I've pushed her away. I'll do whatever it takes to prove to her that she's it for me.

She nods and steps over to her chest of drawers, rummaging through until she pulls out some nightclothes.

"Did you want a shower before bed?" she asks.

I nod, more than eager to wash away the hell from today.

"Yeah, please." I watch on as she enters her bathroom and pulls out some towels from one of the cupboards and leaves them on the side.

"I'll take mine after you," she says, coming back into the bedroom.

Closing the door behind me, I strip and climb into the bath, turning on the shower. I hike up the temperature to as hot as my body can handle. Resting my forehead against the tiled wall, I let out a sigh, the water cascading down my back.

I could stay like this for what feels like an eternity, but I'm conscious that Meg needs one too, and I don't want to use all the hot water. Once I've dried off, I exit her bathroom in only a towel, dirty clothes in my hands, my bag still at the foot of her bed where she's sitting, her head hung low.

"It's all yours," I say.

Her gaze rises to mine, and she pushes herself to her feet. Her eyes roam up and down the length of my body as she passes me, and damn if my dick doesn't react. I wait until I hear the click of the door before adjusting myself and pulling on a pair of briefs under some joggers and a T-shirt. I shove a pillow behind my back and sit up against her cast iron headboard to call Ethan.

"Hey, man," he says on the second ring.

"Hey, sorry I didn't call you back earlier. We were exhausted."

I rest my head back and close my eyes.

"That's understandable. If you want to talk about it, I'm here," he says.

I sigh into the phone. "It was awful, and I can't get the image of her lifeless body out of my head. I tried to revive her, man. I really did." My throat constricts as I try to swallow past the emotion. Seeing her like that will forever be engraved into my memory.

"H, don't do that. You did all you could. How is she holding up?"

I glance at the closed door. "I'm worried about her. But there's something else," I admit, opening my eyes and staring at the bathroom door—the shower is still running.

"About you and Meg?"

"Yes and no. You know Jacob, Clara's little boy?"

He lets out a curse under his breath. "What? Please tell me he's not hurt?"

"No, but he was taken away by social services. But that's not all. I think he's mine… No, I'm certain he's mine. Jacob is my son."

I hear a thud on the other end of the line, followed by an 'oomph.'

"E?"

There's some fumbling around, and then he comes back

on the phone. "Fuck, sorry, I knocked over my drink. What do you mean, he's your son?"

I pick up the picture from the bedside table. "Because he looks just like us when we were little." Sitting up, I lay the photo flat. "Hold on, two secs." I pull up my camera and snap a photo. "I'm sending you a picture."

Chewing my fingernail, I impatiently wait for him to receive it.

"Shut the front door."

I smile at his response. "Well?" I ask, scrubbing my hand over my chin.

"The similarities are too much of a coincidence for him not to be… hold up, did Meg know?"

"No, she said she didn't, and I believe her."

Ethan lets out a relieved sigh. "Fair enough. So what happens now?"

My eyes glance to the bathroom door when I hear the sound of the water shut off.

"I'm going to get proof he's mine and then fight for custody."

"Of course you are. No way is my nephew staying with Emilio. You have my support." My chest constricts… the way he said *his* nephew…

"Thanks, man," I reply, my voice cracking. "There's something else… I'm staying over with Meg tonight."

The moment I admitted to myself I was all in with Meg was when I knew there would be no more hiding.

He clears his throat and I bite my lip, bracing myself for his reaction. "Good, she shouldn't be alone."

"Agreed. I didn't want to keep it from you."

Saying that out loud has lifted a weight off my shoulders, and I'm one step closer to getting everything I want—my son, Meg, and winning this fight.

Meghan

I take longer in the shower than I intended, but my nerves begin to catch up with me. After the way things were left between Henry and me—and now him in my space—it's a lot to process.

Henry is on top of the covers with his eyes closed, one arm underneath his head, the other covering his torso. Pulling back the duvet, I climb into bed and roll on my side, so I'm facing him.

I watch his chest rise and fall—the way his eyes move under his closed lids, his lips parted. Something about being this close to him calms me. His lips curve up into a smile as he opens his eyes.

He shifts under the cover. "Come here," he says, lifting his arm and pulling me closer to his body.

My thoughts keep going back to the images of Clara and the knowledge Jacob is alone, with strangers. And there was nothing I could do to stop it.

The more I try to keep my emotions at bay, the more they begin to surface. I attempt to stifle my sobs, but it's an impossible feat.

"Hey…" Henry's voice is a rough baritone, but it only makes me cry harder. "It's okay, Meg, I've got you." His thumbs wipe under my eyes.

I rest my palm over his chest, the steady beat of his heart soothing.

"I still can't believe she's gone, that she left Jacob. And now we don't even know where he is." Is it wrong to be angry with the dead? Because I am. We still don't know if it was intentional or accidental, the overdose. But either way, it doesn't change the outcome.

And the worst part is, she's not here to defend herself, to tell me why she did it. Or what she was thinking being so reckless. She deserved better than this.

"I spoke to Ethan, told him about Jacob."

My heart beats faster from his admission. "What did he say?"

"He's got my back."

"You're lucky to have each other."

His fingers begin massaging my scalp, and my body begins to relax.

"And I told him I was staying with you."

"Oh."

He kisses my forehead. "He didn't want you to be alone either."

I worry my lip, and Henry frees it from between my teeth.

"What do you think will happen when Emilio does show up? The police will still need to interview him right before they give Jacob back to him."

He shrugs, and my body moves with the motion. "Yeah, Clara's death was unexpected, so he can't get out of talking to them. She was found in their home. As far as him getting Jacob back, he is his legal guardian. But I'm going to make some calls tomorrow, see if anyone I know can recommend a lawyer. And then we'll see what the next step is regarding Clara."

I lean on my elbow so I can see his face.

"We?"

He nods. "I'm not leaving you to deal with this all on your own. Whether we like it or not, Emilio is going to be involved."

Shit, he's right. I hadn't even thought of that.

"Just accept the fact I'm not going anywhere."

Clara is estranged from her parents, so that only leaves Emilio and me. And I'm her next of kin. Jacob is still my godson, and I want his mum to have the funeral she deserves.

"Hey." His finger tilts my chin. "I've got you. I promise."

His lips caress mine in soft and slow pecks, his tongue seeking access. I open myself up to him and surrender.

Chapter Forty-Two

Meghan

When Clara asked me to be her next of kin, of course I agreed without hesitation. I never gave it another thought. Never did I think I'd find myself arranging her funeral. I had to wait for the autopsy to confirm the cause of death for the death certificate before the coroner would release her body.

Henry wasted no time getting in touch with a lawyer and is just waiting on the paperwork for the right to request DNA testing. I haven't been able to see Jacob since social services awarded him back to Emilio. And of course, I had to message him about the funeral arrangements.

I'm beyond stressed, trying to do the right thing for her. I don't want to let her down. Clara tried to reconnect with her parents after she had Jacob, but it was futile. I still contacted them. They needed to know but said they wouldn't be able to make it back for the service. She's their only daughter, and they're not even going to attend her funeral. They didn't even have the decency to ask after their grandson. Clara was better off without them.

I can't fault my dad. He's been great, attentive without

being smothering. He's not questioned Henry spending so much time with me. I've been trying to get together an order of service between clients, probably not the best idea on my part, but needs must.

"You look like you could use a hand."

I snap my gaze away from the computer monitor as Ethan walks towards me, with the same carefree grace he always carries. It's been what feels like forever since I saw him last, and apart from a text after Clara, we've not spoken. And he's had work commitments that have kept him from the gym this past week.

When his lips curve into his signature smile, I'm hit with a wave of overwhelming emotion, and I burst out crying. I move out from behind the counter and straight into his open arms.

"Ah, come on, Meg, stop that unless you want to see a grown man cry."

I let out a snort of laughter and pull back to stare at him.

"I've missed you," I say, studying his face.

"I know, and I'm sorry," he says, his tone contrite. "I was trying to give you space, keep my distance after everything, but H said I was an idiot."

Sniffing back my tears, I bite my lip. "He did?"

"Yeah, he said you need me."

I nod because he's right. It's bad enough I've already lost one best friend. "I do."

"Then you've got me. What can I do to help?"

Henry did offer to help, but he already has enough on his plate, so I'm beyond grateful to Ethan right now.

He wipes my cheek with his thumbs, and his face turns sombre. "Tell me what you need."

"Can you help get the word out with the details of the service?" I step out of his embrace, go back behind the counter, thumb through some papers, and then hand him a printout with all the details.

He pulls out his phone from his pocket. "I'm on it. The only time social media is freaking helpful."

I let out a heavy breath, and for the first time in days, I can breathe a little lighter.

Sensing eyes on me, the hairs on the back of my neck rise, and when I look over Ethan's shoulder, I find Henry watching me. He smiles when my eyes meet his and he winks, causing me to blush, and my stomach flutters to life.

My phone distracts me when it begins to vibrate on the counter, and when I pick it up, the warmth I was feeling seconds ago dissipates, replaced with ice-cold goosebumps.

This is your fault. And I'm going to make you pay.
Emilio.

I don't respond, and before I go to lock the screen, more bubbles appear, so I wait to see what comes next. You know when you're watching a horror film, and you know something terrible is going to happen, but you can't look away? This is what it's like when he messages me.

And don't forget you have something of mine, and I want it back, or else.

"Meg?"

I can't control the adrenaline coursing through my veins as I place my phone face down on the counter. I've been getting good at doing it too, so Henry or my dad won't see the notification banners every time Emilio texts.

"Meghan, I said you look pale. What is it?" Ethan asks, his voice is full of concern, and I'm so tired of covering this shit up.

"It's Emilio," I reply.

He leans over the counter, and before I can stop him, he grabs my phone, his fingers working over the screen. I never did change my password.

His eyes move up and down, his index finger swiping down.

He tears his eyes away and searches for Henry, calling out his name loud enough to draw some attention before they get back to whatever they're doing.

Ethan waves him over, and I quickly try and snatch my phone back, but he holds it out of my reach.

"How long has he been harassing you like this?" Ethan asks, holding up my phone for me to see.

I swallow and brace myself when Henry approaches, staring between the two of us. "What's going on?" he asks.

Ethan's nostrils flare as he passes Henry my phone, leaning into him and pointing out the chain of text messages. I wrap my arms around my middle as I watch his expression harden.

"What the fuck are these, Meg?" he asks, continuing to swipe up. "They go back weeks," he says as his eyes roam over the words.

I bite my lip and swallow, trying to find my voice.

"Meghan?" he says, his eyebrows snapping together.

"Sorry," I whisper, the only word I manage to get out.

His eyes bore into me. "Why the fuck are you sorry? He's the one sending them. Why didn't you say anything?" And that's when I see the hurt in his eyes.

He turns to Ethan with a raised brow.

Ethan holds up his hands. "I didn't know either," he says.

Both of them turn their attention back to me.

"Meg?" Henry says again. This time his voice is softer.

"I didn't say anything because I was worried about Clara."

He scrubs his palm over his jaw. "This is serious, Meghan. He's threatening you. What is it he says you have of his?" he asks, scrolling back through the messages.

I glance around us to make sure no one else is in earshot, and then I draw in a breath and answer on an exhale. "Drugs."

Ethan gasps out loud, and Henry's lips part as his jaw drops.

"What the fuck?"

"I went to see Clara and she was high. There was a bag on the coffee table, and I was worried about her, so I took them off her and stuffed them in my bag. And then Emilio was pulling up, and I left. I forgot about them until he texted me."

Henry begins pacing, his entire body is rolling with tension, reminding me of a caged animal.

"Where are they now?" Ethan asks. I can tell he's trying to be the rational one. Henry, on the other hand, looks like he might snap at any moment.

"The glove box of my car." I didn't want them in my house, and I had no idea what else to do with them.

"When you say a bag, how big are we talking?" asks Ethan.

I shrug. "A small zip lock bag, with about a hundred or so pills."

Rounding the counter, I approach Henry and hold out my hand. He looks at it, confused for a split second, before he looks down at his hand, which has a vice-like grip on my phone.

He hands it back to me with a grimace.

"Do you think Emilio could be using? That he had something to do with her overdose?" I question out loud.

"Honestly, it's a possibility, and I'm sure he was using the night of the fight with Ethan," Henry says, the vein in his neck prominent.

Ethan nods and reaches out to cup my shoulder. "I think we should go to the police."

I shrug him away. "And say what? I have a bag of drugs I stole from him? It's my word over his. And what about Jacob?"

Henrys back stiffens even more. "She does have a point. At least let me get proof Jacob is my son. I don't want him with Emilio when this does all come to light."

Ethan relents. "Fair enough, but we should at least talk to Olly, maybe he knows someone who can help?"

Henry nods in agreement. "But in the meantime, I don't want you going anywhere on your own. We don't know what lengths he'll go to," Henry says.

My head snaps to his. "I'm not some damsel in distress," I say through clenched teeth. No way will I allow Emilio to have any more power over me than he already does.

He sighs. "I never insinuated you were, but, Meg, he already laid his hands on you once before. You're a bad arse trainer, but this isn't some random guy on the street or a drunk prick in a nightclub. He's a professional fighter, and if he wants to hurt you, he will. And I won't see him hurt someone else I care about."

My heart races from his admission, especially since it's in front of Ethan too.

"You know he's right," Ethan replies, pulling out his phone and typing.

I raise my hands and let them fall at my sides. "So now you're tag-teaming me?"

Henry takes my hand, linking our fingers. "If that's what you want to call it, then yeah, we are."

Heat courses through me and straight to my lower stomach. And I'm fully aware of how inappropriate my body's reaction is to him, but it's one I have no control over.

Ethan stuffs his phone back into his jean pocket. His eyes flick between the two of us. "Olly's free now. I'm going to talk to him, see what we can do about Emilio and him possibly doping at the fight." He gives me a chaste kiss on my temple as he moves past me, holding out his fist to Henry. "H, you good to stay with Meg?" he asks. I look heavenward and try to suppress my groan.

"I'm not letting her out of my sight," Henry replies, and it's hard not to admire the tenacity in his words.

"Okay, cool. I'll speak to you guys later," he says and turns to walk away but stops after a couple of metres, glancing back over his shoulder. "And for the record, you two look good together," he says with a wink, looking down at our linked hands.

Chapter Forty-Three

Henry

Between my sets, I barely take my eyes off Meg. And to anyone from the outside looking in, I'm sure I look like an absolute creeper. But I don't give a shit. She's my end game, and my need to protect her is primal. I've never felt something as intense as this before.

I watch her as she makes her way to the kitchen. Her dark plait is the last of her I see before she disappears behind a door. Out of my sight, I stop what I'm doing and stalk to the room, searching for my prey.

She startles when I enter, closing the door behind me, shutting us inside—alone.

"Shit," she says, grabbing her chest.

I hold up my hands. "Sorry."

"No, it's fine." She waves it off. "I guess I'm a little jumpier than I care to admit."

"Come here." I open my arms, and without any doubt of hesitation, she walks straight into them, and I wrap her in a tight embrace.

"Why didn't you tell me about the messages?" I ask,

unable to hide the hurt I felt when Ethan showed me her phone.

She fidgets in my hold and stares up at me. "Because I'm still trying to figure out what we are," she replies.

I move my hands to her face, cupping her cheeks in my palms like a missing puzzle piece, and she fits perfectly under my touch.

"I already know what I want us to be," I say as my eyes skim over her bowed lips, which I'm desperate to taste before I glance back to her penetrating gaze.

She visibly swallows. "And what is that?" she asks, her voice sultry, even though I know she's not even trying to be.

"Together. I want you to be with me. I want you to be mine."

She wraps her fingers over one of my hands. "And Ethan?"

"That depends on whether you're over him or not." This is it, the final dominator. If she's not, she never will be.

"I love him but not like that." Her eyelashes flutter as she speaks. "I want to be yours."

It's all I needed to hear. Our mouths meet in a fierce kiss, and I spin her, sandwiching her between me and the door. My hands are everywhere, touching, feeling, ready to take what I want—what I desperately crave.

"I have to have you," I say against her ear, my tongue flicking out against the sensitive flesh, thrusting into her. She gasps loudly in response.

"Then take me," she replies, her hands fumbling between us as she roughly shoves down my shorts and briefs, grabbing my erection tight in her grip.

My head falls back, and I let out a groan. A small part of my brain still working is aware we're anywhere but private, but my need for her is insatiable.

"You need to be quick," she says, already stripping out of her yoga pants and knickers. She latches onto my bottom lip with her teeth, biting down before sucking it into her mouth, my erection thickening even more.

I grab her leg and she wraps it around my waist. Her wetness coats the bare skin between us. "I'll make it fast, but later, I'm going to spend hours getting lost in your touch. I will worship every inch of your body, every hole, every curve, every fucking inch."

Her whimper is the spark to my fuse, and I am lit.

"Please," she pants.

I adjust myself, bending my knees, knowing she's as wet for me as the pre-cum dripping off the head of my cock is for her.

My gaze locks on hers, and then in one quick move, I thrust up into her, her sheathing me completely. I hold her stare as I pound into her, overcome with so many sensations. The back of her head knocks against the door as she rocks into me, over and over again. Her gyrations are causing friction between my groin and her clit.

Her breathing grows erratic the more I thrust, knowing I won't last much longer. Having her hot channel wrapped around my cock is pure torture.

She's on the brink, but I refuse to let go until I know she's right there with me.

"Faster, oh fuck, please, faster…" Her pleas have me thickening, ready to lose myself in her completely. But I want her to share my pleasure too.

"Can you feel what you do to me?" I grunt.

"Yes," she huffs out between my hard thrusts.

"Then fucking come for me, Meg. Prove you're mine."

She bites down against the flesh on my shoulder, our climax building higher, more powerful. Her channel tightens around me, milking me like an exploding grenade as my hot seed spills into her core.

I rest my forehead against the door, beside her face, as I try to control my ragged breathing. Her hot centre twitches and pulses around me in small aftershocks. I want to stay here, buried in her for an eternity.

Moving my face, I seek her mouth out and convey everything she just did to me in a scorching kiss before I reluctantly pull out, my seed dripping.

She steadies herself with a hand on the waist-height cupboard as she lowers her leg to the ground, and I swear her knees are trembling, and fuck me if I don't get a rush from that thought. I reach over for some hand towels and pass her some, and we make quick work of cleaning ourselves up. Once we're clothed, she drops the soiled hand towels into the wastebasket and quickly ties up the bin liner before pulling it free and dropping it to her feet.

Her cheeks are glowing from our exertions. I reach out and tuck her hair behind her ears, searching her face for any signs of her regretting what just happened. It wasn't what I intended when I followed her in here, but I'm not complaining.

"I should go take this to the outside bin," she says.

I shake my head. "I'll do it."

Her eyes keep shying away from me. I use my finger to tilt her chin towards me.

"I love filling you and watching you come."

She lets out a small gasp.

"I… I love you," she replies, swallowing hard, trying to look away, but I won't let her, not this time.

"Good, because I love you too, Meg. In case you hadn't noticed, I'm fucking crazy about you."

"You are?" she asks.

"Yes, I think I always have been."

Her eyes glisten, and I lean down. My lips meet hers for a slow, breathy kiss.

When I pull back, her smile is my undoing. I wish I'd told her sooner if it meant seeing her light up like this. I thought my favourite thing was bringing her pleasure, but I was so fucking wrong. Her reaction to my feelings for her beats that, hands down.

"Go, get out of here before I bend you over that table and have you again," I say, stepping away from her and reaching for the bin liner. I turn and head for the back door.

But before I open it, I stare over my shoulder and watch her for a moment, her fingers tracing her bottom lip. When she looks up, I wink before pulling the door open, stepping outside and jogging down the metal stairs. I can't wipe the shit-eating grin from my face. She might not know it yet, but I plan to marry that woman and make her mine forever.

Chapter Forty-Four

Meghan

The day I've been dreading is tomorrow. I finally have to say goodbye to someone I never wanted to leave and accept she's never coming back. The thought is unbearable. Dealing with everything leading up to Clara's funeral has kept me busy and stopped me from solely focusing on the fact she is gone. I hate that Emilio will be there. I don't want him to see me while I'm weak and grieving, but it's not like I can stop him from attending.

Henry is adamant he'll be by my side the entire time, and so will Ethan, Nathan and Olly. She was their friend once too, before all the lies and cheating. They're entitled to say their goodbyes.

I still don't like the idea of them being there. After everything with Emilio and the fight coming up, my insides quiver in trepidation. Henry has never been more ready, and it's not his ability in question. It's the lack of integrity from Emilio. He's a weasel, and he'll do whatever he has to do to beat him, and that's what worries me.

"Hey, are you okay?"

I almost forgot Henry was here. Ever since we declared our feelings for one another, he's with me any chance he can get, but I feel selfish monopolising the only time he has free. He does have a life outside of me—of us.

Closing my laptop, I push to my feet, my chair spinning to face him. "Sorry, I was miles away. Hey, you don't need to be here. I know you have a lot going on."

He reaches for my hand. "I want to… unless you need space?"

I shake my head. "No, I want you here."

"That's good. What time is your dad due back?"

I glance at my watch. "About an hour," I reply. He's been trying to get home for dinner most nights.

"Good, because I want to hear you scream my name as I make you come with my tongue."

My body flushes with heat, and my insides squirm when he leans over me.

"Oh yeah?"

His eyes are dark, but his smile is teasing as he reaches for the hem of my top and pulls it off over my head. Braless, my nipples harden from the cold air—or my arousal, I can't be sure. My eyes flutter closed when his tongue traces a luxurious path from my clavicle to the valley of my breasts.

Every cell of my body sparks with pleasure, and I reach out for him, but he pulls back, shaking his head.

"Uh-ah, no touching," he says with a tut, wiggling his finger. "Now, be a good girl and remove the rest of your clothes and get on the bed."

I love this dominant side to Henry, the way he's not afraid to tell me what he wants in the bedroom.

Doing as he asks, his eyes never leave me, not once.

He kneels beside me on the bed. "Now, raise your arms over your head," he says and then wraps my fingers around the wrought iron bed rails of my bed frame.

"Now hold onto it," he says.

I shiver as goosebumps rise and break out all over my bare flesh.

"You aren't allowed to let go until I give you permission. Understood?"

His words have me aroused in anticipation.

"And what happens if I do let go?"

He touches his chin in mock contemplation. "I'll find a way to punish you," he says in a deep baritone which causes my lower region to pulse with want.

"How would you punish me?" I ask. My voice is gravelly.

He slides a finger through my folds, and I arch into him, my fingers tightening around the bars above my head.

"Well, I'll bring you to the brink of coming and then slow down just enough to keep you from an orgasm."

I spread my legs wider as he strokes me. "You know I can make myself come, right? I don't need a man."

He hooks his finger inside me, and I let out a contented moan, writhing under his touch.

"No, you don't, but you want me. There's a difference," he whispers close to my ear.

I swallow hard. "Well, you better get to it if you want me to scream your name."

My eyes dart over his shoulder to my open door, and he follows my line of sight.

A devious smile graces his lips. "It stays open until you come for me."

Oh my God. I buck into him as he inserts another finger, and I close my eyes and relinquish myself to his magic touch.

When his fingers leave me and I let out a sound of discontent, he chuckles. His calloused palms slide up my thighs, pulling my legs over his shoulders.

His hot breath teases my flesh right before he swipes his tongue from my perineum to my vulva. I let out a gasp and thrust against him as he impales me with his tongue. His fingers spread me wide and I writhe beneath him, my hands strangling the bars, the bed creaking from our combined weight as he continues with more vigour than before.

I'm desperate to reach out and grab his head to pull him closer or grip his hair between my fingers and tug.

I gasp when he spreads my arses cheeks; his finger tapping against my back passage.

"I promise, one day soon, I'm going to fuck you right here too."

He pulls my hips higher and begins licking me there. Up until now, the idea of that has never been appealing. His tongue returns to my vagina, my muscles expanding the more he works me over.

"Oh my God."

I'm building higher and higher, aching for him to give me the release I so desperately need.

"I need to touch you," I plead.

"And you will, once you're screaming my name," he says, and then he continues tongue fucking me.

"I need more," I cry, grinding into his face.

He sits up, raising my lower back, so I'm able to arch into him more. Every moan I make, every sound which expels from my lips, urges him on, faster, deeper, and I don't think I can take anymore.

And then I'm screaming his name as I explode all around him. Spots of colour cloud my vision, and I repeat his name like a sacred prayer. My channel continues to spasm around his tongue, his fingers working my clit.

The stimulation of sensations is so overwhelming. I can feel my juices running down my arse crack.

He lowers my body to the bed. His laugh is both sexy and rough as hell.

"You can let go now," he says, and I look up to see my white knuckles.

I release my grip, and my arms fall to my sides limply.

My chest heaves from the exertion, and yet, he was the one being suffocated by my pussy.

I glance down—his arousal strains against the cotton of his joggers, and I swear grey jogging bottoms will be the death of both men and women everywhere.

"Off," I demand, pinging the waistband.

He removes them so fast I can't help but laugh.

Sitting up on shaky arms, I push against his chest.

"Lay back," I say, my voice hoarse.

I straddle him and grip his hard length. His eyes roll into the back of his head as he groans. Moving to my knees, his fingers dig into my hips as I hold myself above him, the tip of his erection just inside my entrance.

His eyes open, heavy-lidded as he looks at me—waiting.

"No touching," I say.

His grin is wicked. "Touché," he says and lays his hands flat on either side of his body. I'm so wet when I lower myself, sheathing him completely, and then I move. Rolling my hips as my hands get their fill, exploring his chest, and then my fingers wrap around his throat, his pulse beating wildly under my touch. I start to ride him, hard and fast.

I can feel him growing harder inside me, and my breathing becomes choppy as I start to clench around him. His fingers have a death grip on the sheets beside him, his teeth digging into his lower lip spurs me on, knowing it's me doing this to him.

"Oh my God, Henry," I huff, my movements unsteady as my body builds for another release. Feeling like it's too much and yet greedy for more, I let out a whimper.

Henry sits forward, grabbing my hips, and in one swift movement, I'm on my back, underneath him so fast the air rushes from my lungs. And then he's pounding into me with the same determination I've seen when he's working out at the gym.

His stamina is unparalleled to my own.

The pressure builds, and I detonate around him. His blunt teeth sink into the flesh of my shoulder as he orgasms. It's all-consuming and euphoric, and nothing else exists beyond the two of us.

Chapter Forty-Five

Henry

Meg opted not to have a funeral procession to the crematorium. The coffin is already here when we arrive. I've seen some old faces from school, but this is not how you want to reconnect with old friends or acquaintances. In your early to mid-twenties, you should be attending weddings and christenings, not funerals.

My main focus, though, is to support Meg. She squeezes my hand before letting go and goes to speak with the funeral director about the imminent service.

Her dad is talking with my mum—they both insisted on coming for moral support, and it would appear some other parents had the same idea. It's just a shame her parents aren't here.

I sense my brother before I see him, and when I turn around, Ethan is stepping up beside me.

"Thanks for coming, man," I say and pull him to me for a hug.

"Of course, I wasn't about to let you go through this

without me. Besides, we all cared about Clara in our own way, and this is about showing a united front for Meg."

I nod. He's right. Clara and I didn't work out for a reason, but she was still someone I cared about, and she was Meg's best friend. It still feels wrong talking about her in the past tense.

"Any sign of him yet?" he asks, and I know he means Emilio.

I shake my head. "Nope. But no doubt he'll make some grand entrance."

As the number of people arriving grows, we're told we can all go inside.

We enter to the background music of *'I'll be missing you'* by Puff Daddy and Faith Evans. Meg chose songs Clara loved.

Taking the front pew to the right of the aisle, we leave the left side for family—that's if they attend, of course. If not, I'm hoping there will be enough people attending to fill the space. No one wants an empty service when laying someone to rest.

"Sorry we're late," Olly says as he and Nathan slide in next to us. Meg stands, and Olly takes her in his arms, squeezing her tight. He whispers something in her ear, and she nods before Nathan pulls her in and then she sits back beside me.

I reach for her hand and squeeze; she links her fingers with mine, giving me a gentle squeeze back. Ethan is on her other side; he reaches over her shoulder and taps my back, but not without her noticing, and when she peers over her shoulder, her entire body tenses. I follow her line of sight—Emilio.

Ethan keeps his arm there to surround her in a protective gesture, and I refuse to let go of her hand. Not only is it Emilio and his family but his motley entourage too.

He's dressed as though he's on a boy's night out and not attending the funeral of his deceased girlfriend.

Locking my jaw, I keep my eyes fixed on him as he comes to a stop at our pew.

"Look what the cat dragged in," he says towards Ethan.

I react instinctively, letting go of Meg's hand and pushing past Nathan, but Olly cuts me off before I reach Emilio.

"Henry," Olly says, his voice low, holding a warning for me to keep my cool.

Long slender fingers wrap around my wrist as Meg pulls me back down beside her.

Emilio dares to laugh as he blows her a kiss and then sits on the adjacent pew.

"Don't let him get to you, man," Nathan hisses under his breath, but I know he's just as vexed as I am. His normal relaxed posture is rigid, tense. But I know he's right. This is what Emilio lives for, to antagonise people and get under their skin like a parasite.

The service gets underway, and I try with great restraint to ignore his obnoxious behaviour. Like now, as we go through the order of service, he lets out a fake cough here or there or a sly comment under his breath, but loud enough to be heard.

Why did he bother even showing up?

To my surprise, Meg is called up to speak. It's what she must have been talking to the director about earlier.

She takes a deep breath, squeezes my hand before letting go, and gracefully brushes past me. Her hair is in a perfect French plait. I can't help but appreciate the care and detail she took while getting ready this morning. Nathan and Olly lean back to allow her out.

I glance at Emilio and study the way he watches her as she makes her way to the front. It makes my skin crawl, and I want to punch his damn eyes out of his sockets.

But instead, I breathe through it and focus on Meg and the way she grips the podium like it's an anchor. She clears her throat and then stares straight ahead.

She begins reciting a poem

"It's okay to miss you, it's okay to cry. Just know I'll never forget you."

I can't ignore the swell of pride that works its way into my chest cavity in awe of her strength. Even though her voice quivers and tears roll freely down her cheeks, she sees it to fruition.

Finished, she steps down, her movements elegant and refined as she walks back towards us, but before she reaches our pew, Emilio grabs her arm and leans in, whispering something in her ear.

Her face pales, and the fear behind her eyes mixes with her grief.

Shoving past Nathan, I'm ready to tear him away from her, but Olly beats me to it, swiftly moving between the two of them.

And I assure you, if looks had the power to kill, Emilio would be in the ground already.

Olly wraps his arm over Meg's waist and guides her back to me, and I immediately pull her to my side. I look back over to Ethan to see he's grinding his jaw—hard—the rage oozing off him. I know because I feel it too.

And honestly, I'm waiting for him to leap over the pew and take the fucker out. I move Meg, so she's back between the two of us, and intertwine her fingers with mine, holding on tight. Instinctively, she seeks out Ethan's hand too.

Even now, she's the one trying to hold all of us together.

How did I ever think I could stay away from her?

There's not even an ounce of jealousy I feel toward her and Ethan, because I see the bond they have with clarity—different than our own, but it's there.

Ethan will be whatever she needs him to be, and I hope in time he finds someone deserving of him, because I'll spend the rest of my life proving I am worthy of Meg.

Emilio doesn't even wait for the curtains to close around the coffin before he makes a grand exit.

I expel a breath, relieved, even though there are a few

whispers about his behaviour. I can't say I'm not glad to see the back of him.

When the final song begins to play over the speakers, we all leave and head outside. The flowers line the concrete, and we walk among them, reading the messages before everyone starts to break away.

Olly booked out the bar at Charlie's Bar for the wake.

Meg is quiet on the drive, but I can't hold back my curiosity.

"What did he say to you?" I ask, glancing at her and then back to the road.

She keeps her eyes on the order of service she saved from the funeral. For a moment, I think she's not going to tell me, but she does.

"That if I care about you at all, I need to give him back what's his. If I don't, you're dead."

I grip the steering wheel.

"He's full of shit, Meg. You know that, right?"

I flick my eyes towards her, and I see her jaw clench before she answers.

"But what if—"

"No," I cut her off and shake my head as we pull up on the side street near the bar, and I turn off the ignition—the engine ticks as it cools.

"You stay away from him, Meg. I can take care of myself. We just need to bide our time, okay?"

She reaches for my hand and brings it up to her lips.

"I just couldn't live with myself if anything happened to you because of me."

I grip her chin and hold her stare.

"Nothing is going to happen to me, Meg. Promise me you won't do anything stupid?"

The thought of her putting herself at risk for me is non-negotiable. I don't want her anywhere near him, not without one of us around.

Instead of answering, she leans over the centre console and silences me with a slow, soft kiss. If she thinks this is the end of the conversation, she's sorely mistaken, but we have a wake to attend.

Chapter Forty-Six

Henry

Emilio has more lives than a fucking cat, and so far, there isn't anything linking him to doping, so it looks like our fight is going ahead. I know the drug testing is rigged, and Olly has a plan to help prove this, but regardless, it's the day before the fight, and today's the weigh-in.

Ethan and Nathan are here, along with my manager, as we wait for Emilio to arrive.

I'm sitting down when the door swings open, and the devil himself walks into the green room. His gaze focuses on me.

"Are you happy, you wanker?"

Moving to my feet, I square my shoulders and raise my brow, crossing my arms.

"Make you feel good taking my son from the only home he's ever known?"

I shake my head. I still can't believe I was awarded custody, and I doubt Emilio's hostility toward me is less to do with him losing Jacob and more to do with him losing.

"He's my son. And there's a reason they never let him stay with you."

Emilio steps forward.

"Because you made me look bad, that's why."

I shake my head. "You did that all on your own."

"If Clara hadn't fucked up and died, they'd still be with me, and you'd be none the wiser, just like before."

Tilting my head, I digest his words.

"Did you know?" I ask, trying to keep my voice calm.

He smirks. "I had my suspicions the little bastard might have been yours," he says with an air of arrogance. "She never could keep her legs closed."

Ethan holds his hand firmly on my shoulder, keeping me in place.

"You are a cunt, aren't you?" Nathan says, surprising the hell out of me when he moves past Ethan and me, getting in his face.

"Fuck off, you gutter rat," he says, shoving him hard.

Before I know what's happening, Ethan's hand eases off my shoulder in an instant, and he's chest to chest with Emilio.

"Boys, calm yourselves," says my manager as he pushes himself between Ethan and Emilio.

I'm barely holding myself in check, and I know if I don't get some air, the only person my manager will need to worry about is me.

Pushing past the arrogant fuck, I swing the door open. I move out into the long corridor and turn back around, thinking the fucker was dumb enough to follow me, but it's Ethan. I can hear Emilio's smug laughter right before the door clicks closed behind him with a heavy thud.

Many things could have gone against me fighting for custody of Jacob, but I made sure I had the best solicitor when I applied to the courts for parental responsibility. Emilio was arrogant, thinking it would all go in his favour, which serves him right for not taking this more seriously. Once the DNA results came back, and with her immediate family not having any contact with Jacob, I was granted parental responsibility.

It also helped with Meg being his godmother. He knows her, and after all the supervised visits, he warmed up to me. During the process, the foster parent looking after Jacob moved in for a week to help with the transition, but tonight is the first night where it's just us, and to say I'm nervous is an understatement. The fact it's the night before my big fight with Emilio is pure happenstance.

"Sorry, man, I couldn't let him think he could push Nathan around like that and get away with it. He's always been a bully."

I nod in agreement. "I was this close to kicking his arse," I say, holding my thumb and forefinger a millimetre apart.

"And you will, tomorrow."

I look up and down the empty corridor, the fluorescent lights flickering above us. "You're still coming with Meg, right?"

"Of course. How is little man settling in?"

I shrug. "I don't know. He still wakes in the middle of the night. I'm completely out of my element even with all the support, hell I practically have army by my side and I still feel useless. But when I manage to coax a rare smile from him, or he reaches out to me, I feel like I might be doing something right, and then I'm overwhelmed by the onslaught of emotions. I never imagined being a dad would feel like this," I admit.

He leans against the wall beside me. "You're doing great, man; you were always going to be a good dad. I'm just sorry you missed out from the beginning. But that little boy is something else. I mean, come on, Jacob has Nathan wrapped around his little finger."

I let out a gruff laugh. Before I'd even been awarded parental responsibility, he'd gone and babyproofed the entire house.

I eye the door, expecting it to open any moment.

"I'm worried he'll never truly settle. To lose his mum and

then the man he thought was his dad… I wonder if I've done the right thing," I admit.

Ethan moves to stand in front of me.

"You know you did, so don't even go there. He will never have a more loving and protective family than ours. Even if Olly is overstepping, acting like his uncle," he says, shaking his head incredulously.

"Yeah, well, he would have made godfather."

He nods in understanding.

"As would you," I say.

Ethan breaks out into a huge smile. "Man, becoming a dad sure has made you soft," he says. "But so that you know, I don't need a flimsy piece of paper to tell me I'm his godfather."

The light outside the door flashes. Time to get my game face on. I now have a four-hour window to hit the scales. This is intended to give us more time to hydrate before tomorrow's fight. Then this afternoon, we have the scheduled television weigh-in. We'll pose on stage; Emilio and I will square off with each other, and they'll announce our weights from this morning.

All I know is that come tomorrow night, everything leading up to this fight will come into play. Everything I've been working toward. Not only wining this title fight, but giving that son of a bitch the karma he deserves.

Chapter Forty-Seven

Meghan

I thought my anxiety was heightened planning Clara's funeral, but it's nothing compared to how I feel tonight. Honestly, part of me doesn't blame his mum for opting to babysit Jacob instead of attending. It's not that she doesn't support Henry and his profession, but after what happened to Ethan, she'd admitted to me she'd prefer not to watch this fight in particular, and I know it's put Henry's mind at ease, knowing Jacob is safe with his mum.

I've not long been here, and I can already sense the unease rolling through both Olly and Ethan, and it's not just because of the impending fight. They're worried he's planned something. It's ridiculous. Not even Emilio is dumb enough to have something happen to me amongst all these people.

"Wow, Olly is just as overprotective about you as he is about me," Lottie says in my ear.

I stare at Olly as he whispers something to Rachel. Her eyes go wide, and she chuckles.

"He's always been like a brother to me. Apart from Clara," I say, my voice catching on her name. "I was a bit of an outcast, and then when we started secondary school, these four older boys took pity on me."

She shakes her head, curling a lock of hair around her forefinger, her eyes trained on something—or should I say someone—walking towards us. Ethan. She diverts her gaze as he arrives.

"I doubt it was out of pity. Have you seen yourself?"

A loud laugh escapes my lips. "Please, they saw me through every awkward phase I ever went through." It's so surreal having a conversation with Olly's sister.

Ethan places the tray down beside me. "I just got you ladies a bottle of Prosecco—thought you could share," he says as he sets the ice bucket in the middle of the table and slides us each a glass.

"And what if Lottie doesn't like Prosecco?" I ask, raising an eyebrow.

He looks taken back by my comment, and an expression I can't quite make out flits across his face, but just as quick, it's gone.

"Lottie loves Prosecco," Olly says, leaning over to pour us each a glass.

She clears her throat. "What girl doesn't love Prosecco?" she says, picking up her glass in salute, and we raise our glasses in cheers. I take a small sip, worried it won't stay down. I glance at Ethan, who's now focused on his phone.

"Everything all right?" I whisper.

"Yeah, of course," he replies, slipping his phone back into his pocket and reaching for his bottle of beer. But something in my gut makes me think there's something he's not telling me.

"Are you sure? You'd tell if something was wrong?"

His eyes soften as he grabs my hand, such a natural action I don't even think he notices. "You know I would," he says, squeezing once before letting go to take a swig of his beer. "Besides, one way or another, after tonight, Emilio's life will change forever." It sounds like an off the cuff comment to anyone else listening, but to me, it's a promise.

Between Olly and Rachel, they manage to keep the conversation going.

"How is Jacob settling in?" Rachel asks.

"It's tough. He misses his mum," I say with a heavy heart. And I see how hard it is for Henry. They're still bonding, and it's not like Jacob understands any of this. "And now he's in a new home."

"He'll settle soon enough," she says, giving me a warm smile.

My eyes roam over the expanse of the auditorium. In the centre, the ring is enclosed by metal fencing, lit up by spotlights and overhead lighting. The air conditioning is high, and the cold bite of air licks at my skin, causing me to rub at my arms absentmindedly.

"Are you cold?" Ethan asks.

"I'm fine." It's a lie, but he pulls off his jacket and passes it to me anyway.

I roll my eyes and slip it on over my shoulders. Rechecking my watch, I begin biting my thumbnail, and Ethan leans over and pulls my hand away from my face.

"Stop it. You'll give yourself an ulcer."

I roll my eyes. "Haha, very funny. What, are you telling me you're not nervous?"

His shoulders rise and fall as if he's taking a deep breath.

"It's more like adrenaline brewing for me, and I'm helpless to stop it," he says honestly. "I miss the buzz," he says with a shrug.

He never talked about it—his career being taken away from him. He never complained, but I know it hurt him, and I hate that he buries it so deep.

"Don't look at me like that, Meg. I know not everything is meant to last forever."

And I wonder if there's a double meaning to his words—

his career or us.

His eyes soften at my expression, and he leans over to kiss my temple, pulling me to his side. "Everything will work out exactly as it's supposed to. Henrys got this, don't worry," he says.

Finally, there's a loud buzz from the surround sound system, and the announcer begins to speak. The crowd goes wild, and we all stand cheering and clapping, ready for the fight to begin.

Henry

I'm buzzing with excess energy, itching to get out there, but I have my headphones blaring. The music keeps me grounded as it fills my ears. I listen to it on repeat. There's something about the build-up, the staccato beat, which has my pulse racing and adrenaline rising.

I take deep breaths as I bounce around, limbering up. I want to be out there already. I think Meg wanted to see me before the fight, but call me a creature of habit, I've always done this a certain way, and I want to keep to my routine, especially tonight.

I chew on my lip, my hands wrapped and gloves on. I flex my fingers, making sure I'm good for grappling. The cold air con kicks up a notch, but it's still too hot in here as my brow begins to sweat.

Nathan comes into my line of sight and holds up two fingers.

"Two minutes," he mouths.

I nod in understanding as the beat picks up speed and I crack my neck from side to side, shaking out my body, and then when the track comes to an end, I pull out my ear pods and leave them beside my phone.

"Okay, man, you ready?"

"Ready."

We make our way out into the main arena. I tune out the yells and catcalls as I make my way towards the cage. Nathan raises my arm in the air, and I acknowledge the audience.

I know Meg is close by with Ethan, and more than anything, I want to make him proud. Emilio took away his hard-earned dreams and ruined his career. Ethan may not voice it, but I know it still hurts him. I can feel it when he's been with me at the gym training these past few weeks.

When Emilio struts out with his entourage in tow and his arrogant fucking demeanour, I already know I have this son of a bitch beat.

Everything about him is all show and ego.

Once we're in the ring, my mouth guard in, I zone in on him, ready to attack.

It's why I love mixed martial arts so much—full body contact, no holds barred, incorporating techniques from various sports and martial arts around the world.

This is what I live for.

I know how he fights, and I'm able to pre-empt his movements. He thinks he's slick, but he's far from it. Bringing my arm forward like a windmill, I target his head and throw an overhand punch. My timing is spot on. He staggers, and then he's throwing out jabs, but he's becoming sloppy, and his technique begins to falter.

My pulse is racing, and my heart thunders in my chest as we grapple. The tension is building on astronomical levels.

The crowd's chorus thrums to white noise as I focus on my faceless opponent. He is no one. So predictable, and I know just when he's going to do it. Everything slows down when his foot goes on the inside of mine, and he grabs me, pushing me to the floor while tripping my foot.

I go down, hard. The smell of our sweat coats the mat beneath me, and I draw in a deep breath and close my eyes.

Chapter Forty-Eight

Meghan

Henry falls to the mat, and I push my way towards the ring. Panic courses through me, but strong arms wrap around my waist and pull me back against a hard chest.

This can't be happening, not again.

"You need to stay calm. He's okay," whispers Ethan. How I even hear him over the crowd or my pulse ringing in my ears is beyond me.

But until Henry is back on his feet, Ethan's words are null and void.

Henry's eyes connect with mine for a fraction of a second before he pushes himself to his feet with ease. And that's when I see it, his smirk. To anyone else watching, they might think Emilio has the upper hand, that he has the advantage, but he doesn't, and it all begins to fall into place.

Everything else happens so fast, and even though I've caught on to Henry's playbook, I'm still unprepared for his level of retaliation. Henry lashes out hard with a swift kick, followed by his knee. Emilio staggers and backs away, but it's too late. I know Henry isn't giving him an inch. This is the significant moment that will change the course of the fight. The charged air crackles across the arena. An invisible force collectively takes our breath away as we all watch on, momentarily suspended in time.

It might only be fleeting, but it's an iconic moment as Emilio is struck with a deafening thud—a deadly strike as it connects with flesh and bone.

I swear I hear it crack even from here. Emilio is separated from his senses. His eyes roll into the back of his head, and he loses control over his body, which grows limp as he drops to the mat.

A perfectly clean knockout.

Air fills the arena, and an almost perverse pleasure ripples through the crowd, the noise overwhelming.

Ethan still has a hold of me, and I turn in his arms and wrap my arms around his neck, squeezing tight.

"Oh my God," I say in his ear. "He bloody did it."

His firm hands rub up and down my back, and it's only then I lean back, I see his eyes are full of so many emotions. I cup his cheek.

"Are you okay?" I ask.

He nods, his eyes darting to the ring, and I turn my head.

Nathan is already inside, congratulating Henry. A medic rouses Emilio, and a look of utter bewilderment covers his face.

Henry is searching the crowd when he spots us, and his smile is a fucking vision. He waves his hand, and I move out of Ethan's hold and shove him in the direction of the ring, but he grabs my wrist, pulling me along with him and into the ring.

Even when Henry picks Ethan up into a bear hug and lifts him off his feet, Ethan doesn't let go of my wrist until a very sweaty Henry moves to lift me off my feet. His hands cup my arse, and his mouth finds mine.

I'm stunned. It's our first public display of affection, and I don't hold back as I kiss him as though he is my last breath.

Lowering me to my feet, he peers back over his shoulder, and my eyes follow.

"E?"

I don't know what it means. Ethan stares at me for a moment, and then he glances back at Henry.

"It's cool, H."

And with that, Henry bends down, his eyes roaming every inch of my face. I've never felt so exposed in my entire life. The crowd is going crazy, voices clapping, cheering, like a swarm of bees.

"I love you, Meg. You're it for me," he says before lowering his lips to mine.

The kiss is slow, and I almost forget where we are until he pulls back. His eyes are sparkling with a newfound hope I've never seen from him before.

"Meg, will you marry me?"

Air catches in my throat, his question completely blindsides me, and I stutter, unable to form a response.

Henry

When I asked Meg to marry me, the last thing I expected was for her to look so confused, and she pulled away completely.

So I begged her to come back with me to the changing rooms, worried she'd bolt otherwise. I shower in record time, even though I want to savour it and hurry to dress in case she's no longer waiting for me.

All I want is to go home, ice my injuries, take some anti-inflammatory, and hold her in my arms. But not without understanding what just happened.

"Meg, I know my proposal was a shock, but you're my end game. You're it for me."

She glances to my face and then to her feet.

"I was worried about you. And then you caught me off guard. I froze. Sorry."

I move in her line of sight and tilt her chin so I can see her eyes.

"I don't want you to be sorry. I want you to say you'll marry me."

Her pupils dilate as she chews on her lower lip to stop it from quivering.

"That's just it, you asked me to marry you, and I hesitated."

Dropping my hand, I take a step back; the tension is palpable, and I feel like there's a huge 'but' about to be let loose.

"But it's just all so fast Henry. You have Jacob to think of, and the last thing I'm ready for is a ready-made family."

She might as well just punch me; a gush of air leaves my lungs.

Adrenaline is still coursing through my veins. I hear *ready-made family*, and, *so fast*.

"Do you think Emilio is going to get over this?" she asks, waving her hand in the air. "He's going to want retribution over the fight, over Jacob, over the drugs. It will keep circling back to me."

Meg bends over, her hands on her knees. I reach out to touch her shoulder, but she swats me away, standing straight, her eyes hard, steadfast. My ears are ringing from the aftermath of the fight, or her admission, I have no idea.

"I think we should both take a step back, and I should give Emilio his drugs back, and hope things calm down."

I pinch the bridge of my nose and close my eyes, drawing in a deep breath.

"So, you're what? Dumping me?" I ask, opening my eyes to find hers shining with unshed tears.

She nods. "If that's what it takes, then yes."

"Fucking hell, Meg, you're not serious?"

I get in her space, but she steps back. "I am, Henry. I need to take a break from all of this, from you."

"No."

Her laugh is incredulous. "No?" she repeats. "It's my life, Henry, and it's my choice."

"You're just in shock. Losing Clara, the situation with Emilio, this isn't you talking," I say and take her hand in mine.

She snatches it away. "It is me, Henry. Please respect me enough to accept my decision."

I shake my head, this isn't Meg.

"Have you been drinking?" I ask.

Meg takes in a sharp breath. "No, Henry, I haven't."

"Then what is even happening right now?" I ask, my voice rising.

A silent tear springs free but I don't dare reach out to have her reject me again.

"Can you just let me go? Give me some time?"

What other choice do I have? She's not my damn prisoner.

"You leave me with no other choice. But you need to promise me that you will not try to return those drugs to Emilio without my help."

Her laugh is unamused. "Yeah okay," she replies, swiping at her face to dry up her tears.

And then before I have a chance to register her exit, I'm standing alone, in a changing room, on what should be the best night of my life.

Chapter Forty-Nine

Henry

My ears are drumming with the force of my heartbeat, the revelation too much to comprehend. He's been tested positive for performance-enhancing drugs.

"Fuck me," Ethan says, wiping his palm over his unshaven chin.

"Yeah, it's true. He's been suspended," Nathan says as soon as he gets off the phone from my manager.

I drop down onto the bench, my arms hanging between my legs.

"Looks like karma finally caught up to him," Ethan says, grabbing my shoulder and giving it a firm squeeze. "Two-fold."

"Yeah, but it was too little too late for you," I say, and my jaw tightens from the thought.

"Well, he's ruined more than his career. You'll see his management team drop him, as will his sponsors. He's well and truly fucked this time."

I doubt he'll go quietly; this is Emilio after all, and he's worse than a blood-sucking leech.

"I think we should celebrate," Nathan says, already pulling out his phone.

"Celebrate what?" Olly asks, approaching us, a smug grin on his face.

"Emilio was suspended, tested positive for drugs," Ethan says with a shit-eating grin on his face.

"Shut the front door," Olly replies, raising an eyebrow.

I stand. "Hold up. Olly, you pulled it off, but how?"

He shrugs. "I went to the head of the board and told them someone was tampering with the testing, and sure enough…" he says, shrugging.

I pull him into a firm hug.

"Seriously, you're the man," I say.

I pull back, and he winks. "What are best friends for?" he says, like it's no big deal.

And the one other person I want to share this moment with isn't even here. Nathan asked me where she was, and I said she had gone home. It's not like she officially moved in with me, even if she has infiltrated my mind, body and soul.

I haven't seen or heard from Meg since she walked away from me on Saturday night, and its now Monday.

My pride took a huge hit, but the more I thought about her reaction, the more I believe deep down she thinks she's protecting Jacob and me. I know Meg loves me, and I refuse to let her go without a fight. So, no less than thirty-six hours after she dumped me, I'm at her place of work, hoping to accost her.

And like the crazy stalker boyfriend I am, I know her schedule, and she should be here by now.

"Has anyone seen Meg?" I ask.

Everyone says no, and Olly scans the gym. I'm reaching for my phone when Olly pulls his free from his pocket and dials.

"No answer," he says, his eyebrows drawing together.

My stomach dips. I dial her next, but it rings out, going to voicemail.

The hairs on the back of my neck stand on end.

"She wouldn't? Would she?" I question out loud.

"Wouldn't what?" Ethan asks, drawing his eyebrows together.

"Return the drugs to Emilio," I say, gripping my hair in my hands.

His eyes bug out, and he's trying her number again.

Shit! I clench my jaw. Surely, she wouldn't?

"Hi," Lottie says with a smile as she approaches us. "Olly, are you ready?" she asks.

But her eyes are darting between us all with a confused expression.

"Sorry, can we postpone, please?" he asks, taking both her hands in his.

"It's ringing out," Ethan says as he begins pacing. "You don't think he'd do something stupid?" he asks, his hand gripping the back of his neck.

"What's going on?" Lottie asks, her voice concerned.

Ethan freezes mid-pace and looks up as though he's only just noticed her standing there.

"It's Meg. She didn't show up for work," I say in answer to her question.

She rolls her eyes. "And here I thought Olly was a tad over-protective. Guys, she's a grown woman, and from what he's told me"—she points her thumb over her shoulder to Olly—"she's also a bad arse trainer."

Ethan's whole posture goes rigid, and I feel the tension rolling off him because it mirrors mine.

"You have no idea what you're talking about," he snaps.

Lottie's eyes flash with surprise as she takes a physical step back.

"Okay, man. No need to be a dick," Olly replies, clenching his fist.

"It's fine," Lottie replies, but she continues staring at Ethan. Her face pales. "I'll catch up with you later," she says.

Olly kisses her cheek. "Thank you," he says.

She nods, glancing back at Ethan. "Of course, text me later," she says before she makes a hasty getaway.

"I'll ask reception if she's called in and spoken to anyone."

"Maybe we should ring her dad too?" Ethan says, gripping his phone.

Reception tells me they haven't heard from her, and a client of hers has arrived—a moot point.

"Henry," Olly says, jogging over to us. "Rachel just rang. She was on the phone with Meg when she heard her gasp Emilio's name and then got cut off. She tried calling her back, but she wouldn't answer."

"Fuck," I say.

"Any idea where they might be?" Olly asks.

"Emilio's," Ethan and I say in unison.

And I know deep in my gut something is seriously wrong.

We all race out to the car park. Nathan is already holding his keys out as he unlocks his car.

There's none of the usual joking or calling shotgun as Olly and Ethan clamber into the back and me into the front passenger seat. Nathan has a mini, and we make a point of giving him shit over his vehicle choice—a mini cooper, he says girls dig it.

I keep trying to phone her while we're on our way, but now it's just going straight to voicemail.

I curse. "Please, man, hurry. I have a bad feeling about this."

Nathan glances at me and then back to the road and puts his foot down.

"Try not to get us pulled over," Olly says, gripping my headrest, but I also don't hear him tell him to slow down either.

It takes an eternity before we finally pull up along the curb outside his house.

I'm unclipping my seat belt and opening the car door before Nathan even comes to a stop, and I sprint to the house and bang on the door, but nothing. I continue, knocking and repeatedly ringing the doorbell.

The guys are all with me now. "Olly, Nathan, go round the back and see if you can get in," I say, crouching down and rummaging around to see if that damn rock is still there.

Ethan bangs on the door with the side of his fist.

Out of my peripheral vision, I see the blind slide back into place in the bay window.

"I know you're in there. I'll call the police," I shout.

And then slowly, the door opens—Meg is standing there, her eyes wide as Emilio holds a knife to her throat.

Chapter Fifty

Meghan

Fear is unpredictable; it can immobilise you and invade every rational thought you've ever had, like right now, when Emilio crept up on me, digging a knife into the small of my back.

It doesn't matter how much self-defence I know or how much training I've had, or how well I fight, because when a knife is concerned, the best option is to run, and here I am, pressed against my car, unable to move.

He snatches my phone and ends my call, slipping it into his pocket. He pulls out a cable tie, my pulse races, and I try to look for help. But he shoves me hard against my car, winding me.

"Don't do anything stupid," he grits out, spinning me around as I try to catch my breath as he ties my wrists together, giving it a hard tug. The cable cuts into my skin painfully.

"Now move," he says, grabbing me by my waist, the knife in his other hand digging into my stomach through the fabric of my thin sports top.

He pushes me up against his car, and it unlocks automatically. Then he's opening the boot.

"Now, get in," he snarls.

"What? No, please, I'll sit in the front with you. I won't try anything, I swear," I say, holding up my bound wrists.

He backhands me, my head slamming into the edge of the open boot.

"Now get the fuck in."

I lift my leg in an attempt to climb, but I'm clumsy and awkward. Emilio growls and pushes me hard. I fall in face-first onto the rubber boot liner, and he throws my legs in. I'm barely inside when he slams the boot shut, leaving me in darkness.

I struggle to catch my breath. I never thought I was afraid of small spaces until now.

And the more I panic, the harder it is to breathe, and then I'm crying, which makes it even worse.

Is this what it's like to suffocate? I try to breathe as Emilio speeds, causing me to be jostled aggressively in the confined space. And the more I think about being trapped in the boot of his car, the more frantic I become. I try to kick my legs out, but the space is too small.

I have a panic attack, and if I can't calm myself down, I'll likely pass out, and I need to stay awake.

I start to count quietly to myself.

The car crunches to a stop, then the engine cuts out.

Blinding light assaults me when the boot opens, and I inhale a lungful of air. He pulls me up with force until I'm half crawling out, and then I'm falling, landing on the ground with a hard crunch.

"Up." He drags me, but my ankle gives way, and I stumble. The pain is quickly forgotten when the sharp tip of a blade presses against my spine.

He shoves me until we're at his front door and pushes the key into my hands.

"Unlock it," he says, his hot breath rancid in my ear.

My fingers shake, and it takes me three attempts to get the key in the hole.

"In," he orders.

I can hear my phone ringing, and he frees it from his pocket, throwing it onto the coffee table.

And then he's on me so fast, shoving me into the wall with such force that the back of my head slams into it.

"Where is he?" Emilio shouts into my face, spittle flying everywhere, the smell of alcohol hard to ignore.

I'm momentarily stunned. He's come completely unhinged. "Who?" I ask and hate how weak my voice sounds.

"Henry, the one you're fucking," he spits.

I try to lean away from him, but he's too close.

"I don't know," I say.

He slams his hand against the wall, the one holding the knife, the blade ragged.

"The fucker thinks he's won. First her and then him, and now this."

He hisses, pushes away, and paces in front of me.

I move to the side, hoping to get back to the front door, but he cuts me off and drags me deeper into the living room, forcing me into the soft padding of the sofa cushions as I land on my side.

Quickly, I right myself as I take in the mess before me. An empty vodka bottle and remnants of white powder line the coffee table.

He goes over to his home entertainment system and turns on his stereo. I can barely hear myself think over the music as it blares from the speakers. He paces some more, smashing the side of his temple with his fist.

"Is it the drugs? I can get you your drugs," I say, hoping to pacify him somewhat.

He crouches in front of me, forcing me deeper into the sofa, his pupils dilated.

"Too little too late, don't you think?"

Bringing his hand up, I flinch, expecting him to slap me. Instead, his fingers trail over my face before gripping my chin roughly.

"I've been suspended because of that cunt. I bet your fuck buddies are celebrating as we speak." He pushes my face away roughly; my neck jarring, and he gets back to his feet.

"I didn't know."

"Yeah, well, those fuckers are going to pay," he says, enraged.

There's a heavy banging on his front door, and he turns to the sound until it ceases and then goes to the window to investigate. Frantically, I look around. I need to get out of here. I know how to fight, but he has a knife, and my wrists are still bound. I get up and walk backwards, keeping my eyes focused on him, hoping I can make it to the back door.

He swings around and lunges, his strides long. I turn and rush to the door. My entwined hands grab at the door handle. He grabs my hair, snapping my head back, and the pain causes my eyes to water. But it's the ice of the metal blade pressing into my flesh that makes me let go of the handle, because this time, he pierces my skin. I can't hide my whimper.

"I will fucking end you. Don't test me," he says in a menacing tone, and I know I am no match for a hunting knife. He spins us around, pulling me tight against his chest.

"Now, you're going to open the door and let your fuck buddies in, and if you try to do anything stupid, this will end badly for your pretty face." And as if to emphasise his point, the tip of the blade scrapes along my cheekbone. I don't dare breathe until it's back at my throat.

He pushes me forward until we're at the door, and he reaches over and unlocks it.

"Let them in," he hisses.

Standing there in front of me is Henry and Ethan. I'm

equal parts relieved and terrified they're here. Emilio brings the knife closer to my throat, dragging me back against his body.

"Get inside. If either of you tries to be heroes, I'll make you sorry."

Henry is visibly pissed, his jaw set. He doesn't take his eyes off me as they enter.

I wish, with everything in me, I was safe in his arms. And more than anything, I wish I had said yes when he asked me to marry him. I don't want a future without him in it.

"Now, shut the door," he says, too close to my ear. I shiver. The metal scratches my throat.

"Just let her go. It's me you want. Let's sort this out between us," Henry says.

Emilio tightens his hold, and I squeeze my eyes shut, expecting the puncture of the blade at any given moment.

"And what about him? Is he going to sit back and watch?" he asks in Ethan's direction.

"Just let her go, man," Ethan says, stepping forward, but all it does is antagonise him even more. Emilio's hold on me tightens.

"Why? You fucking her too? Or you doing her at the same time?"

Bile rises, and I force myself to swallow.

Emilio's words are poison laced with acid. His damp cold lips skim my earlobe, causing me to shiver from revulsion, and his tongue sweeps along my neck. I'd rather him cut me than do that again. And I swear over the racing of my heart, I hear Henry growl.

"Maybe I should have a go too?" he says low, but still loud enough for both Henry and Ethan to hear.

Staring between Ethan and Henry, I mouth one word, "Sorry."

A loud cracking boom echoes behind us, and without forethought, I elbow Emilio as hard as I can, causing him to stumble backwards. His grip on me loosens, and I push my body weight into him, hoping it will give me an advantage, but not before cold metal slices my flesh.

I gasp at the sensation.

Ethan is by my side, his hand reaching for my neck. I swat him away and gasp as Henry charges into Emilio, knocking him hard into the ground. I twist out of Ethan's grasp, trying to see past him to Henry as Emilio bucks him off and continues to slash the knife out in front of him.

I try to push away from Ethan, but he holds firm, his hand still clutching my neck, which is now a searing pain.

His other arm grips my underarm as he tries to lift me to my feet, but my body feels heavy—even to me—and refuses to cooperate.

"Shit, come on, Meg," he roars, worry and torment clouding his features.

He pulls his hand away, and I wonder what he's doing as he strips out of his T-shirt.

Why is he taking his clothes off?

And then he's pushing it towards my skin. Warm liquid oozes over my collar bone. I try to wipe it away.

"Stop it, Meg, you're hurt," he says, anguish in his voice.

"The police are on their way." Nathan? When did Nathan get here? His shadow falls over me.

Sirens howl in the distance, and then my vision blurs, and Ethan becomes two, but another hand reaches for me —Henry.

"Meg?" he says.

"Emi—lio," I stutter, unable to continue my train of thought.

"Meghan, stay the fuck awake."

Darkness comes and sounds around me fade into a distant thrum until there is nothing but silence.

Chapter Fifty-One

Henry

Meghan's eyes roll into the back of her head. "Meghan," I shout, her body limp in my arms.

"Hold this," Ethan says as he lets go of the blood-soaked material.

"Meg, wake the fuck up," I say under my breath. My lips caress her forehead. She's cold and clammy.

"E," I holler. Panic ricochets through me, my hand shaking as I try to keep pressure on her wound.

"Here." He's pulling the saturated material away and replacing it with a pristine white towel. It's not long before it's saturated too.

"Fuck, man, call an ambulance!"

"Olly already has," he says, crouching beside me, his hands covered in claret.

I can feel his hands on me, and I try to push him off me.

"Stop it, man. I'm just checking your arm. He cut you," Ethan says, gripping my forearm.

And that's when I feel the searing pain—heat seeping through my bicep.

"Fuck," I hiss through my teeth.

"Olly, go grab me another dish towel and some scissors so I can get the fucking cable tie off her wrists."

I stare back at Nathan, who has his knee dug into Emilio's lower back. That motherfucker did this to her. I stare back at her skin, so pale.

"I'm going to kill him," I say as I try and hand her limp body into Ethan's arms.

Olly's hand comes down on my shoulder, pushing me back down, and then he leans down, cutting the cable tie.

I want to kill him.

My rage roars in my skull like a mantra.

"Henry, you need to calm down. The police are here," Olly says.

Ethan wraps the tea towel around my bicep and pain shoots through me.

Olly leaves to speak to one of the officers, but I can't focus enough to make out their conversation. I've never seen so much blood, not even in all my years of fighting.

"E, I can't lose her, man. I can't," I choke out.

His blood-stained hand covers mine as I keep pressure on her wound.

"She's going to be fine," he says, but I hear the fear in his voice too, and I know he's as worried as I am.

"Where the fuck is the ambulance?" I call over my shoulder.

Olly says something as Emilio is handcuffed and led out of the house, a police officer talking on his radio.

"Two minutes," Olly says as he kneels back beside us, grunting. I forgot he's still recovering from surgery.

"Come on, Meg," he says, wiping her hair off of her face.

Her breathing is ragged, growing shallow.

"She can't breathe properly." I lay her down.

Ethan leans over, his ear to her mouth.

"Fuck," he says.

Blood is seeping through my fingers.

"Please don't die, please don't die."

Everything else happens like I'm not even present. Olly has to pry me away from Meg so paramedics can stabilise her breathing, and then they're moving her onto a stretcher and into the ambulance.

"Go with her. You need to get that looked at too," Ethan says.

"What?" I ask, confused.

He grabs my shoulders.

"H, you need to go with Meg to the hospital. We'll meet you there." He walks me to the door of the ambulance and pushes me inside. The paramedic points to a seat and tells me to sit. I do as I'm told like I'm on autopilot and watch on helplessly as she continues to treat Meg.

I reach for her hand, so fragile in mine. I squeeze it and hold onto her like I'm her anchor.

"Is she going to be okay?" I ask.

"I don't know, son. We just need to get her to the emergency room and in the hands of the doctors," she says over her shoulder.

"Can't he drive any faster?" I say, frustrated.

"We are going as fast as we can."

Is she for real?

"Really?" I ask, frowning as she looks back at me. I expect her to tell me off, but her eyes soften.

"Listen, we can't put her at any more risk. We need to get her to the hospital safely and without causing injury to anyone else. Believe me when I say we are doing everything in our power to do just that."

I nod and bounce my knee up and down, as if it will get us there faster.

"Talk to her," she says. "Let her know you're here."

"Meg," I say, my voice cracking. "Come on, baby. We're nearly there. You're a fighter. Come on, stay with me."

The paramedic calls ahead to triage and says things I have no idea how to translate. I continue to hold her hand, willing her to hold on.

We come to a stop, and then the doors are being pulled open, and the ramp is lowered with a heavy clunk. I step down and stand aside and allow the paramedics to wheel her down the ramp and straight into ER.

I follow closely behind.

"We'll need you to give some details for her, and we also need to get you checked in so we can see to your injury," says the male paramedic who drove.

I'm about to argue, but he stands tall. "Honestly, she's in good hands." He ushers me away from Meg and towards a large reception desk where I'm asked question after question before I'm told to take a seat, but instead, I pace in front of the plastic chairs.

"Henry Rivera," calls out a tall nurse with a clipboard in her hands.

I walk towards her and she takes me into a room where she looks at my injury.

"Okay, you're going to need stitches," she says and begins cleaning the area.

"Can you tell me how my fiancée is?" I ask. Okay, fine, she's not, *yet*—but she will be.

"Let me get you moved to a treatment area, and I'll see if I can find out," she says as we walk through a door and into a ward full of cubicles, separated by curtains.

"Here, take a seat," she says before pulling the curtain over and disappearing.

She returns moments later with a small trolley.

"My colleague is going to find out about your fiancée. Meanwhile, let's get you stitched up. You're going to feel a pinch," she says as she readies a syringe and pushes it into my skin.

But she's wrong. All I feel is numb as I watch the needle penetrate my skin. How am I meant to feel anything again until I know if Meg is all right?

Chapter Fifty-Two

Meghan

Sound is the first thing that comes back to me, followed by light, and then the pain hits me. And I'm assaulted with vague distorted memories of Emilio and him slashing a knife at Henry. I begin to panic. My throat is scratchy and uncomfortable. I reach up to touch it when I see my dad.

"Dad," I croak out, my voice hoarse.

He sits bolt upright and reaches for my hand.

"How are you feeling?" he asks, his eyebrows knotted together.

"I hurt," I reply honestly. "Where am I?"

"You're in the hospital. Do you remember anything?"

I pause and try to think past the fog in my brain, and I startle when I'm hit with a vivid memory of Emilio wildly slashing a knife. "Oh my God, Henry... where's Henry?"

"It's okay, Meg, he's fine. Only one of us could stay, so we made him go home. They told us you'd likely sleep through, but I'll let him know to come up, and he can stay with you," he says in a placating tone.

He leans over my bed and presses a call button.

The door opens and a stocky woman walks in, her smile bright.

"Meghan, it's good to see you awake," she says, stepping up to the bed and reaching over to turn off the button.

"You are one fortunate young lady," she says as she pulls over a blood pressure cuff and monitor, deftly wrapping it over my upper arm. She takes a reading and then releases it.

"You were very lucky. There was no damage to your trachea, and though you suffered severe blood loss, those with you were quick to keep direct pressure on the wound. If the knife had been even a centimetre to the left, it would have cut your carotid artery."

She doesn't sugar coat it, and I'm aware of how fatal this could have been. I squeeze my eyes closed and try to breathe through that knowledge.

"If you need pain relief, you just press this button. We'll keep you on this overnight, and you'll be put on oral meds tomorrow, once the doctor gives the okay."

I nod my head, but I'm a confusing mess right now. She asks me some questions, but my eyes keep drifting towards my dad. My memories are fuzzy and distorted—puzzle pieces I'm still struggling to connect.

"We have you on a drip, but try to drink too, keep hydrated."

When she leaves, my dad sits forward, taking my hand in his.

"I don't know what I would have done if…" He doesn't finish his sentence. His eyes fill with tears, his throat clogged with emotion. My nose tickles. Ever since my mum walked out on us, he's always been surly, reserved even, and it's rare for me to see such raw emotion.

"I'm sorry, Dad. I'm fine, though, I promise."

He wipes his face, and it's such a soul rendering sight.

"You have nothing to apologise for, I do."

I shake my head, but it makes me dizzy, so I stop.

"No, listen. I know I was always hard on you, but it's only because I love you." I go to respond, but he holds up his hand. "When you said about moving out, my response was selfish. I was a stupid old man, worried you'd leave me as your mum did, but you're not your mum."

He strokes my cheeks; I wasn't even aware I was crying.

"I see it now, how much Henry loves you, and after today, I think he's more than proved he's worthy."

My throat is dry and scratchy, and my dad reaches for the jug of water and fills the beaker. Bringing the straw to my lips, I take a few sips before he places it back on the side table.

"What do you mean 'worthy?'"

"He wants to marry you, and I gave him my blessing."

My stomach is in knots, and my cheeks heat. "You did? He does?"

"Yes. He said you already turned him down once." He wipes the hair away from my forehead. "When he gets here, do him a favour and put him out of his misery."

I laugh and then wince, pressing the button for pain relief, and it's not long before my eyelids become heavy.

"Get some rest, baby girl. Henry will be here when you wake up," he says.

Soft lips caress my cheek, and my eyes flutter open. Henry is above me, searching my face. A small whimper escapes me. I reach up and wrap my arms around his neck.

"It's okay, Meg, it's over now. I'm here," he says, drawing back and cupping my face in his calloused palms.

"I was so worried he hurt you," I say, my voice hoarse.

"I'm fine, it was you who got hurt," he says, tilting my face gently and looking at my throat.

"I love you," I whisper.

He smiles. "I love you more."

Reaching behind him, he drags the chair closer and sits so his face is level with mine.

"You look exhausted," I say, my hand rising to his cheek.

He leans into my touch. "I haven't slept, been too worried about you," he admits.

"What happened to Emilio?" I ask.

"He's been charged with attempted murder and drug-related charges. I don't think things will end well for him," he replies.

"This was all my fault."

His eyes go wide. "Are you serious? This isn't your fault. It's him. He's to blame, no one else."

I lick my cracked lips and look to the side table but don't see any of my belongings. Henry releases my hand, pulls my bag from the bedside cupboard, and rummages through it until he finds my tube of lip balm.

He twists the lid, and I go to take it from him, but he shakes his hand and scoops a sliver onto his pinkie before gently coating my lips.

I rub them together. "Thank you."

"I have something to ask you."

I stare at him and wait in anticipation. He shuffles in his chair and reaches into his pocket to reveal a small black trinket box.

"Meghan, I can't imagine my life without you in it. You are everything to me. So, I'm asking you *again*. Will you marry me?"

I smile, not even caring if it makes my throat hurt.

"If you'll still have me, then a million times yes."

He opens the lid and resting between a soft cushion is the most beautiful ring I've ever seen.

"Oh my God, it's beautiful," I say, unable to look away.

He pulls it out and picks up my hand and slides it onto my ring finger.

"I don't want to waste any more time Meg. From this moment forward, everything I want is to be with you."

Holding my hand out in front of me, I stare in awe at my engagement ring—so perfectly me. An emerald cut sapphire-blue graduated halo diamond ring. And I know this because it's my dream ring, and there is only one other person who knew about it... Ethan. And it warms my heart, knowing he must have had a part to play in helping Henry choose the perfect ring for me.

When I wake up, Henry is no longer here; instead, sitting in his place is Ethan. His head is lowered as he taps away on his phone, but his brow is furrowed. He raises his eyes and notices me watching him.

"Hey, how are you feeling?"

I swallow. "Like I lost a fight with a knife."

He shakes his head. "Not funny."

"Sorry. Where's Henry?" I ask, looking past him.

"I sent him home to change and see Jacob."

Ethan looks like he hasn't slept either.

I reach out for his hand. "Hey, are you okay?"

Tilting his head, the corner of his mouth rises. "Shouldn't I be asking you that?"

Rolling my eyes, I let out a sigh. "Don't deflect, Ethan."

He groans, and his fingers stroke my hand. "Nice bling," he says, eying my engagement ring.

"You helped him choose it, didn't you?"

"I did. I couldn't have my best friend wearing anything mediocre, could I?"

I swallow. I don't know if it's the dressing or the actual wound which feels tight.

"Ethan, you joke, but are you okay about Henry and me?"

His lips rise into a genuine smile. "Yes, you're right for

each other, and this," he says, waving his hand toward my throat. "Only proves it. Because as scared as I was for you, I've never seen Henry so terrified. He'd be irrevocably broken without you."

I think my mouth gapes open. "Wow, Ethan, have you been reading romance novels?"

He holds his free hand to his chest. "You wound me," he says in mock horror.

"Seriously though, Ethan. I'll always care about you. You're my family."

He cups my cheek before he tucks my hair behind my ears.

"I know, and I love you, my soon to be sister-in-law," he says, wiggling his eyebrows.

I swat his chest, trying to suppress my smile. "Yeah, like that won't be too weird, right?"

Ethan shakes his head. "No, not weird at all."

Chewing my lip, I voice my thoughts. "So, you don't think we're moving too fast?"

His eyes search my face. "I think the question is, do you?"

I shake my head once. "No, no, I don't."

"Then there's your answer, and neither do I."

I bring our joined hands to my mouth and kiss the back of his. "I never did deserve you. But there is someone who does, and she better treat you right."

He clears his throat, and I see the heat rise in his cheeks.

"Wait, are you blushing?" He leans back in his chair and shakes his head, but I know he's lying. I sit up and pull on his hand.

"Oh my God, Ethan. Have you met someone?"

He shrugs. "It's complicated," he replies. "I think I might have messed up."

"Then what the hell are you doing here?"

He draws back his head as though I've slapped him. "Are you serious? You could have died, Meg."

I roll my eyes. "I'm fine." But the truth is, I was lucky. "I'm okay, I promise. Now go and uncomplicate whatever you complicated."

He smiles and leans over, kissing my forehead.

"Fine, but you tell Henry you wanted to rest if he gets here and finds me gone or I might be in a room next to you."

I swat his arm. "Ha-ha, very funny. Now go, and when I'm out of here, I want details."

Walking to the door, he shakes his head and glances over his shoulder. "Maybe some things are best kept private," he says with a wink before he exits.

Chapter Fifty-Three

Henry

It's been almost two months since Emilio kidnapped Meg, and though she's healing physically, I know she's still struggling mentally. She wakes in the middle of the night, almost suffocating from the nightmares. I coax her out of her panicked state, reminding her repeatedly that she's safe and that she's home. *Home.* As soon as she was discharged from the hospital, I brought her back here, and we moved her stuff in gradually.

At least Jacob is sleeping through the night now. He even called me "Dada" the other day, and the swell of pride I felt was more monumental than anything.

Not even winning title fights came close to this.

Well, except for Meg agreeing to be my wife, but there is one more thing I want, and that's for her to adopt Jacob once we're married.

Of course, I'll make sure he knows who his birth mother is. Meg and I agreed he would know how much Clara loved him, because regardless of her faults, she loved him unconditionally.

I know he'll never be without a mother while Meg is in his

life. She's been there in every way possible since I was granted parental rights. She stepped in without complaint and blew me away. Nurturing comes so naturally to her. And I'd be lying if I said it didn't make me excited for our future together.

Because I know I'd love nothing more than to give Jacob a sibling or two, okay… maybe three, and yes, I'm aware I need to slow my rolls. I don't want to scare her away.

"Can't you sleep?" she asks, facing me.

"No, I was just thinking," I say, rubbing her silky hair between my fingers. "I love this hair colour on you. It reminds me of the irises my mum grows in her back garden."

She strokes over the pink scar tissue on my bicep.

"Those beautiful wine-coloured ones?" she asks.

"Yeah, but she calls them"—I click my thumb and middle finger as I try to remember—"midnight something… that's it, Midnight Embers."

"Oh my God, Henry, that's it, the colour scheme I want for our wedding, Midnight Embers," she whispers, and I can hear the smile in her voice.

"I'm down." I don't add that I'd marry you tomorrow if I could because I want her to have the wedding of our dreams.

"Have you thought any more on a date?" I ask, my hand stroking the length of her spine. When I hook her thigh over mine, she shivers, trailing my fingers over the back of her knee.

Her breath hitches. "May… I want to get married next May."

I grab her hand and bring it to my lips, kissing the pulse point on her inner wrist. Her breathing picks up, and I roll onto my back, bringing her with me.

"Yeah?" I ask, smiling.

She rubs up against my length, and I sit forward until she's straddling me.

"Yeah, I can't wait to be Meghan Rivera."

I let out a growl and pepper kisses over her scar and down her neck.

"You're taking my name?" I ask. It's not something we spoke about until now.

She nods. "Of course, I'll take anything you're willing to give me."

I don't miss the double innuendo in her answer as I grip her arse cheeks and squeeze, causing her to arch into me and throw her head back. I'll never get tired of exploring her body. But mostly, I'm thankful every day she's still here, and she's mine.

"How about a baby?" I ask.

She freezes, and I realise I've spoken my thoughts aloud; I loosen my hold and lay back. "Fuck, me and my big mouth." I close my eyes and turn my head to the side.

Her hands cup my face. "Look at me," she whispers.

Unable to deny her, I open my eyes and find hers shining.

"You want to have a baby with me?"

I nod. "Yes. I've already seen what an amazing mother you are."

She kisses my face and pauses at my lips.

"I want you to adopt him," I admit, deciding I might as well go all in.

After all, I've never been any good at staying inside the lines.

"You do?" she asks, and her voice cracks with emotion.

I bite down on her lower lip and tug it gently before releasing it.

"Yes."

She pushes my shoulders back and hovers over me. Her hair falls over her shoulders, tickling my bare chest.

"So that gives us plenty of time to practice between now and the wedding," she says.

I bite down on her shoulder. "Practice?" I ask, my tongue sweeping down to the valley between her breasts.

"Practice making a baby," she replies with a soft giggle.

In one swift movement, I pin her beneath me, her lips parting on a sharp intake of breath. She loves it when I do that. She's a fucking vision laid out before me, her long locks fanning the pillow. And I have a moment of worry if this is the colour theme we go with for our wedding, I may spend the entire day with a boner.

But if it's what she wants, who am I to deny her.

"Are you saying what I think you're saying?" I ask, peppering her face with kisses.

Meg reaches up and cups my arse.

"I am, now what are you going to do about it?" she teases.

Gripping her knee, I raise her leg, smiling as I align myself with her entrance.

"I'm going to show you," I say.

Letter to Reader

Thank you for making it this far, and I hope you enjoyed Henry and Meghan's story. If so, please consider recommending Midnight Embers to your book friends and leaving a review. It doesn't have to be much—one sentence will do—but I'd be forever grateful. Remember, your voice matters, and without you, authors like me are invisible.

Forever Embers is Book 3 in the Embers standalone series and is available to pre-order on Amazon.

Acknowledgments

Mum—Thank you for being the best friend a daughter could ever have and always supporting my dreams unconditionally.

Cassie—My lobster, thank you for being you and constantly pushing me to be better.

Crystal—Thank you for your endless support. And always willing to proofread at the drop of a hat, I couldn't do this without you.

Amber—Thank you for your kindness and always talking me off that ledge. If there is any author out there who deserves the very best, it's you.

Kirsten—You are, without a doubt, incredible. I couldn't do this without you as my Beta Bitch.

Dusti—Thank you for beta reading when my novels are at their roughest and loving them anyway.

Julie—I love your guts, always.

Ruth—Thank you for always being so supportive and full of light and always cheering me to carry on.

Kayleigh—Thank you for always being ready and willing to read my books.

Indie Authors—Who support without motive or agenda, I see you.

My famalam—Special shoutout to Grace, Tam and Dave. Jon, we miss you every day.

Friends who are my extended family—Victoria and William. Laura, Andy, Evie and Zach, and our mountain goat, Ethel.

My family—I love you to the moon and back.

Harley—My most loyal companion, gone but never forgotten.

Also by L.S. Pullen

Where the Heart Is

Dysfunctional Hearts

Hearts of War

Burning Embers

Midnight Embers

Forever Embers Pre-Order

About the Author

L.S. Pullen, aka Leila, was born and raised in North London, but now resides in Peterborough, England. When she's not walking her adopted pooch Luna, you'll likely find her squirrel spotting or taking care of her adopted guinea pig, Maurice.

She is passionate about everything books, lover of photography and art. And in true English cliche fashion, loves afternoon tea. No longer working the corporate life, she is currently writing full time and managing a small craft business Wisteria Handmade Crafts and Indie Author's Book Services.

facebook.com/lspullenauthor
instagram.com/lspauthor

Printed in Great Britain
by Amazon